WRITTEN IN THE STARS

Kate could not be certain that the excitement bubbling up within her had more to do with Edmund's company than watching a play by Shakespeare. Unfastening her cloak, she turned her attention to the actors.

Kate understood full well why the playwright had Valentine and Proteus debating the merits and pitfalls of love. Somewhere in her laughter she sighed for Julia and her misadventures masquerading as a male. Kate understood the quickness and frustration of Silvia and thoroughly relished the drama and comedy, the story of friendship and love.

Because she lived a drama of her own. Loving the man at her side, and knowing she could never reveal her love. Feeling the warmth of his body close to hers, the excited skip of her heart whenever Edmund smiled at her.

She'd misplaced her gloves and so had not worn any. During act three, when Edmund caught her rubbing her cold hands together, he caught them up in his, clasping them both. With one hand he enveloped both of hers, warming them, sending sparks of pleasure through every limb, sparks that curled her toes and tingled in her fingertips . . .

Dear Romance Reader

In July of 1999, we launched the Ballad line with four new series, and each month we present both new and continuing stories set everywhere from medieval England to the American West—the kind of passionate, romantic stories you love best, written by the most gifted authors. At the back of each book, we tell you when you can find subsequent books in the series that have captured your heart.

First up this month is **Just North of Bliss,** the second book in the fabulous new *Meet Me at the Fair* series by Alice Duncan. An ambitious photographer thinks he has no interest in a certain Southern belle except for her pretty face—until he learns that love knows no boundaries. Next, Sandra Madden introduces Elizabethan-era siblings *Of Royal Birth* with **A Princess Born.** Everything changes when you discover that you're a princess . . . except the man you love.

Also this month, Tracy Cozzens presents another fabulous new series called *American Heiresses.* **Flight of Fancy,** the first of five books about the wealthy Carrington sisters, takes readers from New York to Paris to London—and straight into the heart of passion. Finally, ever-talented Sylvia McDaniel begins a provocative new series called *The Cuvier Widows* with **Sunlight on Josephine Street,** in which the wife of a philanderer discovers that she's not her deceased husband's only widow—and she's suddenly prepared for a second chance at love.

From Bourbon Street to Elizabethan England, these are stories we know you'll love!

Kate Duffy
Editorial Director

OF ROYAL BIRTH

A PRINCESS BORN

SANDRA MADDEN

ZEBRA BOOKS
Kensington Publishing Corp.
http://www.kensingtonbooks.com

ZEBRA BOOKS are published by

Kensington Publishing Corp.
850 Third Avenue
New York, NY 10022

All Kensington titles, imprints and distributed lines are available at special quantity discounts for bulk purchases for sales promotion, premiums, fund-raising, educational or institutional use.

Special book excerpts or customized printings can also be created to fit specific needs. For details, write or phone the office of the Kensington Special Sales Manager: Kensington Publishing Corp., 850 Third Avenue, New York, NY 10022. Attn. Special Sales Department. Phone: 1-800-221-2647.

First Printing: May 2002
10 9 8 7 6 5 4 3 2 1

Printed in the United States of America

ONE

The Year of Our Lord, 1596
Astrological signs indicate a tranquil spring

Thump. Thump. Thump. Her heart thudded against her chest.

'Twas not what the stargazer predicted.

Alone in the garden, Kate watched in terror as the wild beast bore down upon her.

The animal came barreling out of nowhere bounding toward her like a fiend from the netherworld, a large creature with lolling tongue and foaming mouth. Her body stiffened. Immobilized by uncommon fear, she waited breathlessly. Unable even to shift her gaze, Kate spotted the canine's prey from the corner of her eye. The fearsome hound chased a small hare, which hopped toward the hawthorn at great, and enviable, speed.

Oh, fie!

No sooner had the inevitable flashed through her barely functioning mind than it happened. It had to happen.

In one wild and desperate move, Kate threw herself into the dirt, hoping to avoid a nasty collision. Her frenzied movement caught the dreadful brute's attention at the last possible moment. He made a mighty leap, soaring above her but nonetheless spraying Kate with freshly tilled soil.

Sputtering, she pushed herself to a sitting position and gingerly picked the dirt from her mouth. More of the malodorous manure covered her person than lay under the rosebushes. Chunks of dark, damp earth clung to her hair, splattered on her face, and lodged in scattered clumps on her borrowed gardening attire.

Although never one to mind a little dirt, Kate did not deign to roll in it. She had donned her ailing papa's thick woolen trousers and jacket to work in the garden. She enjoyed gardening. The rich black soil smelled of spring and hope. She'd breathed deeply of it as she planted several new centifolia bushes. Had she been born a man, she would have become a gardener just like her papa.

As she brushed the dirt from her jacket, Kate looked about cautiously. Satisfied the beast had disappeared, she let out a sigh of relief, a heavy, unladylike whoosh of air.

And then she heard the whistle, sharp and piercing. Her breath stuck in her throat, causing a strangled gasp. She knew that whistle. Surely, it could not be . . . But it must be.

Oh, double fie! After all these years, to meet Edmund again when she wore more grime than the rushes on a tavern floor. The whistle came again. Kate turned toward the garden path, hoping against hope that it was not Lord Stamford.

But it was.

God save her, she smelled like the stable!

She considered making a run for it, but the sight of him stopped her. Riveted to the spot, she watched him approach.

Tall and solid as a rugged English elm, Edmund strode toward Kate in a hurried, off-step gait. No matter what changes time had made upon his physical person, she would know him anywhere. Her heart fluttered madly. Dressed in simple country attire, his white linen shirtsleeves billowed from beneath a buff leather jerkin; wearing deep russet venetians, and polished black boots, the earl cut a striking figure.

A surge of joy shot through Kate, sweet and strong. Trembling within and without, she started slowly to her feet, never taking her gaze from the dark-haired man almost upon her. Drawing a deep breath to steady herself, Kate struggled to regain her composure, or at least to quiet her quaking body.

Kate Anne Beadle had not seen Edmund Wydville for well over ten years, and she wished to greet her old childhood friend with some semblance of dignity.

Instead, her shaky knees gave out and she plopped back on her bottom. Branches snapped and thorns pierced her derriere as she hit the dirt. Biting her lip to prevent a yelp, she fought back tears of humiliation as the Earl of Stamford reached her bed of roses.

"Good morrow, Gardener."

His great, warm smile struck her heart directly, as if he had taken special aim. For so long, her heart had been a very still and silent part of Kate, but now it skipped in an alarming fashion.

She forced a quivering smile.

"Are you hurt?" he asked. His forest green eyes darkened with concern.

Kate, still rendered incapable of only the merest movement, shook her head. "Nay," she whispered.

Grasping her wrist, Edmund pulled her to her feet. She could feel the warmth of his hand through her papa's heavy, soil-stained cotton gloves. A warmth that burned like the touch of fire.

The rust-colored beast returned, and Edmund took a firm hold of the chain circling the panting animal's neck, even as Kate took a wary step back.

"Ah, Percy, only see what you have done. Thrown more dirt over this poor gardener than is to be found in the entire garden."

Percy barked in reply. A deep, ferocious sound akin to a lion's roar. She held her breath, eyeing the beast with fresh apprehension.

With his gaze focused on her dirt-covered garments, Edmund did not seem to notice her distress. "I fear your clothes are beyond repair. I shall see that you have new—"

" 'Tis not necessary, my lord." *Just hold your dog,* she thought.

As a child, Kate had been bitten by what had appeared at first to be a harmless greyhound. The bite had gone deep and left her with a distrust of dogs ever since, no matter how playful or innocent they appeared. Edmund, though, had always loved animals. Dogs, cats, ferrets, or birds, he had time for whatever species crossed his path.

"Aye, it is quite necessary," he insisted. "Percy has badly misbehaved on our first day back at Rose Hall."

"I believe he spotted a hare."

"Percy enjoys the hunt, but I shall keep him at heel."

Kate prayed for Edmund's success.

His brows slashed into a frown. "Forgive me. I have not introduced myself," he said, dipping his head briefly. "The Earl of Stamford, at your service."

"Good day, sir."

She could hardly credit it was truly Edmund standing before her.

He did not boast a boring chiseled perfection like some men. The planes of his face were broad and generous, just as his heart. The square set of his jaw projected strength, both of body and spirit.

While Kate contemplated Edmund in dreamy adoration, he stared at her papa's big, ugly boots. Ashamed to be caught wearing them, she shifted her weight as her old friend's bold study moved to the thick woolen trousers and oversized jacket she wore.

Painfully aware of her unsightly appearance, Kate felt ready to sink even as giddy elation spiraled through her. What must he be thinking? When would he recognize her?

The musky heat of the striking earl swirled in the space between them, reached out and wrapped around her, warming Kate like a woolen cloak on a summer's day. His inspection paused briefly on her dirt-adorned face before rising to her wide-brimmed straw hat.

She attempted to smile, but her lips merely twitched.

He did not recognize her. As if he could through all the dirt!

"Bloody hell!" Edmund folded his arms across his broad chest, studying her with a bemused expression. "Despite your dress, I believe you to be a woman."

"I am indeed a woman," she assured him, suppressing the need to both stifle a giggle and crow with delight.

Against all the rules of polite society, and Kate *did* know her manners, she would keep him guessing all day if she could. After all, he had plagued her relentlessly when she was a child.

But the desire to torment Edmund a bit was quickly

dampened by a flicker of impatience. How long would it be before he recognized her? She had recognized him easily enough, although he hadn't had such broad shoulders when he was a green young man of eighteen.

Edmund shot Kate a wry smile before his gaze traveled the length of her once more. "Pray pardon, but do you always dress like a man?"

"I find men's work clothes so much more comfortable for gardening," Kate replied sweetly.

"An uncommon attitude unless . . ." His voice trailed off. Cocking his head to one side, he craned his neck slightly forward, narrowing his eyes as if he would then be able to see behind the dirt and the oversized clothing concealing the woman before him. "Unless you are—"

"I am Kate," she blurted. "Do you not remember me?"

"Kate?" Edmund's mouth dropped open, his eyes widened, and his dark craggy brows spiked up in astonishment. "Kate Beadle?"

"Aye!"

"My Kate?"

"Aye, my lord."

Obviously stunned, he stood in silence for a moment before the beginnings of a grin creased his quite agreeable lips. His meadow-green eyes sparkled, crinkling at the corners, as Kate remembered.

"I thought it might be you," he confessed. "For what other woman would dress so?"

"No other, indeed!" she responded jubilantly, not at all offended by his remark. Teasing her had been his way when they were young.

"Kate!" He shouted her name with a deep, rumbling exuberance that certainly could be heard clear to the village, miles away.

And Kate released the joy and laughter locked inside since she'd first caught sight of him. The thrill of seeing her old friend spilled from her like the burst of a waterfall over a mountain bluff.

Before she knew what was happening, Edmund joined her laughter as he scooped her into his arms, twirling her around and around. Their laughter echoed in the quiet countryside.

The earl's behavior was completely inappropriate, and Kate loved it. She loved feeling his strong arms about her, loved hearing the deep laughter erupting from his chest.

Kate had loved Edmund ever since she could remember.

Perhaps she'd loved Edmund since he'd first taken her along on his fishing expeditions. To her mama's chagrin, Kate had been rather a hoyden. She preferred to fish with Edmund than attend a tea party with his sister, Jane. Besides, Jane let it be known in not-so-subtle ways that she found playing with the gardener's daughter sorely beneath her.

Even though there was almost a ten-year age difference between them, Edmund had always treated Kate with kindness. In retrospect, she must have been an annoyance following him about as she did. Anytime she spotted the gangly young man, she would take up his company without leave. She trotted behind him, adoring his every step. To Edmund's credit, he never lost patience with her that she could recall.

They shared a love of the outdoors, and more.

The earl had been an unwelcome addition to his family; Kate had been abandoned by hers. It had been their secret, unspoken bond: two unwanted children who found comfort in each other's company.

Edmund's beast jumped and barked beside them, growing louder and more excited by the moment. When at last her feet touched the ground, she braced herself momentarily against Edmund to keep from falling.

"I fear you have made me quite dizzy, my lord."

"But you shall forgive me? You always did."

With reluctance, Kate stood back from him, from his warmth, from the strength of his arms and the shelter of his spirit. "Do you not think that I may be a different person than when we were children?" she asked.

It was difficult to flirt with a man when one resembled a street urchin. In truth, Kate had no idea why she was behaving in such a bird-witted manner. Edmund had been her childhood friend and could never be anything more. 'Twas useless playing the flirt.

"I shall not allow you to be any different at all." Edmund chuckled, shaking his head in a gesture of wonder. He smiled down at her.

A smile that captured and held her rapidly beating heart.

"I hope you have not changed overmuch," he said.

"Why is that?"

"An independent spirit is rare in a young girl—and admirable."

"Admirable, only to you, I fear." No one else thought it amusing that Kate railed at destiny for having been born a girl instead of a boy.

His lips quirked in amusement, but his gaze remained steady and soft, locked on hers. "I thought never to see you again," he said quietly.

"Nor I, you," she admitted in the barest whisper.

Kate had been a brokenhearted child when Edmund went off to Cambridge. He had not always returned on holidays. Too soon she had been sent to an Italian convent for study. Eventually, she had resigned herself to the idea that she would never be in Edmund's company again.

"How do you fare, Kate?"

"Well. Very well."

"When last I asked after you, Aunt Cordelia told me you had accepted a position as a children's nurse."

He'd thought of her! He'd asked about her!

"Papa has been ill," she replied above the sound of her boisterously pounding heart. Could Edmund hear its thunderous beating? "I was obliged to return home to care for him."

"I confess I am glad for your return, but regret the reason."

"Aye, but Papa has made great strides."

"Have you been doing his work?"

"Nay. I had some idle hours, and if you remember, I always loved the roses."

"And digging in the dirt."

She laughed. "You do remember."

His voice softened. "I remember much, Kate."

She felt a great flapping of gossamer wings in the pit of her stomach. 'Twas the tenderness of his voice to blame, the gleam of his wondrous green eyes. "You were always kind to me, my lord."

"Would you ride with me on the morrow?"

Such an outing would be highly improper. "I would enjoy that very much," she replied quickly.

"We shall ride to the stream and fish for trout."

"The same trout we could not catch years ago?" she asked.

"The very same." His mouth turned up in the same

disarming grin he'd had as a boy. "The fish will jump and taunt us, but we shall be engrossed in conversation. I am eager to know every detail of your life during the past seven years."

It had been more than ten years since Kate had last seen Edmund, but she did not correct him. "You shall discover that my life has been uneventful, my lord. And I do not wish to bore you."

"You have never bored me, Kate," he said with a droll twist of his lips. "I shall have Cook prepare us a basket."

Kate realized only too well that the Earl of Stamford could not ask her to dine with him at Rose Hall. It simply wasn't done. Certain protocol might be overlooked when they were young, but not any longer. A nobleman of Edmund's rank and station could never form an alliance with a gardener's daughter. Kate remained well beneath Edmund's touch.

Edmund's thoughts were on Kate as he rode over his East Midland estate that afternoon with his steward, Joseph Trumble. As a child, the gardener's daughter had been sassy and sweet, a mixture he'd found amusing. From time to time over the course of the years, he'd wondered about her. He'd speculated on what had happened to the impertinent little girl who believed she could do anything a boy could do—an uncommon attitude that at the time had caused Edmund to fear for Kate's future.

He wondered if nature had favored her. It was impossible to tell through the layers of dirt and manure if she had become a comely miss or an ill-favored wench. The years might have wrought many changes in Kate. His invitation to ride with him had been an impulsive one, one he hoped he would not regret.

For the first time since his arrival, Edmund felt happy to be back at Rose Hall. He did not come often to his country estate, located just north of Leicester. He preferred London's city life and the company of his burgeoning group of companions there. Although he dutifully took his seat in Parliament and was a regular at court, Edmund's heart belonged to gaming and sporting with his intimates. He could think of nothing better than an afternoon of hawking, bowling, or billiards—unless a worthy tennis opponent challenged him to a match.

When Parliament adjourned for the Easter recess, Edmund had journeyed to Rose Hall. He had neglected matters of his estate for too long. Another compelling factor forcing his return was his dear aunt, Cordelia. In her last communication to Edmund, she claimed to be on her deathbed. She warned that if he did not visit soon, he risked never seeing her again.

Edmund expected the old woman had the constitution of a team of oxen and would outlive him by a number of years.

The smell of spring freshened the air and sharpened the puffs of snowy white clouds ambling across the sky. As Edmund rode beside Trumble, he realized he'd forgotten the beauty of the country. Astride his favorite gray, he surveyed the rolling hills, scanned the herds of grazing sheep, and listened to Trumble list the needs of the estate. Percy pranced like a pup beside his mount, barking at anything that moved, including rich green blades of grass stirring in the breeze.

As the afternoon wore on, Edmund felt a deepening sense of peace, a feeling he'd not experienced for quite some time. Hours later, unexpectedly energized by what he could only attribute to the country air, he strode into the great hall where he knew he would find Aunt Cordelia.

"Edmund, where have you been all the day?"

"Reacquainting myself with Rose Hall." Smiling, he brushed his lips against his aunt's parchment cheek.

Evidently, she'd misjudged her toilette and had applied an extraordinarily thick layer of powder. The white talcum filled the crevices of age and gave her complexion a deathly pallor. Her dyed lips presented a startling crimson contrast to her ghostly flesh.

"Why must you spend the day with Trumble when you have not paid a visit to me in many months?"

"And why have you refused my invitations to come visit me in London?" he countered.

She hung her head. Faded yellow ringlets bobbed with a sigh so heavy it weighted the room. "I cannot travel. I am dying."

Edmund rocked back in surprise, stifling a chuckle. "Dying!"

For most of her life Aunt Cordelia had suffered from an acute case of one malaise or another. Aware that imagination seldom led to death, Edmund had never been overly concerned.

"Aye. Dying."

"Forgive me, Aunt, but you appear to be in excellent health. One might say . . . robust."

Aunt Cordelia's double chin and plump figure were not hidden by the wide ruff and volume of her dress. She did not look remotely like a woman withering away from a fatal illness. Further, he knew his aunt kept a close secret. Cordelia sipped sack throughout the day, from dawn's light till midnight.

"Do not be deceived by thine eyes." She blinked at him in an accusing manner.

"My apologies."

"The surgeon cannot discover what ails me. I have been bled and blistered to what end, eh? I continue to feel weak and indisposed day after day."

"Do you take daily walks in this good country air?"

His aunt recoiled as if Edmund had suggested throwing herself on a bed of nails. "Nay! I could catch something dreadful in the outdoors."

Before Edmund could respond, the door to the drawing room opened. He looked up and experienced his second shock of the day.

"Edmund," Cordelia asked, "do you remember little Kate?"

The air rushed from his lungs.

Little Kate. This was not the smelly, dirt-covered girl he'd discovered earlier that day in the rosebushes, nor the small child with the big round eyes who years ago followed him to his castle in the trees.

The Kate who stood just inside the drawing-room door regarding him with a soft, enigmatic smile was a tall, slender beauty.

Edmund could not be certain he was breathing as he beheld his former fishing companion. A mixture of awe and appreciation fixed him in a near mesmerized state.

Who would have guessed Kate would blossom into a beauty with high, regal cheekbones the same soft pink shade as the garden roses? Who could have known the smattering of freckles he remembered would fade, leaving a flawless, creamy complexion? The child's mass of tangled blond curls had been captured and tamed by the woman. Kate's sleek honey mass had been pulled back and covered by a net caul at her crown.

She wore a simple open gown of violet silk over voluminous petticoats. The low square neckline of her cream-colored bodice displayed a delicious view of full, round breasts. Porcelain mounds pushed up—and out—in a tantalizing spectacle.

Edmund felt warm of a sudden. Without ruff or farthingale, Kate managed to be more attractive than any lady of his acquaintance dressed in the height of fashion.

"My lord," she said. Her lips parted in a teasing smile as she made a slight curtsy.

Edmund drew a ragged breath.

"Edmund?" his aunt repeated.

Jarred from his stupor, he grinned and strode across the room. "Mistress Kate! What a delightful surprise." He winked as his eyes met hers. Clasping her hand in his, Edmund slowly brought her fingers to his lips, brushing them softly.

"I fear I keep appearing where you least expect me," she said. Her wide amber eyes sparkled like spun gold.

The pulse at his wrist raced.

"I am charmed, nevertheless," he replied, lowering his voice to an intimate aside. "But I must confess I hardly recognized you without your gardening attire."

"Or dirt?" she asked with a saucy grin. Her lips were scarlet and dewy, as if she'd just run her tongue across and wetted them.

Fleetingly, Edmund wondered if Kate's lips had ever been kissed. She smelled of rosewater. The sweet flower scent drew him closer. "You have become a beautiful young woman," he said, rather hoarsely.

They stood inches apart. The urge to gather Kate

into his arms and whirl her about again struck Edmund with amazing force.

"You flatter me, my lord. Time has made changes."

Edmund nodded, willing his body to cool, his eyes to look away. "Time has blessed you."

She gave him a brilliant smile. "You appeared surprised when first you saw me."

Kate had always spoken what was on her mind. 'Twas a disconcerting habit Edmund had hoped she had outgrown. Apparently, she had not.

"Not at all," he mumbled.

Embarrassed, Edmund took Kate's elbow intending to hurry her to his aunt's side. But she balked. She scanned the room, searching for someone or something.

"Is something amiss?" Edmund asked.

"Is . . . is your hound about?"

"No. Percy waits downstairs."

"Did you find my comfrey?" Aunt Cordelia asked, unmindful of Kate's apprehension.

"Aye. 'Tis here." Kate held up the ivory vial and carried it to where the old woman waited impatiently. " 'Twas in your bedchamber, just as you suspected."

"God reward you," Cordelia declared. "In my delicate condition, 'tis necessary to keep the comfrey close at hand, eh?"

Edmund gave a nod without taking his eyes from Kate.

"Sit here, Kate." Cordelia blinked as if the dim room had suddenly flooded with sunlight. She patted the bench beside her box chair. "Kate has been a fine companion to me since she came home to nurse her papa," his aunt explained to Edmund.

"I am certain that she's an excellent companion.

She always was," Edmund replied as he met Kate's eyes.

"Fortunately, Papa has not required all of my time, so I have been able to visit regularly with your aunt."

"Kate plays the lute, you know," Cordelia said, flicking a speck of lint from her black wool shawl.

"Nay, I did not know."

"And she plays draughts with me."

"A woman of many talents," Edmund offered.

"Aye. And, oh, my dear, when I have the headache, she gives the most comforting strokes about my forehead, and here at my temples." Cordelia demonstrated with her own gnarly fingers while she talked. "Kate all but chases the pain away, eh? She is more effective than any herb."

Edmund imagined Kate's slender fingers caressing his brow with the soft, feathery touch of an angel. He could almost feel her fingers trailing down to his chest, splayed against his heart. With his eyes wide open Edmund could even dream of her hands drifting still further down.

Bloody hell! What was he thinking? Such devil thoughts were blasphemous in the company of his spinster aunt and a lovely young virgin. But was Kate a virgin?

Bloody hell! Had he lost his mind? The state of Kate's virginity was no business of his. Had he been brought to the brink of madness by the country air? Or was it something in the gardener's daughter's smile? He knew not.

"I shall miss Kate when she leaves," Cordelia lamented.

"When she leaves?" Edmund repeated. "Where are you going, Kate?"

"Since Papa has recovered, I have applied for another position as nurse."

A small part of Edmund relaxed. Her departure did not appear imminent. "Will you be happy as a nurse?"

"Aye, my lord. I am quite fond of children."

Her smile was warm enough to melt an iceman's heart.

"Then why not marry and have children of your own?" he asked.

'Twas a forward question, but the thought of his childhood friend laboring as an unappreciated servant rankled Edmund. Even worse was the thought of what untoward demands might be forced upon Kate behind the stairs. Many of his fellow noblemen were infamous for taking liberties with the more fetching help. If Kate was a virgin now, she might not be for long.

Pursing her lips, heavenly lips in Edmund's opinion, Kate considered the question. "Someday I shall. I look forward to having children . . . but I am not yet ready for marriage."

"The vicar is smitten with our Kate," Aunt Cordelia offered in an exaggerated whisper before heaving a sigh. "But I can hardly see a future for her with him, eh? Dudley is twice her age and has a dreadful overbite."

"Are you matchmaking for Kate, Aunt Cordelia?"

"Not at all," she snipped. Visibly affronted, she quickly changed the subject. "Will you stay to hear Kate play or are you off to join Mister Trumble once more?"

"Forgive me, but I must meet often with Trumble while I am at Rose Hall."

"But I shall see thee before nightfall, Edmund, eh?"

"Most certainly, Aunt." Edmund shot his aunt a reassuring smile and then turned to Kate. "I look forward to our next meeting, Mistress Kate."

She lowered her head demurely, but not before he caught her enchanting smile and the sparkle of gold in her eyes. "As do I, Lord Stamford."

TWO

Throw caution to the wind; no harm shall befall you while Mercury is in retrograde

The next morning, as soon as she and Edmund cleared the stables, Kate gave a whoop, a gentle nudge of her knee to her mare, and rode off in a cloud of pebbles and dust. She raced as if the devil-hound Percy was at her back.

The hood of her cloak fell back almost at once, and the biting wind tore her hair from her caul, loosening the mass in a wild cloud of honey-kissed curls. Chills swept through her body. Her skin prickled and stung. She hadn't felt such exhilaration in years!

Taken by surprise, a laughing Lord Stamford caught up to her in moments. He looked so fine, so very masculine in his snug buckskins and polished black boots. Astride his enormous black gelding, Edmund appeared every inch an earl. His raven hair curled at the nape of his neck, with one loose shock falling across his brow in a rakish manner.

With a teasing wink and a devastating lopsided grin, her childhood friend suddenly surged ahead. Kate gave chase.

The early fog had lifted, but a mottled gray sky threatened rain. She could smell it in the air. Although she had not visited their former fishing spot in many years, Kate had not forgotten the route. The clear, winding stream was little more than two miles down the back road and off through a meadow bursting with the first golden primroses of spring.

Urging her mare to one last surge of speed, Kate galloped past Edmund. His startled expression evoked a burst of laughter from Kate. She was unable to stop laughing, and tears soon streamed down her cheeks. When at last she felt herself under control, she looked back to determine if the astonished earl was gaining on her. 'Twas a mistake.

She did not see the low-hanging sycamore branch ahead of her. *Wop!*

Kate landed on her back in the dirt.

Two of Edmund leaped from their mounts and ran to her side.

Two Edmunds! How wondrous!

But alas, she knew it to be only double vision from the blow to her head.

"Kate! Kate! Are you all right? Can you see me? Can you hear me?"

He was shouting in her ear. "Aye, aye."

Slipping an arm beneath her shoulders, Edmund lifted Kate to a sitting position. His emerald-green eyes reflected concern as he examined her for visible signs of damage. A cowlick stood upright in his dark, windblown hair.

Surely Kate could reach up and straighten the cowlick?

But no, what would he think of her?

If she were younger and unaware it was not the thing, Kate would not have hesitated to reach out and push back the unruly lock. As she would like to do now. The urge to touch him had possessed her ever since he'd taken her in his arms and whirled her about the day before. She yearned to be in his arms once more, crushed against the power and strength of him. How delicious his warmth would feel against the cool morning air!

And oh, how her feelings so quickly betrayed her. Kate closed her eyes as she felt her body warming and the blush rise to her cheeks. A body bruised and battered! How could she be thinking such scurrilous thoughts when she was more than likely near to death?

"I daresay you ride well for one who claims to be 'sadly out of practice,' " Edmund said, sweeping a distracted hand through his hair. The wayward midnight lock settled into place.

"Aye." Kate sighed as her fingers gently searched for the painful lump she felt protruding from the side of her head.

" 'Tis the last branch one must watch out for," Edmund added drolly.

"Aye."

"We are not far from the stream. Can you walk if I help?"

"I, I believe so."

But she did not walk. Apparently having a change of heart, Edmund scooped her up in his arms. Kate's pain vanished.

"I shall carry you to the stream," he declared. "As a precaution."

"God reward you," she whispered with all due humility.

Hey-ho! She was in Edmund's arms once again! Her heart danced a rousing galliard, leaping and twirling as hearts are not wont to do.

He carried her with ease, as if she weighed no more than a mayfly. Held close to Edmund's chest, Kate basked in the feeling of his lusty warmth—for some twenty paces.

Ever so gently, Edmund lay her down beside the stream after fashioning a pillow from his folded jerkin.

Dappled light filtered through the trees in hazy splotches. Taking care not to move her head abruptly, Kate scanned the wooded area. If she listened well, she might hear the laughter of a young girl and a growing boy, woven through the winds of spring for all time. She and Edmund had returned to a place and time where happy memories dwelled.

Ancient oaks offered a canopy of sheltering branches on either side of the stream that splashed a greeting as it ran off into an even thicker copse and disappeared. This shaded spot where lush ferns, hogweed, and dusky wild dog rose flourished was where Edmund and Kate had often fished for trout together. The Garden of Eden could not have been more idyllic.

"Would you like to return to Rose Hall, Kate?"

"Nay, my lord." The lump on her head throbbed unmercifully. A spot below her left cheek ached. "I shall be fine with a bit of rest."

"Would you mind if I fish while you rest?"

"Nay." As long as she did not have to bait his line, as she had in the past.

Edmund had always been an avid fisherman.

An hour later the earl had caught a twig but no trout. Kate had recovered sufficiently to watch his efforts. She leaned against a tree trunk, struggling to maintain a stoic expression. For some reason, she found his frustration humorous.

"The fish are not biting today," he growled, throwing down his pole.

"Aye, but look, my lord," she pointed to a stately

oak several yards to the south of where they fished. "Your tree fort still remains."

Constructed haphazardly, the weather-beaten structure perched in the thick old tree was no more than a ramshackle ruin with only half a roof wedged between two giant limbs. At least two floorboards had rotted away.

"Fort?" Edmund repeated, feigning offense. " 'Tis my castle, wench, where I ruled as king."

"A thousand pardons."

"And pray, Kate, when we are alone, call me Edmund. 'My lord' sounds odd coming from you."

"Aye . . . Edmund."

The Earl of Stamford regarded the remains of his youth, and chuckled. "I am astounded that even parts of my castle still stand. Mayhap I possessed some structural talents in my youth."

"You were always most clever."

His eyes met hers, and his lips parted in a crooked grin.

Kate's heart fairly jumped from her chest. Disconcerted, she placed a protective, staying hand over the general area.

"I fear only you would say so, Kate."

"You never allowed me up into your tree . . . castle."

"King Arthur could not allow females entry to his private chamber."

"You pretended to be King Arthur?"

"Aye. Who else?" He grinned, the sheepish grin of a boy caught stealing comfits.

Assuming the identity of a proud mythical knight of honor suited Edmund. As a girl, Kate had believed he possessed the most worthy qualities of a valiant knight. She still did.

"Who else?" she repeated, returning his smile, meeting the deep forest green of his eyes.

A languid warmth spread through her, leaving a bright burning spot at her core. 'Twas as if the sun had broken through the overcast sky in a fiery blaze. For a moment, even the lump on her head ceased its throbbing.

The knight of her girlish dreams contemplated Kate with narrowed eyes and a mocking half smile. "Did you ever trespass in my castle, Mistress Kate?"

"Never." Many times. Kate had found comfort by trespassing in Edmund's tree castle after he left Rose Hall.

"Would you like to climb with me into my castle?"

"Methinks a delicate female should not climb trees."

Edmund pressed his lips together and swiped back the wayward lock of sloe-black hair that had fallen across his forehead once again.

"Where is this delicate female, Mistress Kate?" he asked with twinkling eyes. "Who would she be?"

Undaunted by Edmund's merciless teasing, Kate laughed. " 'Twould most certainly not be me, for I am not known to be delicate," she replied. "And that's the shame of it."

"No shame," he countered with a roguish grin.

A grin, Kate was certain, that brought the ladies of the court close to a swoon. Edmund possessed charm enough for ten men. His playful manner and beguiling smile made the Earl of Stamford a dangerous man. A very dangerous man.

A thrum of excitement spiraled through Kate. 'Twas the thrill of challenge, she expected. "I should like to climb to your castle, Edmund."

"You are a rare female, Kate. But are you certain you feel steady on your feet?"

"I am fully recovered." Two broken legs would not have kept Kate from being with Edmund in his castle.

"I will go before you."

She watched Edmund climb, admiring his quickness, his strength and agility. When he reached the platform, he planted his hands on his hips, appearing full of himself and quite like a conquering crusader of old.

"If you will turn your back, I shall climb up and be settled in a matter of moments," she told him.

Once more, the dashing earl flashed a smile that transformed his rugged features into a striking, heart-pounding force. Edmund's pleasure showered down upon Kate like tingling beads of crystal rain.

'Twas not an easy climb in her cloak, heavy broadcloth gown, and voluminous petticoats. Fortunately, Edmund had not built his castle on the loftiest branches, and Kate had not far to go.

At the last moment, he turned, clasped Kate's hand, and pulled her up.

She stood before him on the platform, gazing at his extraordinary face, making each well-hewn feature familiar to her once again. Free from moustache or beard, the firm, square line of his jaw suggested an invincible masculinity.

The silence between them deepened, at once comfortable and uneasy. A ripple of pleasure skimmed down her spine. Kate longed to touch her fingertip to the vague cleft in Edmund's chin.

"Someone has been here before us," he said softly, breaking the spell.

Kate looked to the spot where he pointed. Obviously, Edmund's personal attendant had come ahead to deliver a small basket and folded blanket.

Edmund had promised refreshment, and he was a man of his word. A man who made Kate feel more like a queen than a gardener's daughter. Queen of a castle perched high in a tree.

She spread the blanket, and Edmund set out the contents of the basket.

" 'Tis a feast," she declared, eyeing the generous chunk of cheese, crusty bread, jug of ale, cold roasted duck, and ginger cakes.

"Would you expect less from a king?"

Laughing at his feigned pretentiousness, Kate settled on the rough platform next to her childhood friend. She kept a discreet distance from him, something that would never have occurred to her when she was still a child.

Kate and Edmund sat but feet apart, yet they were worlds away from each other. A fact she must never forget.

A cool breeze rustled through the leaves of the trees. Kate caught a glimpse of granite sky through the heavily laden boughs. But the weather could not dampen the sunshine within her heart. Warmed by the ale, Kate slowly sipped from a pewter goblet.

Reunited with her childhood friend, 'twas a moment beyond all praise. A moment unforeseen by her astrologer. Alas.

"Are you not pleased with being an earl, Edmund?" she asked in a cajoling tone. "Must you be king?"

"Pleased?" He gave a wry twist of his lips. "At the time I constructed my castle, I had no thought of ever becoming the Earl of Stamford. My brother, Reggie, was the heir."

"Ah, then the good virgin queen has nothing to fear from you."

"Nothing, I assure you." Edmund sounded annoyed, like a man trapped in ill-fitting garments.

"Have you a contented life?"

"Life is . . . as it is. I take my pleasures at court and with friends."

"Do you fill your time with only the pursuit of pleasure?"

"There is no better pursuit."

Kate laughed at his glib reply, assuming he teased her.

The boy she had known possessed a quick intelligence and a keen curiosity about the world. He would not suffer long in a tedious state of indulgence.

There was so much she wanted to know about the man Edmund had become, about his life since last they had been together; she could not dwell on one frivolous reply.

"Do you attend Parliament and make certain our poor country peasants are not forgotten?"

"I fulfill my duties, Mistress Kate."

She raised her goblet of ale. "To Lord Stamford."

Edmund touched her goblet with his. He could scarcely credit that the beautiful woman beside him was the same gawky girl he had known as a boy. A gullible girl who had unfailingly supported him in deed or idea.

Each time Edmund looked into Kate's bright, tawny-gold eyes, whenever his gaze fell to her full berry lips, he felt a wave of fresh astonishment.

He remembered when Kate's two front teeth had been missing; he recalled when she was an awkward miss who fell over her own feet. He had known her when she had no flesh on her bones. Her body had been as thin and straight as the shaft of an archer's arrow.

But even then Kate had been different from other females. She'd flaunted a bold, free spirit even some of his male friends lacked. At the time, he'd believed her brazen behavior had something to do with being the gardener's daughter. He knew little about her class, a class he was forbidden to associate with. Nevertheless, he found the girl intriguing.

Kate knew all about flowers—and pollenation. On one memorable afternoon, the young Kate passed on a lesson recently learned from her papa. She prosaically instructed Edmund on the virtues of stamen and pistil.

She displayed courage for her sex, as well. Occasionally Edmund took notice of her vulnerability. At those times Kate reminded him of a fledgling newly on the wing. He could not turn away from her, even when she annoyed him with her endless questions.

"Edmund? What are you thinking?"

Was there no end to her questions, even now?

"About you, Kate," he answered truthfully.

Her tentative smile broadened to brilliance. "Aye?"

"Aye. You have a bruise beneath your left eye. 'Tis changing color."

"Aye?"

"Black-and-blue."

"Oh, fie!"

"Eh?"

"Nothing."

Edmund smiled. She did speak her mind. Too often, before thinking.

Kate had been a foundling. She'd come to John and Nell Beadle long after they had given up on having a child of their own.

"Why are you seeking a position as a nurse, when you should be seeking a husband?" he asked, knowing it was an impertinent question.

She did not remark on the impropriety of his question. She simply answered it. "A husband does not interest me . . . as yet."

"Every female is interested in securing a husband."

"Ah, but 'tis written in the stars that I first must find the woman who gave birth to me."

"The stars?"

"Aye. In every way but one, Nell Beadle was my mother. She mended my bruises and kissed away my tears. She nursed me when I ran a fever and taught me to mend with a deft stitch. I called her Mama, and I could always feel her love, even when she scolded me, when I had disappointed her. But now that she is gone . . . resting with the angels, as Papa says, I must find my natural mother and follow my destiny."

Kate's golden eyes shone with determination.

Edmund frowned. He feared only heartache lay ahead for Kate if she pursued such a course. "You may find only disappointment."

"Papa has voiced the same concern. But I am willing to accept whatever I discover."

"I remember the story of how you came to the Beadles."

She smiled shyly. "The wisewoman?"

Called wisewoman by some, witch by others.

Edmund was not superstitious, but many of his friends and family were.

"Aye," he replied. "You told me that one night a wisewoman brought you in a basket to the Beadles' door. You were bundled in silk swaddling and sprinkled with rose petals, a gift for John and Nell Beadle to treasure."

" 'Tis a lovely story, is it not?" Kate pulled up her knees and wrapped her arms around them.

Edmund had seen her take the same position years ago as a young girl. Now, with a wistful smile, she looked out beyond the limbs and leaves, to a place back in time.

"My mama said that when she drew back the blankets I smiled at her. She told me I was round and pink with a whisper of blond fuzz covering my head. She knew at once she must always love and care for me with all her heart, else the wisewoman would return and take me away."

"Nell was more a mother to you than my own ever was to me," he said quietly. Edmund knew well he had been an unexpected inconvenience to both his mother and father.

Kate lowered her head. For an instant, her long, dark lashes curled against her porcelain cheek. "No one shall ever replace Mama in my heart, Edmund. You can be certain. But when she died last year, I knew I must find my natural mother. There are so many questions here"—she tapped her temple and then placed her hand over her heart—"and a hollowness here."

Quite unexpectedly, the thought of Kate feeling anything but content distressed Edmund. He thought to reach out and take her hand and promise his help. Instead, he nodded his understanding and sipped his ale.

He dug back deep in his memory. "You used to wear a chain around your neck with a special ring that you believed gave evidence of your birth. One day you even let me hold it. Do you still wear the ring, or was it lost long ago?"

"Oh, my, no!" she cried. "I have not lost my ring.

And to this day, you are the only person who has worn the band except for me."

Edmund started as his heart seemed to turn around in its chamber.

Kate held out her right hand. He gazed at her lovely long fingers and the gleaming ring. "Now that I'm grown," she explained, "it fits on my finger. According to Papa, the only stipulation the wisewoman made when she brought me to the Beadles was that I must wear this ring at all times."

Kate leaned toward him then and whispered in a conspiratorial manner. "I yet believe my ring identifies me in some way and will lead me to my true mother."

Kate's rose scent went straight to his head. Edmund felt quite light-headed as he studied her ring. Etched entirely in heavy gold, the ring featured the stem of a rose wrapped around a crown. Only a small portion of the crown could be seen, as it was overlaid with the finely crafted rosebud. Edmund had never seen a design quite like it before or since.

" 'Tis a beautiful ring, and a rare design," he said. "It may very well aid you in your search. But are you not interested in finding your true father as well?"

"In all likelihood my mother was a poor underage girl with no knowledge of my father."

Bloody hell! Kate believed her mother to be a strumpet. There was a strong probability that she was correct. Still, as a gentleman, Edmund could not agree.

"Have you not thought your mother might be gentry. A woman mayhap, who'd been indiscreet?"

" 'Tis possible," Kate conceded.

"The odds are against you finding your true mother," Edmund pointed out gently. "England is a large country. You might have been born in a remote village."

She shook her head vehemently and argued passionately, "I shall find a way to travel the length and breadth of the land if I must. Somewhere there is a person who has seen and knows of this ring, or one similar. I shall begin with goldsmiths. I will visit every goldsmith in Britain if I must. My hope lies with this ring."

"If there is any way that I can help—"

"Thank you, Edmund. You have always treated me with kindness."

Any acts of kindness toward this beautiful young woman now might be misconstrued. "Kate, I am not the boy you remember," he warned.

"I shall never forget the pony you gave to me. Do you remember Star?"

"Do I remember? You were so excited your screams could be heard all the way to Hyde Park. Your face grew so red and round I thought you would explode. I worried how I would explain such a phenomenon to my mother."

Kate's laughter filled the secluded wood, a light pealing sound that caused Edmund to smile, to feel a warmth wash over him that he did not understand. For so long he had felt . . . untouched. His emotions always in check, confined behind a locked door waiting for release, waiting for someone with a key.

"I loved Star," Kate whispered, lost in her memories.

Her eyes sparkled like golden jewels. Edmund felt as if he were being drawn into them, diving into deep pools of hope and promise. His mouth went quite dry as he dragged away his gaze.

He lowered his eyes to her mouth and locked on

her lips, lips parted in a sweet, wistful sigh. Edmund's heart slammed against his chest, demanding he taste Kate's open, inviting lips.

"You, not me, own the kind heart," he murmured.

His voice was husky and soft as he gave in to temptation. Bending his head, Edmund leaned closer to Kate's upturned face, her remarkable eyes . . . until his mouth came down with a sudden urgency and covered hers.

Kate thought she would swoon on the spot. *Oh, hey-ho!*

Edmund's mouth smothered hers, warm and wet and delicious!

God save her!

While her mind spun, Kate's lips welcomed Edmund. A fierce heat rushed from her heart to her belly and to the tips of her fingers. So many emotions swirled through her, she could not savor all at once. Edmund was kissing her, causing her heart to skip and leap in a frightening, wondrous spine-tingling fashion. 'Twas her first kiss!

A kiss that could lead to naught.

Kate tasted and savored the salt of Edmund's lips, inhaled the sandalwood-and-leather scent of him, and touched the rough bristle of his cheek with her hand. Ripples of white-hot pleasure shot through her. Warm and trembling, her lips quivered beneath his. She feared she would dissolve in tears of happiness at any moment.

She knew she should stop him, but she could not. How could she stop a dream? She felt his hunger and was filled with an urgent desire to satisfy him.

And then she felt him draw away. "Kate . . ." His breath came in ragged gulps; the timbre of his voice sounded hoarse. "I . . . I don't know what came over me. Pray, forgive me."

Forgiveness was not at all necessary. She would like nothing more than for him to kiss her again. And again.

"Pretend this never happened," he pressed.

How in the world could she pretend such a heart-searing kiss had never happened? If Kate had a kingdom to give, she would gladly turn it over for another of his kisses.

Nevertheless, she nodded her compliance. He needn't know she would remember the taste of his kiss for as long as she lived.

"Aiye!" Kate shrieked.

"Kate, what is it?"

"Ants!"

Ants were everywhere. Absorbed in each other, Kate and Edmund hadn't noticed the quiet assault. The ants had attacked the bread, covered the cheese, and those with a failed sense of direction were marching up Kate's legs.

She jumped up, swatting her skirts, ignoring the fine show of ankles Edmund must be viewing. All she cared about at the moment was removing the silent army of ants from her person.

Edmund pushed himself up. From the corner of her eye, from the edge of Kate's hysteria, she saw the earl observing in silent fascination. She knew he was unable to help, for fear of touching an inappropriate part of Kate's anatomy.

"By your leave, Kate, is there anything I can do?"

Tears of humiliation burned behind her eyes. She bore a lump on her head larger than a goose egg, an unsightly black-and-blue eye that gave her a blurry view, and now . . . ants.

What type of impression had she made on her old friend?

"I should, should like to return to Rose Hall," she stammered.

An hour later Edmund made determined strides toward his steward's office in the west wing of Rose Hall. His steps echoed in the large marble hall, as did the *click click* of Percy, who trotted at his side.

Before she had been assaulted by the ants, Edmund had prepared to whisk Kate from his boyhood castle. He feared he might ravish her if they lingered, so powerful was the impact of their kiss.

The sweet, soft lips of his childhood friend had sent him into a tailspin. A rare heat had rushed through his veins like a firestorm until it lodged deep in his loins, simmering there . . . to this moment.

At the time he could think of only one way to rid her of the ants, and that was to rip off Kate's garments. Highly unsuitable, so he stood by helplessly, afraid to touch her.

On the ride back to Rose Hall, the heavens unleashed a torrent of rain, but he dared not stop and wait for the storm to abate. 'Twas in Kate's best interest to ride through the rain. He surely would have taken her right there on the sodden meadow, unmindful of the storm, of anything but his heat and her bruised beauty. Even a black eye could not diminish Kate's allure.

When Edmund and Kate arrived back at the stables, they were soaked to the skin and she appeared slightly dazed.

He prayed she would not take ill.

Bloody hell, he'd acted the fool.

He'd taken his leave of Kate with an abrupt fare-thee-well. And when her amber eyes dulled, Edmund had experienced a loathsome sinking in the pit of his stomach. What could he do but put distance between them immediately? 'Twas for her own good.

THREE

A great calm shall come over you and serve you well while the moon is in the seventh house.

Kate was torn. Irritable and confused. Other than that, she might have taken pleasure, as she normally did, in the half-mile walk from her papa's cottage to the main house. Ever since Lady Cordelia's gentlewoman had run away with a traveling jester, it had been Kate's habit to visit her in the afternoon.

The disturbing interlude with Edmund on the previous day still preyed on her mind. Kate could not imagine what had come over him. Although it was she who had asked to return to Rose Hall—overcome by a throbbing headache and a legion of ants—it had been Edmund who insisted they ride through the rain. He could not wait to be rid of her company.

Was it the kiss that put him off?

She was not experienced in the art and feared she had disappointed him. But Kate had not been disappointed. Not at all. The memory of Edmund's lips on hers still lingered. The initial shock, the heart-pounding thrill of his eagerness . . . or was it a fierce hunger? A demand? Whatever he'd had in mind at the start, Edmund's bruising kiss gave way to a soft and tender caress. And oh, how she'd savored the deep masculine heat of him that filled her being. She'd reveled in the warmth flowing through her veins, the sweet ache that settled between her thighs.

The wonder of Edmund's kiss made Kate lightheaded just to think of it!

But this is where she felt torn.

What gave Edmund the right to take such a liberty? Did he believe just because he was the Earl of Stamford that he could have his way with her? Did he think of Kate as simply some old possession of his that belonged, like the rose garden, with his country estate? 'Twas no way to treat an old friend. His high-handed arrogance appalled her!

To make matters worse, she'd made a fool of herself by abandoning herself to the moment. Instead of fighting off Edmund's improper advance, she had surrendered to the utter delight in his kiss. He might now be under the impression he could take such liberties with her whenever he chose. If he ever chose again.

By his hasty flight back to Rose Hall, she thought it highly unlikely.

Alas, Kate could not be dangling after Edmund. There could be no future for her with the Earl of Stamford.

She strolled the narrow rear path through tall, deep green boxwood hedges to the clearing where the maze began. Even from the rear approach, Rose Hall loomed as grand as any country estate in England. Its beauty struck her anew each day. Walls of windows, projecting bays and classical ornamentation enhanced the towering brick building. Four solid floors surrounded a courtyard of eglantine roses. She failed to understand why Edmund spent so little time here when he had loved his country home as a boy.

Kate entered by a side door and hurried through the cavernous main hall, larger by far than her papa's cozy thatch-roof cottage, to the low parlor chamber.

"Kate." Lady Cordelia greeted her on a feeble note.

"Good day, Lady Cordelia."

With a rabbit fur draped across her lap, Edmund's aunt lay supine on a daybed of loose purple velvet cushions. A fire burned in the massive fireplace.

"I burn with fever," she complained. "I think I have caught a chill."

If anyone had caught a chill, it would be Kate, riding in the rain yesterday with Edmund.

Kate placed the back of her hand over Lady Cordelia's brow. "Nay, you are not feverish. Mayhap the fire burns too bright?"

"Aye?"

"Aye."

"How fares your dear papa today?" Cordelia asked, in a tone eager to compare ills.

"I am happy to report he is at work in the north gardens."

John Beadle's heart had broken when her mama, Nell, died. Kate had begun to wonder if it would ever mend. Sometimes, when she thought of how very dearly her papa had loved the woman he'd lived with for over twenty-five years, Kate wondered if any man would love her as much. The planets were yet to promise her a love match.

" 'Tis heartening to hear someone is well, eh? The pain swells up in me and will not go away, no matter how much sack I swallow."

"I shall play my lute for you." Kate never played for long. Lady Cordelia usually fell fast asleep during the first melody.

Edmund's aunt had come from London to live at

Rose Hall upon the death of Oliver Wydville, her brother and Edmund's father. Kate long suspected it might be country life that did not agree with the long-suffering woman.

"Kate?"

"Aye?"

"Do you have a black eye?"

"Aye."

"How did you come by a black eye?"

"I . . . I walked into a low-hanging bough."

"Were you not looking?"

"My mind was elsewhere."

"Aye."

Miracle of all miracles, the old woman let it go. Kate could only think Lady Cordelia was eager to nap.

"Play something soothing, Kate."

She was.

With a sigh of relief, Kate took up the lute. At least she did not have to explain the lump on her head. Lady Cordelia's failing eyesight kept her ignorant of small things such as dust, mites, and lumps.

Kate knew the music so well she did not even have to think about the notes or strings. Her fingers struck the notes as if they had a mind of their own. "Rose, rose, rose red, will I ever see you wed?"

Lady Cordelia had just begun to snore when the door burst open.

Startled, Kate strummed an off chord.

Lady Cordelia bolted upright.

It was Edmund. His towering form filled the doorway; his raw energy charged the room. Even the wall painting, a ribald hunting scene, seemed to come alive.

"Good day, ladies." He inclined his head slightly before casting a wide, heart-stopping grin.

"By your leave, Edmund, you gave me a fright!"

Lady Cordelia exclaimed, patting her straw-colored curls as if they might be in danger of falling out.

"I do apologize Aunt Cordelia. But I have hit upon a famous scheme and could not wait to speak with you."

"Impatient as ever," she mumbled.

The corner of his eyes crinkled in a most appealing manner as he turned his riveting smile on Kate alone. He seemed not at all put off by her black eye. And she had no defense for Edmund's smile. Delicious warm waves of pleasure skipped down her spine.

Lady Cordelia reached for her silver goblet of sack. "Pray, do not keep us in suspense, eh? What is thy famous scheme?"

"My work here is concluded and I must return to London to be on hand when Parliament resumes."

"Go on," the old woman urged.

"You and Kate must accompany me."

Lady Cordelia's arm froze in midair; her goblet of sack halted midway to her lips. She blinked rapidly as if the room had suddenly gone dark.

For Kate's part, she was certain she had not heard correctly. She tilted her head. "Me?"

Edmund nodded eagerly as he approached her in his odd, loping gait. "Aye, Kate. Until you have secured a position as nurse, I am proposing you come to London as Aunt Cordelia's gentlewoman."

"But I am not gentry born," she protested. "I cannot hold such a position."

Clearly dubious, he hiked a dark brow. "You cannot be certain. You may well be gentry born, Kate."

"What makes you think I wish to go to London, Edmund?" Lady Cordelia's parchment-paper brow folded in a bewildered frown as she set down her goblet.

"My dear aunt, I shall feel very much better if you consult the finest physicians . . . who can only be found in London."

After but a moment's thought, Cordelia heaved a weary sigh that shook her abundant bosom. " 'Tis true, healing care is lacking in the country. Everyone knows it to be so."

"You are at a country surgeon's mercy by remaining at Rose Hall, Aunt Cordelia," Edmund intoned gravely.

"Mayhap a truly knowledgeable physician could cure my rheumatism and give me a remedy to ease these bilious attacks that continue to plague me."

Kate feared 'twas the constant stream of sack that plagued Lady Cordelia but dared not say as much. Besides, her own head spun with Edmund's proposal.

London? Kate had never been to London. The city offered many goldsmiths. Perhaps the one goldsmith who knew the origin of her ring plied his craft in London.

But the thought of living under the same roof with Edmund caused her pulse to pound. 'Twould be dangerous.

"What say you, Kate? We will reward you well to serve as you already do from the goodness of your heart. You shall officially become Aunt Cordelia's gentlewoman."

"I . . . I do not know . . ." Kate's voice trailed off in confusion. How could he demand such a hurried decision? There was much to consider. What to do? What to do? She must consult her stargazer at once.

"You hesitate. Do you find my dear aunt much too trying?" Edmund asked with a rakish wink.

Kate's heart fluttered.

Lady Cordelia cried out in protest. "I am not the

least bit trying. But do I not have any say in this matter?"

"Of course, Aunt. What say you?"

"I . . . I should like Kate to be my gentlewoman."

"I thought as much." Edmund turned his broad grin on Kate. 'Twas a dazzling grin that immobilized her mind. "Kate?"

"I, I . . ." Her voice trailed off. She could not think.

Edmund's great charm was not his only means of persuasion. "If you are residing in London, it may help with the business we discussed at our last meeting," he noted.

"What business?" the older woman asked, slicing a questioning glance at Kate, who quickly lowered her eyes.

Cordelia Wydville had never been bashful in taking an interest in the affairs of others. The country not only lacked physicians, it lacked titillating gossip as well.

When Kate raised her eyes, she found Edmund's gaze challenging her. "Kate expressed the desire to visit a London goldsmith, did you not?"

"Aaaaayyye." He was quite influential, in a thoroughly male way.

"This may be the opportunity you have been seeking. 'Tis also the opportunity to help my aunt . . . and me," he pressed.

Kate's heart beat far faster than it had ever done before. A bubbling excitement curled through her, spiraling from the caul at her crown straight down to her toes.

"You have suggested a most interesting proposition," she allowed, calmly and quietly, while a jumble of mixed emotions whirled within her. How could she be expected to come to such a complicated decision by herself? "Before I can give you an answer, I must talk with Papa."

And consult the planets.

A veil of cold damp mist clouded the late-afternoon air as Edmund escorted Kate back to her papa's thatch-roof cottage.

With nothing urgent to occupy his time, other than his bowling and tennis matches, which were of import to him, Edmund had resolved to rescue his childhood friend from an uncertain serving life as a nurse. He knew the liberties taken by unscrupulous employers. To think of Kate unwillingly seduced by a noble rogue bent on a dalliance beneath the staircase set his teeth on edge.

And why should she labor in any home but her own? Edmund had no doubt Kate's beauty and intellect would win the heart of a wealthy merchant in less than a fortnight.

As they strolled the gravel path of defining hedgerows, sheltering oaks, and beeches, he meant to convince Kate of the wisdom of his plan.

"Only think of the people you will meet, Kate. And the goldsmiths whom you shall be in a position to question."

Her softly arched brows knitted in a troubled frown. "I don't know—"

"I understand my aunt can be tiresome at times, but if you weigh the advantages of spending time in London against one unfavorable—"

"Lady Cordelia is not tiresome," Kate interrupted. "She is lonely."

"I can assure you, my aunt shall not be lonely in London. As a matter of fact, I expect you will have more time to yourself as Cordelia flits from physician to surgeon to apothecary."

Kate looked up at him. Her tawny-gold eyes danced with laughter; her bright smile chased the afternoon chill, made his steps feel light and uplifting.

Edmund's gaze focused on her lips. The cool, damp air had deepened the color of her lips from an innocent pale rose shade to a sultry scarlet.

Momentarily distracted from his mission, Edmund recalled how her lips had felt beneath his the day before, soft and pliant, warm and . . . welcoming. He had tasted her, seeking to satisfy an urge, a curiosity. Now he found himself needing to savor the tangy cinnamon flavor of her just one more time.

He felt a tightening in his gut.

Her cheeks glowed crimson. The corners of her mouth turned up in a soft smile.

A smoldering heat curled through him.

Bloody hell! Why did his body react so strongly to Kate? Had he acquired some country malady?

"Have I said something to amuse you?" he asked, more gruffly than he'd intended.

Kate did not appear fazed by his tone. She continued to regard him steadily, with her knowing smile. "No, not at all."

"Why do you regard me in that manner?"

"What manner?"

"As if you know something I do not?"

She laughed then, a light, echoing peal of merriment that sent fiery sparks shooting through Edmund's body. "Perhaps," she admitted. "I was remembering the impatient boy I used to know and realized he'd grown into an impatient man."

She had the temerity to laugh again.

Edmund stiffened. No one addressed the Earl of

Stamford in such a manner. Except Kate. But that was before she knew what was expected of young ladies. Since then, she had supposedly studied under fine scholars and mavens of protocol at the Italian convent. She should know when to hold her tongue.

Unfortunately, however, she was right. Edmund had not learned patience in all these years. He demanded an answer immediately. And he only wished to hear one reply. Kate must come to London as Aunt Cordelia's gentlewoman.

"Edmund, I did not mean to wound you. Forgive me. Impatience is the mark of an intelligent man. What's more, I am certain your aunt has friends in London as well as physicians."

"To be sure. Aunt Cordelia and Lady Mason will fall in together at once to compare ills. There is also my sister, Jane, to commiserate with her." He stopped in midstep.

Kate continued to smile in that disconcerting manner.

Strands of sun-brushed curls had come loose, framing her face and teasing the shoulders of her dark blue cloak. Edmund experienced a sudden and extraordinary longing to free the rest of her golden mass and weave his fingertips through the silky locks.

Bloody . . . What sort of milk-livered man was he? Once again he'd allowed Kate to divert him from his undertaking. Obviously, he must avoid looking at her. To that end, Edmund strode off at a rather brisk pace with his eyes straightforward, locked on the smoke rising from the gardener's chimney. When it became apparent she intended to continue strolling, he slowed.

"My aunt shall be pleased to introduce you to everyone she knows," Edmund coaxed, renewing his effort. His gaze fixed upon the smoke. "Aunt Cordelia and I are acquainted with a good many people, aristocrats and gentry alike. One of our acquaintances may have seen a ring similar to yours, or will recognize its crest and rose."

Kate lightly kicked a pebble in her path. "You make it difficult to say nay."

"Then you must agree." The tightening of his chest seemed less. Although they were fast approaching her father's cottage, and his time to persuade her was running out, Kate appeared to be bending his way. "If you say aye, I shall be forever in your debt."

"Prithee Edmund, allow me time to consider such a change in my plans . . . and to gain my papa's counsel."

"Mayhap by the morrow you will have come to a decision?" he pressed. "I must know before I return to London."

Kate gave a fretful puff that Edmund found endearing. "A maiden woman living in the house of a bachelor?" she mused.

"I promise you, as my aunt's companion your reputation shall not be tainted."

"Are you certain?"

"Absolutely."

"And our presence, Lady Cordelia's and mine, will not put a damper on your . . . on any romantic liaisons you might have?"

Taken off guard by her question, Edmund's breathing slammed to a stop. After clearing his throat and gathering his wits, he took a deep breath and replied stoically, "Not at all. There is no romance in my life."

"By your leave, should you not be thinking of marriage soon?"

"You take great liberties with our old friendship to ask the question," he replied stiffly.

"But you must have an heir," she stated simply.

"You begin to sound like Aunt Cordelia. Aye, I shall do my duty and provide an heir. Lady Judith Witherspoon has great hopes that I will offer for her before the summer is out. And I may."

"Are you . . . in love . . . with Lady Judith?"

Kate's voice sounded faint and far away. Edmund looked down to make sure the gardener's daughter still walked by his side. She had paled considerably. "No, Kate. I shall never marry for love."

"Prithee, why not?"

"A man who loves becomes as weak as a house of cards."

"Nay, I believe love makes one stronger."

Only a woman could think that.

Edmund sighed. He had no true reason to put her off. 'Twas clear Kate retained the quick and curious mind she had possessed as a child. She would discover answers to her questions one way or another. Nor did he have any reason not to trust her. She inspired his confidence. Edmund felt quite certain that he might share his thoughts and plans with her as openly as he had in the past.

"Kate, I was wounded when the Spanish attacked Cornwall. I was one of the casualties at Mousehole."

She gasped. "Edmund!"

He'd been shot in the foot by one of his own men, wounded by a flintlock musket. It was a most inglorious war injury. When he spoke of it, however, he lowered his voice and made the wound sound mysterious and deadly. His considerable pride would not allow him to confess he'd been shot in the foot. Even to Kate.

"A slight misstep is not such a horrible price to pay when I think of my fallen comrades."

"Oh, my, no!"

"I took up residence at Stamford House in London with my father and brother. Fearing I might be crippled for life, I was determined to recover in the hands of only the finest physicians—those residing in London."

"It must have been a difficult time for you," Kate offered, an angel's compassion reflected in the mist of her extraordinary eyes.

Edmund turned away, renewing his resolve *not* to look at her.

The healing period had been difficult. But following his recovery, Edmund adopted the life of a wild young aristocrat. He became a first-class rake. In no time, he became one of the most popular young men about town, carousing and sporting with other young aristocrats his age, like Christopher Carew, the Viscount of Lavingham, and Robin Wells, Earl of Cheltham.

Stopping just short of scandalous behavior, Edmund took up gambling, games, alcohol, and the company of the fair sex. A courtesan named Minnie had been his favorite.

"There were days when I despaired," he answered Kate honestly. The memories of late mornings when he awoke with terrible headaches and stomach upset were still painful.

"How long was it before you recovered?"

"Several months. But still I walk with a lopsided gait as you can readily witness."

" 'Tis hardly noticeable."

"During those months I became acquainted with my father. He'd removed from Rose Hall to the city with Reggie when I was just a boy, long before you would have memory of him in residence at Rose Hall. He only returned to the country for holidays."

"I used to see him walking in the gardens."

"My father kept to himself. My mother made life at Rose Hall unbearable for him."

"I did not realize." Kate laid a gentle hand on his arm. "I am so sorry."

Edmund felt her touch clear through his shirtsleeve. A tingling warmth traveled slowly up the length of his arm to the nape of his neck and slid like fire down his spine, warming him through and through.

"Do not be sorry for me. 'Twas my father who suffered."

One evening, in the drawing room of his London town house, after several tumblers of claret, Oliver Wydville, the Earl of Stamford, felt it incumbent to warn his son. In his cups, he confessed that he had married Edmund's mother, the cool and beautiful Margaret Grayson, because he loved the lady to distraction. 'Twas a love match.

Oliver pampered and spoiled Margaret, and before he realized what he'd done, he had created a shrew. A fetching shrew to be sure.

The earl admitted morosely that he became little more than his wife's chattel. She viewed him as a weakling for so willingly doing her bidding, and rarely bothered to hide her contempt. He had been completely emasculated by love.

" 'Tis not easy for a boy to grow up without his father. I did not understand at the time how you must have suffered," Kate said, peering up at Edmund beneath her long, dark lashes.

"Suffered is putting it a bit . . . too strong," he replied. "I was not old enough at the time for my father to take me along to London."

"But not Reggie."

"No, Reggie was his heir, and five years older than I. Father feared my mother's influence might damage Reggie irrevocably."

"What a sad affair!"

And there was more to the story he could not tell the innocent Kate.

Oliver Wydville brought his spinster sister Cordelia to Stamford House. She ruled the household and acted as hostess when social obligations demanded a woman's presence. In order to make up for the female companionship his wife had deprived him of, Oliver took several mistresses over the course of time.

"Forgive me if I am being too forward," Kate said, interrupting Edmund's dismal musings. "But what . . . what happened to your mother?"

Kate *was* being too forward, but that had never stopped her questions in the past.

"While I fought the losing battle with the Spaniards in Mousehole, my mother left England to live with her sister in the Americas."

When the news of her husband's mistresses reached Margaret Wydville, she was beyond humiliation. She packed as many belongings—Rose Hall's most precious items—as could be shipped to her new home.

"Does she communicate with you?" Kate asked softly.

"She writes occasionally."

His father warned Edmund never to marry for love. He declared time and again to his sons that a more casual arrangement, like those he kept with his mistresses, brought a man true happiness.

" 'Tis a sad affair," Kate repeated woefully. "But I am certain your mother misses you."

Edmund was not certain his mother thought of him at all.

The sad affair became grimmer still. His aunt frequently relived the drama that brought her back to Rose Hall, so he felt confident that Kate had heard the story.

Shortly after the earl bared his soul to Edmund, another tragedy struck. Reggie was killed in a duel.

His headstrong brother had ignored their father's admonition not to fall in love. Worse, he became embroiled with a woman whose husband took exception to Reggie's attentions.

Not long following his eldest son's death, Oliver Wydville's heart gave out. He died, leaving Edmund as his heir and the new Earl of Stamford.

The Earl of Stamford, a position Edmund never expected nor wished for.

While perfectly willing to fulfill his duty by marrying and producing an heir, Edmund meant to avoid love at all costs. He knew only too well what a dangerous emotion love could be. He'd vowed never to make the mistakes of his brother and father. As last of the line, he could ill afford to be doomed by love.

"Edmund, we are here."

"So soon?" He looked up from the contemplation of the path.

The gardener's cottage lay directly before them. Instead of winning an answer from the beauty by his side, Edmund had been woolgathering.

When he turned to Kate, he found her gazing up at him. Smiling. Captivating. She made him feel as if he were the only man on earth, that she would be looking only at him even if a regiment of handsome, broad-shouldered soldiers passed them by.

"I thank you for walking me home, Edmund."

"Promise me you will consider all that we have discussed?"

Her expression became serious, sweetly serious, as she twisted the ring on her finger from side to side in an absentminded fashion. "Aye, Edmund. I shall consider all."

"And you will say aye?" he coaxed.

"Must you have your answer on the morrow? I should like more time—"

"I must return to London. My business is finished . . . except for the poaching. Nasty business. Trumble has suggested mantraps."

"No!"

"Aye. His solution seems an excessive measure to me."

"Open your preserves, Edmund. Give the tenants and villagers a month, perhaps two, to hunt each year. They will have no need to poach, then. As it is, they are hungry men, and poach only to feed their families."

"I shall think on it." Kate had offered an interesting solution, one that in all likelihood would not have occurred to him.

"Are you humoring me?" she asked.

"Are you coming to London?"

"I cannot promise. 'Tis a decision I cannot make lightly."

"I shall only hope, then." Without thinking, Edmund made a slight bow, as he would to any lady. "I will take my leave now. Give my regards to your good father."

Kate bent her knee. "Good day, Lord Stamford. you shall have my answer as soon as I know it."

He tipped his head, offering his most winning smile,

and departed. He whistled all the way back to Rose Hall.

She must agree, for he would not take nay for an answer.

Edmund meant to find Kate a husband.

FOUR

The new moon promises harmony

Edmund had chosen a bride! How horrid the thought!

'Twas inevitable, but difficult to contemplate. Who could love him as well as Kate?

Edmund had asked her to come to London! How wondrous!

'Twas impossible, but truly tempting.

Kate could not make a decision of such import without first consulting her astrologer, Jutta.

The moment Edmund strode out of sight, whistling a merry but unrecognizable tune, she hurried into town. Her mind was awhirl, her thoughts scattered like a deck of playing cards caught in the wind. She could not latch on to even one for more than a moment.

Worse, her emotions fluctuated between a dispiriting sadness and light-minded excitement. When at last Kate reached the village, she was in a rare state of turmoil.

Jutta, the baker's wife, lived above her husband's shop, where she interpreted the position of the planets for the curious. Loyal patrons, like Kate, customarily purchased a loaf of cheat bread from the stargazer's husband before they departed.

A mass of untamed coarse, wren-brown hair mushroomed from her head. Otherwise, the middle-aged astrologer's only notable feature was her receding chin, which sloped into her neck at a rather startling angle.

In the normal course of events, Jutta charted the constellations and counseled Kate once a week. Kate always knew how the alignment of the planets would affect her health and fate.

But nothing had been normal since Edmund's return to Rose Hall. Kate had no choice but to pay a second visit to Jutta.

"London, Jutta! The Earl of Stamford has asked me to travel to London as his aunt's gentlewoman. Why did the stars not reveal this course beforehand?"

"I know not."

"What say they? Do I go or stay?"

But Jutta behaved as if she had not heard the question. The stargazer regarded Kate with mouth agape.

"Your eye is black."

"I walked into a low-hanging bough."

"Aye?" The stargazer hiked a sparse brow.

"Do you see a journey for me in the stars, Jutta?"

Jutta looked down at the parchment chart that lay between them on the crude wooden table. "Your sign is Cancer, a family sign."

"My family is here." At least the family Kate knew.

"But you are a moon child, vulnerable to the changing phases."

"Are you saying I am meant to travel to London? Change is predicted?"

"You shall see the way by the light of this eve's moon."

"No more? They say no more?"

"Your sign rules here." Jutta rubbed her belly. "If

you do not take regular meals there will be a disturbance."

Kate felt the disturbance as she headed for home deep in disappointment. A mass of butterflies frolicked in the pit of her stomach.

Kate begged her papa's forbearance and retired early to her small room. But when darkness fell the moon was shrouded by clouds. She spent a ragged night, alternately tossing and turning on her small feather bed, and then staring from her window to wish on any number of stars. Stars hidden in the hazy mist. Kate wished the same over and over: that she might make the correct decision. Jutta had been no help, and nothing was forecast in the midnight sky. Kate was left to weigh the wisdom of such a great change by herself through the long, quiet hours.

The hope of a London goldsmith identifying her ring filled her with an edgy excitement, a prickly anticipation. To discover her true identity would be the answer to her prayers.

Alas, the rub: to live beneath the same roof in London as Edmund. Kate feared the folly of such an arrangement. Instead of becoming closer to him, she should distance herself from the earl's simmering virility and spellbinding eyes.

Still, when might she have another opportunity to search London for her natural mother? The moon gave her no sign, the stars did not shine, and the stargazer's chart remained unclear.

By dawn's light Kate had not yet made up her mind.

She sought her papa's advice. Soon after dressing for the day, Kate carried a ripe red apple, a chunk of cheese, and jug of water to the south garden where John Beadle worked.

The finest gardener south of Newcastle, he looked

more like a member of the gentry than a gardener, even when down in the dirt readying the spring soil. His complexion had long ago been darkened and leathered by the sun, and his dark hair had been sprinkled with gray. Kate loved his forthright hazel eyes and his calm, quiet dignity.

Calm and dignity that she did not possess. Ever since she could remember, Kate felt a restlessness, a constant churning deep inside her. She did not understand its cause or know its cure, but she felt sure it had to do with the past.

Although dissimilar in temperament, John's patience worked in good stead with Kate. By example, he had instilled in her a love of gardening and given her an unequaled knowledge of rose gardening. From John Beadle she had learned strong, firm values. She'd been more fortunate in the parents who took her into their home and hearts than Edmund had been with his natural mother and father.

Her papa had lost a great deal of weight following her mother's death. He appeared thin and wan. Kate worried about him, wondered if she should even ask his advice. But then, her dilemma might take his mind off his sorrow, if only for a little time.

"Good day, Papa."

"Kate." He looked up, surprise mixed with pleasure in his ready smile. "What brings ye here, me girl?"

"I brought you refreshment, so that you might take a rest."

He waved her away, his attention returning to the soil. "No need to worry over me. 'Tis better to work."

"Papa, I miss her, too."

He continued to stare at the dirt. "I know ye do. How is your eye today?"

"As you can see, the normal color is almost restored." And the lump on her head, which he could not see and did not know of, had lessened in size as well.

Kate hunkered down to his level, squatting on her heels. "Papa, you know that I have been keeping Lady Cordelia company in the afternoons."

"Aye."

"Lord Stamford has asked me if I would accompany Lady Cordelia to London as her gentlewoman. It would only be until I gained a position as nurse, and I would be well compensated for my time."

He looked up at her, plainly perplexed, if the scowling bunch of his brow was any indication. "Would ye like to be Lady Cordelia's constant companion? She does go on with an endless list of complaints."

"Aye, the lady's ailments are numerous," Kate agreed. "But I am accustomed to her, and she is good to me. I am thinking that living in London might offer me opportunities not available in the village . . . like the theater."

"And Edmund?"

"Oh, no, Papa!"

"I've seen the look in ye eye the last few days, me girl."

"Edmund and I have always been the best of friends."

"But he is the Earl of Stamford now. And ye are just . . ." His voice trailed off. Averting his gaze to the garden wall, he pressed his lips tightly together.

"Papa?"

He turned back to Kate. His words came slowly. "Ye are me girl. Ye cannot be friends with the man in the same way ye were friends with the boy."

Stung by the truth stated aloud and plainly, Kate

tilted her chin. "I am fully aware of our differences, Papa."

"As I am certain the earl is. Ye have grown to be a beautiful young woman, me girl."

"Edmund and I used to play together. We forged a bond that has nothing to do with . . . your meaning."

"Aye? Kate, do not be naive."

"I am not."

"Ye are the gardener's daughter. The earl may think he owns ye, like one of his hounds or horses." Her papa's tone was ominous. " 'Tis the way of the world."

"No! Do not even suggest that Edmund would take advantage of me, Papa."

"Lord Stamford to ye, me girl."

The implication that Edmund would use her unjustly wounded Kate. Her papa's suggestion echoed her own suspicions, which Edmund's kiss had elicited.

"Ye would not be the first young girl lured to ruin by a member of nobility."

"Papa! We are speaking of Ed—Lord Stamford. He has only been good and kind to me since I was a child."

"Ye are not a child any longer, and he is a man," her papa pronounced in a dire tone. He emphasized the word "man," making it sound as if Edmund were a monster to be feared.

"Do you not remember the pony he gave me?"

John Beadle's dark, heavily lined face folded. His voice rumbled in a threatening tone Kate had never heard before. "Has Lord Stamford offered ye gifts?"

"No!" Increasingly uncomfortable, Kate decided to change the direction of the discussion. "There will be opportunities in London for me to make inquiries about my ring."

"We were warned not to make inquiries."

"You and Mama vowed not to make inquiries. I did not."

"No good can come of questions," he insisted.

"No good ever comes of ignorance either, Papa." She smiled then, reaching out to take his gloved hand. "Did the wisewoman have such magic that she plucked me as a babe from the air?"

"Ye know she did not," he replied, his voice weary.

Paying no mind to her dress, Kate fell to her knees beside him. "I do not like to leave you, but we could use an extra shilling or two, could we not?"

Her papa was silent for a long moment, long enough for an exceedingly tight knot to lodge in Kate's throat. "I have been thinking of going to me sister," he said at last. "Letty has invited me to come live with her in Nottingham."

Kate reacted to the news as she would a blow. She swallowed air before replying in a hushed tone, "I did not know."

"Aye, I was waiting for ye to obtain a position before I made firm plans." Love, clear and bright as precious stone, shone in his eyes as his gaze met hers. "Ah, me girl, what a fine nurse ye will make."

She took his hand again. "Only because of the many sacrifices you made. There were no other gardener's daughters who had been sent to Italy to study at the convent school. You gave me a fine education."

"That's not quite the way of it," he said, giving her a doleful smile. "The wisewoman left funds for ye. We were told we must educate ye, even though ye were a girl child."

"I have been blessed."

"Mama and I were blessed to have ye," he confessed, lowering his eyes, but not before she saw the tears glimmering in them.

Kate kissed his cheek. "I will always love you, Papa."

With his gaze still fixed on the ground, John Beadle nodded his head.

Understanding her papa's discomfort with such mawkish talk, Kate changed the subject abruptly. "What would you do at Aunt Letty's?" she asked softly.

"I might find work at an estate in the shire or take odd jobs."

"Ah, you have given thought to this move, then."

"Aye. Will Richards could take over as head gardener here at Rose Hall. He's a good man."

"Indeed."

Whatever Kate was about to say next was forgotten as soon as she heard the bark. She looked up, and for the second time in a matter of days saw the wild beast called Percy bounding toward her.

This time the devil canine did not appear to be chasing quarry. He ran toward Kate with seeming purpose.

Oh, fie!

She stared, transfixed. Numb from her nose to her knees, she could not even feel her heart beating—until Edmund's hound was upon her. Wildly unpredictable of late, Kate's heart lurched into a new tempo, too rapid to count.

The animal made a flying leap. His giant paws found their way squarely to Kate's shoulders, knocking her to the ground.

She fell with a thump as John Beadle jumped up, too late to intervene.

Before she could stop him, Percy licked her face with his rough, drooly wet tongue. It would only be a matter of time before the beast opened his mouth and began to chew on her. Kate's attempts to push the slobbering hound away were to no avail.

"Stay calm, me girl. I'll pull the wretched cur off of ye."

"Let me help."

Upon hearing Edmund's voice, Percy backed off.

Splayed on the ground, Kate winced. The bump on her head throbbed anew. Her heart still raced. She dared not move.

"Percy, stay."

At last. Kate released her breath. Her lungs ached. She'd begun to turn blue.

"Ye fine bloodhound surprised us, Lord Stamford," John Beadle explained. " 'Tis a frisky animal."

Edmund chuckled. "After only one meeting, Percy has become exceedingly fond of your daughter, John."

The grinning earl extended a hand to help Kate up. Once again, she was covered with dirt.

His eyes twinkled as she bristled.

"Is that what you think?" she demanded, brushing the dirt from her dress. "He likes me?"

"Calm yerself, me girl," John Beadle urged. "It's Lord Stamford ye're talking to."

From his stance, he could not see Kate roll her eyes.

But Edmund could. He appeared more amused than affronted, however, continuing to grin at Kate in a most maddening manner. Discomfited, she averted her gaze. She wiggled her nose to dislodge a particle of wayward soil from its tip. When next Kate looked, the earl still grinned.

Perhaps her papa was right. Lord Stamford had chosen to amuse himself with her. Vexed anew at the disturbing thought, she huffed her displeasure.

"Percy does not go around kissing all the girls, I assure you."

"I do not welcome his affections, my lord." Kate spun on her heel and marched toward the refuge of the Beadles' cottage.

Edmund matched her step. "My apologies once more. By your leave, I shall do better at keeping Percy at bay."

"As you will."

"I have come for your decision, Mistress Kate."

Kate stopped in her tracks. In a whirl of bombazine skirts she confronted the persistent earl. "Will your ill-mannered, flea-bitten hound be living with you in London?"

"Nay." Edmund shook his head slowly. His glorious green eyes twinkled mischievously as he gave Kate a roguish wink and grin. "Not if you are."

FIVE

Nothing shall impede your progress

The journey to London by coach proved so jarring that two days later Kate's bones still rattled. Lady Cordelia required copious amounts of sack to restore her tranquillity and quiet her querulous claims of broken limbs.

Rather than rush straightaway to the goldsmiths of London, as she was wont to do, Kate found herself stroking her lady's temples and playing soothing melodies on the lute. From first light to dusk she assured Edmund's agitated aunt that no one had ever died from the strain of travel between the East Midlands and London.

Kate's growing impatience to go about her business caused a constant tightness in her belly and a frequent clenching of teeth.

Another pressing matter deepened her distress. Edmund, who had either been attending Parliament or playing wind ball since their arrival, had planned an evening's entertainment for the family.

Kate waffled. She thought to plead illness in order to avoid the gathering. While she would enjoy the musicians, Kate did not anticipate renewing her acquaintance with Edmund's sister, Jane. The lady had been rude to her in the past. She could not expect a warm welcome now, 'twould be out of character.

But the opportunity to see Edmund—especially after another long day spent in Lady Cordelia's company—won out. Kate missed her old friend's company, though she knew it was just as well the earl distanced himself from her. Without the influence of his boyish charm, his arresting jade eyes, his warming grin and compelling figure, she yet might rid herself of her schoolgirl yearnings. In time, she might banish the sweet tingle that skipped down her spine whenever she thought of him.

She must. Edmund and Kate could never be more than friends.

Aye, and she could ill afford to be distracted from her mission. She must solve the mystery of her birth. Using her ring as a key in this city occupied by a multitude of goldsmiths, Kate held hope of finding her natural mother.

Further, rejecting her papa's suggestion, Kate wished to believe Edmund had only the most noble intentions toward her. After all, he soon would ask for Lady Judith's hand in marriage.

Edmund's kindnesses to Kate were simple ones. True to his word, he had left his beloved hound behind at Rose Hall in the care of Joseph Trumbull. Knowing how the earl cared for Percy and how aggrieved he would feel without the drooling beast at his side, she was excessively grateful for what amounted to a sacrifice of some import on Edmund's part.

More than a week before Lady Cordelia and Kate departed Rose Hall, Lord Stamford had traveled ahead to London. He bid them a fare-thee-well, explaining that before Parliament was seated he meant to oversee the preparations for their arrival at his town house.

Stamford House was an imposing structure located on the fashionable Strand. Edmund's London home boasted mullioned windows, wainscot paneling, waxed and polished oak floors.

Sculpted friezes depicting the tales of mythical Greek gods adorned each chamber. The furnishings were sparse but innovative, including daybeds carved with the Stamford arms. Ornamental wall coverings of maps and richly embroidered tapestries reflected the wealth and interests of the Stamford men who had made this house their home.

Owing to the lack of floor rushes, strowing herbs of hyssop and meadowsweet filled a multitude of baskets placed in every chamber. While Aunt Cordelia was in residence, Edmund was determined to overpower any malodorous city scents that might waft through open windows. He did not desire the blame for any new malady his aunt contracted.

Edmund waited for Kate and Aunt Cordelia in the private dining parlor. He'd quickly taken up the latest departure of dining separately from the servants, and was quite pleased with the smaller chamber.

He rubbed the back of his neck, although nothing ached or itched. 'Twas his nerves unraveling. Edmund had never attempted matchmaking, known by all to be women's work. He excelled in sport, as a man should. He defied custom for Kate.

If his efforts succeeded, Kate would be none the wiser and happily settled with an adoring husband before summer's end.

"Edmund!"

His sister's voice reminded him that he did not wait alone. Jane and her husband, Alexander Bowers, the Viscount of Chumley, had arrived, as well as the guest of honor, Richard Digby, the noted family limner. After greeting them, he'd left the threesome in conversation while he watched the door for Aunt Cordelia and Kate.

Jane sidled up to him. " 'Tis been ever so long since you have invited the viscount and me to dinner."

"And I regret my oversight."

"It seems you favor the shades of wine and gold. I should have chosen marigold for the draperies rather than wine velvet."

Edmund did not spend a great deal of time with his sister for good reason. Her critical tongue annoyed him. She noticed every detail and remarked on each.

"I shall consult with you in the future," Edmund replied with a forced smile.

Up until now he'd been pleased with the appearance of his home. Edmund had been under the impression that he'd accomplished pleasant surroundings with little time or interest beyond making Stamford House a welcoming respite for his sporting companions.

"You would be wise." Slanting him a satisfied smile, Jane tipped her head.

"A wise man am I," he jested.

Jane possessed piercing green eyes and little sense of humor. "I do hope you did not find Rose Hall in disrepair," she said.

"Rose Hall flourishes," Edmund reported without hesitation. Which was not quite the truth.

In his diligent pursuit of good sport, Edmund had neglected his properties. He thrived on winning whatever game he played, be it billiards, tennis, archery, or bowling.

As a boy Edmund had been alone and overlooked. By excelling in sport, he'd become a man of consequence whose ability was applauded and whose company was sought after by many. He desired nothing less than the admiration of all he met.

Except, mayhap, Jane.

Seeking escape from his sister's disapproval, Edmund looked to where Jane's bird-watching husband, Viscount Chumley, conversed with Richard Digby.

He wondered what they discussed, willow tit and mistle thrush?

"What is keeping Aunt Cordelia?" Jane asked, her tone decidedly petulant.

"Our aunt suffered from the journey. She is rather weak."

"Pray pardon, but Aunt Cordelia has never been weak a day in her life."

At that, Aunt Cordelia, resting heavily on Kate's arm, appeared in the doorway. "I have come to dinner," she announced with a blink and a smile.

Suppressing a grin, Edmund's gaze flickered to Kate, who also suppressed a smile, if he weren't mistaken. The twitch of her lips gave her away.

Wearing the simply styled gown of a merchant-class woman, Kate's overdress of peach sarcenet with its snug bodice and slim sleeves flattered her tall, graceful figure. The soft shade of her gown heightened her roses-and-cream complexion. With every movement, her underskirt of ivory silk rustled gently like the song of a siren.

Kate's natural beauty captivated. She required no ruff, farthingale, or ropes of pearls to capture a man's eye.

From across the room, her wide-eyed gaze met his, causing his heart to bolt. 'Twas as if he'd been thumped by a tilting lance during a jousting contest, though he seldom took part in the tournaments any longer. He considered them old and tired competitions.

Was that promise gleaming in the deep amber pools of Kate's eyes? Nay, not for him. There could be no promise of anything between the Earl of Stamford and the gardener's daughter.

With great effort, he dragged his gaze away, turning to his sister, who jostled him as she sailed toward their ever-suffering relative.

Jane had reached her full height at the age of fourteen, and she'd had the misfortune to have doubled in weight since the birth of her daughter, Frances. As a consequence, she moved more like a wherry than a sleek seagoing vessel.

"My dear aunt, it gladdens my heart to see you," she fawned.

" 'Tis been too long, dear Jane, eh?"

Cordelia shifted half her weight from Kate to Jane, allowing both women to escort her to the table.

Edmund quickly stepped up to assist. "Do you remember Kate, Sister?"

"Kate?" Jane regarded Kate with a tilt of her head and a blank stare. "I do not believe so."

"By your leave, allow me to make introductions, as Mistress Kate Beadle is serving as Aunt Cordelia's gentlewoman."

Jane's eyes narrowed ever so slightly as she leaned across her aunt to examine Kate. She applied the same sharp scrutiny she might to a strand of pearls she considered acquiring.

"Kate Beadle." Jane said the name slowly, as if searching her memory. "Surely you are not the gardener's daughter?"

"Aye, Lady Chumley. I am the gardener's daughter."

Edmund's throat went dry. Every muscle in his body tightened. Dismissing his tension as natural with a new game, in this instance matchmaking, Edmund made fast work of finishing the introductions.

As they made for the table, Jane drew him aside. Her dark, highly arched brows gathered in a menacing frown. "Could you find no other suitable to serve as Aunt Cordelia's gentlewoman?" she hissed beneath her breath.

"Kate *is* suitable," Edmund informed his sister softly. He did not wish to make a scene in front of Digby and hurt Kate's chances with the man. "She has earned our aunt's affection."

Pulling away, he directed his guests to their seats at the table. Digby was seated next to Kate, and opposite them, Jane and her husband. Edmund sat at the head of the table with Aunt Cordelia to his right, so that she might readily converse with Jane.

A white cloth covered the oak table set with salt cellars, trenchers, silver tankards, goblets, and spoons. Placed in the center of the table, long tapers of beeswax shed flickering candlelight. Roasted beef and pheasant were served on pewter platters along with bread, cheese, and berries, all supervised by the chief usher. The yeoman of the buttery and the cellar stood at the ready with beer and ale, and sack for the ladies.

'Twas a sumptuous display, yet Edmund lacked appetite. He experienced a curious rocking sensation in the pit of his stomach. Bloody hell! Matchmaking was proving to be more delicate than a chess game played with a master.

"Following our meal, mayhap Kate will entertain us," he suggested, ignoring Kate's start. Her eyes widened as he directed his comments to Digby. "She plays the lute so fine you would believe the angels were singing."

"An artitht!" Digby declared.

"Pray, sir, not quite," Kate demurred.

Kate would never find a husband displaying such modesty. Edmund felt quite right in coming to her aid. "By your leave, you are too modest, Kate. you have much in common with Digby here, who is an accomplished limner. He has painted our portraits of late, Jane and mine and Viscount Chumley's. Digby's artistry is oft likened to that of Sir William Segar and Issac Oliver."

"I will look forward to viewing your paintings," Kate said, casting a hesitant smile at the artist.

Ah, such a sweet smile. Edmund felt certain the limner's heart had already been lost. What man could resist Kate's smile?

Flashing an apish grin, Digby flicked a wrist. "Fair maiden, pray allow me to capture your thmile upon my canvas."

The poor artist had a speech impediment. Edmund had forgotten. He wondered if Kate noticed.

A matchmaker's road was strewn with obstacles.

"I doubt Kate will be staying in London long enough to sit for a portrait," Jane remarked offhandedly. "How long do you intend to stay in London, Aunt Cordelia? You understand the city air cannot be advantageous for your . . . conditions."

"I shall consult several physicians and seek out a fortune-teller, eh? As well, I should like to shop at the Royal Exchange and visit with my friend, Lady Mason."

"Ten days should be quite long enough," Edmund's sister declared.

But Aunt Cordelia paid no mind. "Did I mention

court? I must be presented at court. You will make arrangements, will you not, Edmund?"

"Certainly, Aunt," Edmund said, uncertain what he'd agreed to. His attention had been on Kate and Digby, who were engaged in whispered conversation.

Once again Jane cut Kate and gave Edmund a set down. "You understand Kate will not be allowed at court?"

"She has expressed no desire to attend court."

"Brother, do not be taken in by a comely face." Jane lowered her voice to warn him in a whisper, "There is no doubt Kate is a beauty, but meant only for meaningless dalliance."

"I do not dally," Edmund bit back between his teeth, understanding her insinuation full well.

"Why did you not invite Alicia Witherspoon this evening?"

"I thought to enjoy family on this night."

"Yet you invited Digby?"

"Do you not consider the limner family? He has been in our homes for months, painting our portraits."

Jane's lips withered to two narrowed, murrey lines. "No, Digby is not family."

"Ah, but Frances is family," Edmund said in a smooth change of subject, one he knew his sister could not resist. "If you please, tell me how your daughter fares."

Jane told him in minute detail for the remainder of the meal.

After dinner, the gentleman usher provided basins, ewers, and a towel for the lords' and ladies' ablutions. Edmund then led the way to the music room.

Jane, Aunt Cordelia, and the viscount drifted to the far corner where a harp, yet to be played, stood in waiting. The small group discussed plans for how best to spend time between Cordelia's visits to city physicians. Instead of listening to their ruminations, Edmund strained to hear what passed between Digby and Kate, who sat on stools in the opposite corner.

Unable to hear a word of their conversation, he chafed with frustration. He detected an intimacy had sprung up between them. A favorable sign for a matchmaker. But he felt no elation. Unwilling to interrupt only to ask Kate to play the lute, Edmund nonetheless felt out of sorts. Disgruntled. 'Twas disconcerting how quickly and easily Kate and Digby got on together.

Having little choice but to join his family, Edmund ambled in their direction. He wondered if Kate might be put off by the portrait artist's foppish manner of dress? Perchance he could find a better husband for Kate than the limner—someone without a speech impediment. Richard Digby had been the first eligible man to come to mind. With further thought, Edmund felt certain he could do better. Kate deserved better.

The music chamber boasted a harp in the back corner and a virginal in the front corner. A lute, dulcimer, tabors, and a viol occupied places of prominence.

Kate was enamored of the room at once, though she thought it unlikely, from the looks of them, that any of the musical instruments had ever been used.

Several high-backed benches and low stools provided seating. A rich, multicolored Turkish carpet covered the polished oak floors, and thick, deep blue velvet draperies framed the lone, tall window standing partially opened.

Still, the chamber felt close and Kate uncomfortably warm. She'd misplaced her best, and only, fan. 'Twas a disagreeable habit of hers, forever misplacing the very item she needed most.

Digby flicked his parrot-green feather fan in rapid motions. The artist's finery would put a peacock to shame. Kate was hard-pressed where to look. His snug, paned trunk hose and overly decorous canions would not permit the eye to rest. His screeching green satin doublet, studded with gold points and pearls, caused Kate to blink in the habit of Lady Cordelia.

And much to her surprise, Digby wore a codpiece, which was no longer fashionable. From its rather alarming size, Kate could only think a great deal of horsehair padded the piece. As a final dramatic touch, from his shoulders Digby had flung a collarless short coat of searing orange velvet around his high, stiff ruff.

A gleaming assortment of accessories and jewels dangled from his gold-link girdle. Rings encircled every finger.

The limner's mules were fashioned of the same green silk as his doublet but adorned with orange rosettes.

"I thall give you the names of the finethst milliner and theamstreth in London," Digby said. "With the proper gownth you will dathle all of London, my dear."

"You are too kind, Master Digby."

Kate did not wish to offend Edmund's friend, but she did not care to meet either his milliner or his tailor. She had no wish to emulate an artist's affectation.

"You thhall have knights and nobleth falling at your feet, Mithtress Kate."

"But I do not care for men falling at my feet."

The artist's darting, otter eyes appeared startled. He leaned closer to Kate. "Do you not favor men?"

His breath smelled of ale. While not ill featured, Kate could not find him attractive. The limner wore his wispy walnut-brown hair long but with a fringe cut along his high forehead. A trim moustache grew below his narrow, turned-up nose. His beard consisted of a tuft of hair on the point of his chin.

"Indeed, I favor men," she assured him, marveling at the question.

Digby appeared to relax. "Ath do I. Women ath well. But Lord Thtamford ith above all a most thtriking male."

"Aye, he is exceedingly handsome," Kate agreed. "I have always thought thus."

"Lovely eyes."

"Aye." She sighed, studying Edmund's invincible presence. His sensuous mouth, his remarkable eyes.

Unmindful of Kate's observation, Edmund stood across the room, arms folded, deep in conversation with Viscount Chumley. Did they discuss wood lark or warbler?

"Lord Stamford's eyes remind me of glistening emeralds," she murmured at last.

"Exthellent dithcription! You do potheth an artithst'th eye."

Digby's girlish enthusiasm made Kate feel as if she were sharing observations with one of her own gender. However odd, she was thankful not to be forced into conversation with Jane, who'd sent disapproving glances her way all evening.

"And my lord cuts a dashing figure," Digby added, still waxing poetic over their host.

"Aye."

"His thoulderth are ath broad ath an armored tholdier." The limner sighed. "His legth beyond compare."

Kate could not but agree. Edmund's black stockings displayed shapely, muscular legs to full advantage. She felt certain that the Earl of Stamford's well-honed physique had been enhanced by his devotion to sports. His body shimmered with masculinity, virility.

Kate's breath caught in her throat.

She smoldered and burned, stunned to realize she could no longer ruminate upon Edmund's attributes, it seemed, without suffering consequences. Of all times to be without a fan! Resisting the impulse to snatch Digby's, she inhaled deeply.

"Do you not apprecthiate Lord Thtamford's legth?"

"Oh, aye. Aye."

Kate appreciated everything about Edmund, including the cut and color of his garments. He oft wore black, and the darkness of his figure alluded to a potent force. But he was never without a touch of color. This eve, Edmund's gold brocade doublet relieved the black.

"Methinkth I thould like to paint another portrait of Lord Thtamford. A full-length pothe."

A portrait Kate should like to own.

Fearing further conversation with the limner might give her feelings for Edmund away, she shook off her dreamy reverie.

"Would you like me to play the lute?" she asked.

"Aye, Mithtreth Kate. 'Twould make a pleathing interlude. I thall join Lord Thtamford and hith family to lithten."

Soon, all conversation ended, and the music chamber filled with music.

Long after the guests departed and Aunt Cordelia had settled in her chamber, Kate still could not sleep. A restless mixture of weariness and excitement kept her awake.

Donning her cloak over her shift, she made her way to the small, gone-to-weed back garden. Although the candle she carried shed little light, 'twas enough to detect a mass of tangled, twisted dead bushes and dried grass. The garden suffered more than Lady Cordelia. Kate thought to take it upon herself to transform the neglected patch, thereby occupying herself with thoughts that did not flit between finding her mother and seducing Edmund. She blushed in the dark.

A trying evening had Lady Jane attempting to cut Kate down at every turn, Edmund paying her no mind at all, and Richard Digby apparently unable to talk about anything or anyone except the riveting earl.

Kate clutched her worn cloak tightly around her as she sat on the cold stone stoop to contemplate the stars. The city noise had quieted to muted sounds of horse hooves on cobblestones, babies crying, and drunken exclamations drifting on a cool breeze. The moon was merely a narrow crescent of hazy silver in the sky. A blurred spray of stars winked in the blackness.

And there her fate was written, written in the stars.

"Kate!"

"Edmund?" She looked up to find him looming above her. He held a torch, which cast flickering shadows and golden ribbons of light across his face and chest. "You gave me a start."

"I did not mean to."

Kate looked back into the garden.

He sat beside her, his long legs dangled two stone steps beyond. "I went to Aunt Cordelia's chambers to be certain she, and you, had all that you needed. But I discovered you gone."

"I could not sleep."

"Is the bed not comfortable?"

He smelled faintly of sandalwood and deep, lusty maleness. His fine lawn shirt exposed a tantalizing patch of crisp raven chest hair.

She should not look. He should not have removed his doublet.

"Aye, the bed is fine," she said. " 'Tis excitement that keeps me from sleep."

Edmund cocked his head, eyeing her closely. A stubble of beard darkened his strong, square jaw. "Has your excitement anything to do with Digby? Did you favor the limner?"

"He is likeable."

"Pray, what did you talk about?"

"You."

Edmund's brows shot up in surprise. "Me?"

"Your limner is quite fond of you, Edmund."

"Oh." His brow gathered in a bunched, ill-humored frown before he spoke. "Think no more of Digby."

In fact Kate had not given the limner a thought since her conversation with him. "What truly excites me is the prospect of visiting at least one goldsmith on the morrow."

"I shall see to it, then."

Kate's joy was tempered by the realization that if Edmund moved only a bit, he would brush against her. If that were to happen, she would surely burst into flame.

"If only I could read the stars like Jutta does," she said, diverting her shameful thoughts and feelings. "Then I might know what will happen on the morrow. I could foresee my future . . . and my past."

"Do you truly believe the stars can be read?"

"Does not the queen have her own astrologer in George Dee?"

"She does," Edmund conceded. "But I doubt if our queen consults Dee daily on affairs of the kingdom."

"He chose the most propitious day for her coronation."

"Did Dee also select the time for the defeat of the Spanish Armada?"

"I do not know. I only know that the position of the stars affects our body and mind, the crops and the tides."

"There are scholars who doubt these theories, Kate."

"Do you?" She looked up and into Edmund's eyes. As her gaze came to rest on his, her heart swelled up and against her chest, pressing painfully against fragile walls.

Oh, fie! The Earl of Stamford would be the death of her—in a most pleasant manner.

With his deep green gaze still locked on Kate's, Edmund's lips turned up in a wry, half smile. "Let us just say I have reservations."

She sighed. He'd been a cynical soul even as a boy. She, on the other hand, was not limited by suspicion or doubt. "I should like to find an astrologer to consult while in London."

Edmund sighed, a resounding sigh of resignation. "Aunt Cordelia plans to see a fortune-teller; you should accompany her."

"A fortune-teller is not the same as an astrologer," Kate reminded him. " 'Tis guesswork involved in fortune-telling."

"But an astrologer—"

"Astrology is a science."

"You would lead your life according to the stars?" Edmund asked.

"I cannot entirely," she admitted. "I do not know the

exact date of my birth nor the time. Jutta warned me that my chart will never be true unless I discover—"

"Who is Jutta? An astrologer?"

"Aye, the village stargazer." When indecision plagued Kate, Jutta's insight helped her determine the proper course.

"Did Jutta advise you as to what would happen to you during your stay in London?"

"She counseled me to be on guard."

"Being on guard is sage advice for those visiting a bustling city where beggars and pickpockets abound," he said.

"I believe the warning goes deeper. Jutta's words were: 'Be on guard without and within.' "

Edmund rubbed the back of his neck and made a grunting sound beneath his breath.

Kate waited silently, expectantly. 'Twas the perfect setting for him to steal a kiss. But since he'd kissed her in the country, he no longer appeared interested. 'Twas her lack of experience to blame. Not that she wished to be taken advantage of and then discarded as her natural mother must have been. Still, for one more kiss . . . oh, hey-ho!

Beside her Edmund whistled softly. He idly pulled at weeds, twisting their blades absentmindedly before tossing them aside. The uneasy silence, save for the low whistling, fell between them like an invisible curtain. Could Kate go around the barrier, leap over it? Was it even penetrable? What to do? What to do?

This odd silence was a prickly new phenomenon Kate had never experienced in Edmund's company. All had been playful and harmonious with them in the past. Silences had been sweet.

Edmund's whistle ceased. "Are you feeling weary?"

"Aye." Kate yawned to emphasize the fact. She would say or do anything to escape from the breath-quenching nearness of his body, the unnerving silence. "I shall sleep till past dawn."

"Come. I'll see you to your bedchamber door. Early on the morrow, we shall visit my goldsmith. The search for your natural mother begins."

SIX

Look for a warm, early summer

The old Scottish castle was cold, the corridors damp, the walls crumbling. Donald Cameron, the Duke of Laird, could no longer delay making the necessary repairs. The remote Downes Castle lay south of Moffat on the road to England. Perched high on a bluff overlooking the village below, it discouraged all but the most desperate visitors. Which he had been.

The aged structure was several days' travel from his own palatial estate in the highlands. Laird Manor nestled in the shadow of Stirling. Donald might never have known of Downes's existence but for a twist of fate.

Seeking shelter from an approaching storm, he had approached its doors with his entourage almost twenty-five years ago.

Donald had been a regular visitor ever since. He stopped at Downes Castle whenever traveling to England as an emissary of his king, James the Sixth. He came to see the beautiful Englishwoman who had lived in Downes all of her life, never straying beyond the bailey walls.

Beguiled by the mysterious lass at first sight, Donald looked forward to his visits but found himself at the mercy of Anne's whims. Sometimes he stayed for days at the castle without ever seeing the reclusive woman. Enamored beyond good sense, he suffered, without complaint, the eccentricities of the fragile lass who had quickly become his lover.

Donald had lost his wife the year before he first passed through the portals of Downes Castle. He had been content in his marriage with Caragh for near ten years. In his grief, he thought never to care for another woman, never to know contentment again. Unexpectedly, he found more than contentment with Anne.

He was invited to sup with her on the eve he sought shelter at Downes. One expected a hag to be hidden away, but not a fair, gossamer beauty. Donald had stammered like a schoolboy; he lost his heart before the first candle flickered out.

Over time, Anne shared her feelings with Donald, her opinions, her talents, and her heart. She shared all but her past and her future.

A year after their meeting, the pale, blond beauty asked him to make love to her. Donald had been shocked at her invitation, but did not hesitate. He'd never made love to another woman since.

Anne did not always see him, and Donald was forced to deal with Sally, the old retainer who doted on her mistress. Whether Anne remained in seclusion because of a low mood, ill health, or simply because she was unwilling to see him, Donald could never be certain. After several years of perseverance, the duke developed a trusting relationship with the plump, cherry-cheeked guardian of his cloistered lover.

For Anne's own safety Donald resolved to start the repairs on Downes Castle immediately. He would not ask her permission and risk refusal; he would tell her.

"Weel na, Sally, I must see me lady today."

Belying her jovial appearance, Sally possessed a somber demeanor. "Lady Anne is indisposed, my lord."

"Aye? An' what ails the lass?" he asked suspiciously. Anne frequently avoided him claiming ill health. While she did indeed look delicate, Donald believed her claims were often ruses. She was a wily one. Unlike other women he'd known, the mysterious English lass enjoyed solitude. "Has milady caught a chill from this damp prison she calls a castle?"

" 'Tis a fever she does not wish to pass on to you, my lord."

Donald felt like a swine. "Wish milady a swift recovery."

"Aye, my lord."

He started away and then stopped. "Be a kind lass and convey my intent to begin repairs on this ruin as soon as I return from England."

"Aye, my lord."

"Tell her I must leave for London at dawn. I am expected at court and canna delay."

"Aye, my lord." The old woman shuffled off.

Although Sally never showed disrespect, 'twas evident early on that she held a duke in no higher regard than any other man.

"There is more."

Sally stopped, gazing at him over her shoulder.

Donald lowered his voice. "Tell me lady Anne, I hold her close to me heart. An' I pray to find her in good health upon me return."

Sally smiled.

Edmund guided Kate through the bustling Cheapside section of London. Street vendors hawked their wares and dust billowed from the road to smite the eyes. Above them, thick smoky, gray clouds rolled across the sky in silent warning of rain to come.

"I would not take you away from your duties at Parliament, Lord Stamford."

"And I would not have you venturing about alone on Goldsmith Row, Mistress Kate."

Kate's eyes were large with the sights and smells of the city. "Lady Cordelia means to shop on the morrow. I could have waited," she replied, her gaze on several large penned peacocks, brilliant of plume and proud of bearing.

"Last eve you sounded impatient to begin. I feared for your wits were you to wait another day," Edmund teased. "What better time than now, whilst Jane's personal physician is attending Aunt Cordelia? You will not be missed."

In order to escort Kate this afternoon, Edmund had declined an invitation from the Earl of Cheltham to play billiards. He and Robin played once a week. The loser provided dinner to the winner. But as Edmund accompanied his childhood companion along the street, taking in the sights through Kate's marveling eyes, he did not miss his game nearly as much as he'd anticipated.

Kate held her pomander close to her nose. Unused to city smells, she more than likely suffered from an unsettled stomach—not that he expected her to admit as much. 'Twas common for country visitors to react badly to the city stench. She slowed as they reached Goldsmith Row, passing the elegant shops of London's foremost jewelers.

"I did not expect so many goldsmith shops," she confessed a bit breathlessly. "How long will it take me to visit every shop?"

"Mayhap you will not need to visit each shop. Come, this is the shop of my goldsmith, Beacham." Edmund held the door for her.

Pausing to give Edmund a small, tremulous smile, Kate entered the shop.

"Beacham, good morrow."

"Good morrow, Lord Stamford."

"I have brought a friend seeking information about a ring she wears."

" 'Twill be my honor to help if I can," the young jeweler replied. Edmund did not miss the light in his eye as Beacham dipped his head to Kate. "How do you do, milady?"

Edmund did not have the heart to embarrass Kate by correcting the goldsmith. Although not a lady, Edmund fancied others would make the same mistake regarding the gardener's daughter. 'Twas the proud angle of her chin, the Cleopatra smile upon her lips, and the curiosity shining in her eyes that made Kate appear manor born.

In the garden last eve 'twas all Edmund could do to keep his hands to himself. He'd torn countless weeds to shreds in the effort to exert self-control. He had taken far too much liberty when he had kissed her in his tree castle. The soft, moist warmth of Kate's mouth still haunted him. The faint cinnamon taste of her had left him with an unfulfilled craving, a forbidden craving. One he could not satisfy.

Remorseful ever since, for taking advantage of his childhood friend, Edmund vowed not to impose upon the woman she'd become again. He'd vowed not to even think of her lips—as he was now.

Compounding matters was his mistake in selecting Digby as a potential suitor for Kate. A fop with a speech impediment.

Edmund knew it to be in his own best interest to make a proper match for Kate as soon as possible. Bloody hell, how much longer could he be expected to resist the temptation of her? He was a man of hearty appetites.

"I am well," Kate was saying. "And you, Mr. Beacham?"

Beacham appeared taken aback to have a lady inquire of his health. Though his mouth dropped open as if he would speak, he only nodded.

Edmund stepped between the two. "Prithee, Beacham, will you examine my lady's ring?"

"I cannot remove it, Edmund," she whispered tersely, tugging on his sleeve.

"Why? Is it too small? Or have the stars said nay?" he asked, unable to resist the jibe.

Kate raised her chin a notch higher. "Mama and Papa Beadle vowed I would never remove the ring."

"May I remind you?" One day long ago, she had allowed him to hold her precious ring.

"I may have removed it once, when I was too young to understand."

For you, were her unspoken words. She had removed it for him. Inexplicably, Edmund's heart pitched against his chest.

"But now with full understanding," Kate continued, "I am breaking one of their promises by seeking my ring's origin."

"They promised?"

"Aye, but not I. I did not promise."

Edmund nodded. "Show the goldsmith."

Kate stepped toward Beacham, splaying her hand to better display the ring. "Have you seen this ring before, sir? Or one like it?"

As the goldsmith examined the ring, Edmund observed Kate. Each time they were together he discovered something new and bewitching about her. The light velvet lilt of her laugh. The unruly golden wisps of curls that framed her heart-shaped face. The heightened color of her cheeks when she grew excited.

Her worn, lightweight woolen cloak might appear shabby on another woman and distract from her figure. But on Kate, the cloak mattered little; it went all but unseen. Kate's beauty commanded the eye's attention, a beauty that shone from within and was captured in the deep amber of her eyes, eyes sparkling like stars of gold.

" 'Tis a rose wrapped round a crown," Kate explained as if the goldsmith could not see for himself.

He shook his head. "Nay, milady. I have never seen such a ring before."

"Do you know where my lady's ring might have been fashioned?" Edmund asked. "Perchance in another country?"

"Perhaps, milord. 'Tis fashioned of the finest gold. And since the crown is barely to be seen I would suggest a noble or royal connection."

"Royal?" Edmund repeated.

"Royal!" Kate scoffed.

A tightness gripped Edmund's gut. Unlike the goldsmith, he'd never considered a royal connection. Crowns were common on a coat or arms, why not a ring? Edmund believed as Kate did. He assumed her to be the illegitimate by-blow of a lesser noble and a peasant woman.

"My thanks, sir." He placed a shilling in Beacham's hand before taking Kate's elbow and steering her out the door.

"Oh, Edmund!" Disconcerted, Kate spoke faster than a man could listen. The words fell in a wretched tumble from her mouth. " 'Tis as I expected. My father was of noble blood. He bedded a poor innocent servant girl. And when the girl discovered that she was with child, she stole his ring so that her babe would have a token."

She bit her bottom lip. The golden light in her eyes faded, replaced by dark shadows of conjecture. Her shoulders sloped; her steps slowed.

Edmund longed to comfort her, but other than taking Kate into his arms, which he could not do, he did not know how.

" 'Tis . . . 'tis a common happenstance." *Bloody hell, I am a blathering fool!*

"Perhaps my mother was a bawdy house woman who lay with many men and—"

"Kate, your imagination flies away with you."

She stopped midstep and gazed up at him. "There is only one way to still my imagination."

Edmund feared to ask the question, yet knew he must. "And what way would that be?"

"To find the truth. Let us go to another shop . . . to all the shops on Goldsmith Row."

Declaring her intent, she marched off.

He quickly caught up. "Kate, on the merest chance that there is a noble family behind your ring, we must be discreet."

"A by-blow." She spit out the word. "I truly am a by-blow."

"You cannot be certain."

"What other explanation can there be?"

"Mayhap you were born to peasants too poor to raise a child though they loved her very much. They made the supreme sacrifice by giving up their golden girl. 'Twas the only way to give her a better life."

She stared up at him. "Do you believe such a story?"

"Do you not believe it could be so?"

"Aye," she allowed at length, and grudgingly. "But explain the ring and the funds marked for my education."

"I cannot," Edmund confessed. "But I shall think on it. In the meantime, I understand there is a new Shakespeare play at the Rose Theater. I suggest we go."

"Now?"

"You must calm yourself before pursuing this matter further."

Kate heaved such a heavy sigh before replying that Edmund thought he felt the ground tremble. "I have read many of Shakespeare's plays, but I have never attended a performance of one."

"Come," he insisted. "We shall take a wherry to Southwark."

"A wherry?" Kate asked, lifting the pomander to her nose.

"A small boat to carry us across the Thames. We shall return to Goldsmith Row on the morrow."

"Do you promise?"

"I promise." His first promise to a woman, and the earth did not fall away from beneath his feet.

"Very well."

Pleased with himself for suggesting the perfect diversion, Edmund led Kate toward the river. At least for a time she would not be in despair over the origin of her birth.

In all likelihood she would never find her natural mother nor her father. 'Twas clear to him they did not care to be found.

* * *

The Rose Theater's presentation of *Two Gentlemen of Verona* was in progress when Kate and Edmund arrived. Several bleacher seats, reserved for the aristocrats and gentry, were empty. With the slightest touch to the small of her back, Edmund guided Kate to a stone bench high above the pit, where a full view of the stage could easily be seen.

A mix of emotions tangled in her blood. The excitement of actually witnessing a play by William Shakespeare and the leaden disappointment that settled like spoiled mutton in her belly.

Kate had always realized hopes of finding her mother quickly were futile; still she had hoped. Worse, Edmund's goldsmith confirmed her fears. 'Twas plain to even a stranger that she'd been born a by-blow and abandoned. The planets had not been in auspicious alignment when she was born.

As she made herself comfortable on the stone bench, Kate conjured another story. Perhaps following Kate's birth her poor mother sought another position safe from the noble grasp. Mayhap the servant girl had married a farmer, birthed more children, and even now was searching for the child she'd given away.

With that happy thought Kate turned away from the mystery of her origins and turned her attention to the play.

Master Shakespeare had gathered untold accolades for his dramas and comedic plays alike. She could hardly believe she was sitting in a theater watching a performance with Edmund, Earl of Stamford, beside her. In her wildest imaginings, she had not dared to dream such a scenario. And Jutta, her astrologer, had never predicted it.

"Edmund, the women in attendance are wearing veils."

"Do you mind being seen? If so, we can return to Stamford House for a veil."

"We should miss the performance."

" 'Tis your choice."

Kate did not waffle over this decision. She would not miss the performance, for in all likelihood, she would not have the opportunity to see another during her stay in London.

Kate slanted the hero of her young girl's heart a sideways glance. Edmund towered over the other men present at the theater. Dressed in black silk and velvet, he exuded a commanding presence—and a pleasant scent of sandalwood. His wayward lock of ebony hair fell across his dark brow as if it were directing attention to the silver-green light in his eyes and the merry way they crinkled at the corners.

Kate could not be certain that the excitement bubbling up within her had more to do with Edmund's company than watching a play by Shakespeare. Unfastening her cloak, she turned her attention to the actors.

Kate understood full well why the playwright had Valentine and Proteus debating the merits and pitfalls of love. Somewhere in her laughter she sighed for Julia and her misadventures masquerading as a male. Kate understood the quickness and frustration of Silvia and thoroughly relished the drama and comedy, the story of friendship and love.

Because she lived a drama of her own. Loving the man at her side and knowing she could never reveal her love. Feeling the warmth of his body close to hers, the excited skip of her heart whenever Edmund smiled at her.

She felt his gaze upon her; she expected his sidelong glance was to determine if she were enjoying the play. Now and then his gaze lingered, and Kate felt the intensity of his scrutiny. Why? What did he seek? Edmund knew her better than any man. During those awkward moments, Kate shifted uneasily on the hard bench.

She'd misplaced her gloves and so had not worn any. During act three when Edmund caught her rubbing her cold hands together, he caught them up in his, clasping them both. With one hand he enveloped both of hers, warming them, sending sparks of pleasure through every limb, sparks that curled her toes and tingled her fingertips.

Barely able to catch her breath, Kate missed most of act four. By the fifth and last act, while gloriously aware of her hands engulfed by Edmunds', she'd resumed normal breathing and could once again concentrate on the actors.

"Lord Stamford?"

"James!" Edmund dropped Kate's hands as if they'd burst into flame, and rose to greet the gentleman who had approached him.

The handsome fellow was but a few inches shorter than Edmund, of fair complexion, and dusky blond hair, trimmed beard and moustache. His eyes were the shade of indigo velvet, reminding Kate of the purple-blue columbine growing wild in the wood. Dressed finely in blue brocade doublet, breeches, and stocks, he could easily turn a woman's head.

Jutta had never mentioned meeting a tall fair-haired man in London. Had the stargazer missed an important planetary conjunction?

"James Moore," Edmund repeated his greeting. "In faith!"

"I thought it was you. Missing your game with Cheltham?"

The smile vanished from Edmund's mouth. Within the blink of Kate's eyes he acquired a solemn visage. "Unfortunately. I had pressing family business to attend to."

"I see," James Moore said, looking straight at Kate, entrancing her with his blue eyes and enigmatic smile.

"May I introduce you to Kate Beadle, my aunt's gentlewoman? I accompanied Kate to an appointment with my barber surgeon earlier."

Barber surgeon! Edmund lied. She had no toothache. Why would he lie? But no sooner had she asked the question to herself than the answer came to her.

An earl did not escort a gardener's daughter to the theater.

She could not fault him; she could only weep later. Alas, much later.

Moore swept off his plumed hat and bowed low. "I am enchanted, Kate Beadle."

"And I am pleased to meet you."

"James Moore is my barrister, Kate," Edmund explained, while rubbing the back of his neck. "He handles all legal matters for Rose Hall and Stamford House."

The barrister gazed past Edmund to Kate. "The city is blessed by your presence."

Oh, the honey dripped from Mr. Moore's lips.

James turned his attention back to Edmund. "Did you discover any business during your visit to Rose Hall that needs my attention, Lord Stamford?"

"No. Er, yes. Yes, indeed. Pray, could you attend me on the morrow at Stamford House?"

"I shall be happy to call upon you, my lord."

"After our business is finished, pray stay and sup with us," Edmund added. " 'Twill be a small party, only my aunt and Kate."

"I would enjoy that above all," the barrister replied.

And once again, his eyes locked on Kate's in a most mesmerizing manner.

" 'Tis done," Edmund said, giving Moore a hearty slap on the back.

"I shall see you on the morrow . . . and you, Mistress Kate."

As soon as Moore was out of earshot, Edmund lowered his voice. "James is an intelligent man and does quite well at business. I am certain you shall like him."

"He is exceedingly comely," Kate offered.

Edmund hiked a dark brow. "Do you think so?"

"My eyes tell me so!"

"Hmm. My barrister does not have a wife as yet," Edmund told her.

"Shhh!" a nearby patron admonished them.

Kate paid no mind. "Moore may take a wife at any time he wishes," she declared.

"Do you think so?"

"Yes, my lord, like you. You may take a wife whenever you choose."

"When my business is finished, I shall take a wife. And you, mayhap, should think of marriage, too, ere you are too long in the tooth for an upstanding man."

"Edmund!"

"We are old friends. Cannot I speak the truth with you if not with anyone else?"

" 'Tis done. And I pledge to you that when my business is finished, I, too, shall look for a husband." Though she knew it would be impossible to love anyone as well as she loved Edmund.

"Shhh!"

"James Moore might prove to be the man for you."

"Do not play matchmaker, Edmund," she warned.

"Shhh!"

"Hush, Kate."

"Pray?"

" 'Tis frowned upon to talk in the theater—unless you are speaking to the characters, of course."

"Oh, fie!"

Kate's anger at Edmund's arrogance slowly dissolved as she watched the remainder of the play. To think he would serve as matchmaker for her. She was more than capable of finding her own husband, when the time came. When she was ready.

Though some of the members of the afternoon audience threw rotting garbage upon the stage at the play's end, Kate applauded with gusto.

"Did you enjoy the performance, Kate?" Edmund asked.

"Aye! Did you not think it most diverting?"

His eyes met hers. His smile broadened. "Aye, Kate. Aye."

Seeking warmth, the crowd of play goers attempted to leave the theater at once. The late-afternoon chill nipped at Kate. Even with her hood raised, the tip of her nose stung and her ears burned. Although Edmund had a firm hold on her hand, she was buffeted in the swarming mass.

"My Lord Stamford?"

'Twas a woman's voice that stopped Edmund in his tracks.

Kate turned with him to regard the small veiled woman who stood behind them, firmly protected between two male escorts.

"Lady Judith!"

Judith Witherspoon. The marquis's daughter that Edmund meant to marry.

SEVEN

Circumstances will favor you . . .

Oh, fie! Face-to-face with Edmund's future bride.

Confronted with the woman who would one day become the countess of Stamford, Kate could barely catch her breath. Her lungs squeezed shut.

Oh, how she longed to be elsewhere. Anywhere else. She yearned for the magic of a cunning woman able to make herself invisible. To be turned to dust, or to simply faint away and slip into the dark abyss of ignorant bliss.

"Lady Judith!" Edmund exclaimed. " 'Tis an unexpected pleasure to greet you."

Unexpected, aye, thought Kate. *Pleasure? Nay, nay.*

One glance pronounced Judith Witherspoon a proper lady. Attired in the first of fashion, her heavy popinjay blue damask gown featured a stiff ruff that forced the lady's chin to a height that could only be described as unnatural and haughty. Wearing a farthingale that spread her skirts as wide as her shoulders, the lady appeared . . . stretched in different directions.

Despite her costume, Lady Judith remained small in stature. The plume of her small velvet hat barely reached Edmund's chest. She stood rigidly, as if fearing the many gold chains, pendants, and broaches adorning her person would fall away with the slightest movement. Or perhaps they weighed her down so that she could not move.

For Lord Stamford's sake, Kate hoped the lady possessed a heavenly countenance and the smile of an angel, that beneath her heavy crepe veil, Judith did not hide the face of a frog.

Kate bit down on her lip, intending to inflict a measure of pain upon herself for having such a mean-spirited thought. Lady Witherspoon came from an aristocratic family. Her blood might run cold, but it was noble.

Lady Cordelia had told Kate that the Witherspoon family was a powerful force throughout Britain. Edmund would be fortunate to win the lady's hand, for her family would provide needed allies in Parliament and court.

But alas, Kate feared her childhood friend might pay the price for allies by spending the rest of his life in regret.

She clamped down on her lip a bit more forcefully.

Lord Stamford withdrew a muckinder and dabbed at beads of sweat on his brow. An odd condition on a mild, overcast afternoon. Kate wondered if he'd taken ill. But before she could ask, Edmund recovered.

With eyes only for Judith, the corners of his mouth turned up in the warm, heart-fluttering grin that made Kate's insides ache. 'Twas the sort of smile that made a woman feel as if she were the center of his world, the only woman in his life. And it was aimed at Judith Witherspoon.

Edmund's great charm poured forth in glowing words as he complemented Lady Judith on looking so lovely. More than once, he declared his pleasure upon meeting by chance.

Kate thought she would gag.

"You have not introduced your companion, Lord Stamford."

Lady Judith squeaked like a mouse when she spoke. She sounded more child than woman.

Kate bit down on her lip once again, this time drawing blood.

"Lady Judith, I am pleased to present Mistress Kate Beadle, a long-time acquaintance just arrived from the country. She is Aunt Cordelia's gentlewoman."

To her credit, Lady Judith did not ask why Lady Cordelia's gentlewoman was attending the theater with the Earl of Stamford. Nevertheless, feeling the frosty glare from eyes she could not see, Kate dipped into a polite curtsy.

"A country miss," Judith squeaked.

And proud to be, Kate silently replied.

Stretching her neck to gain added height over the little woman, Kate greeted Edmund's lady. "Pray, Lady Witherspoon, I am honored."

"Is Lord Stamford entertaining you well?"

"Lord Stamford is a most excellent host," Kate said.

Lady Witherspoon turned abruptly to Edmund. "Did you approve of the Shakespeare play?"

" 'Twas an interesting tale, full of humor."

"I prefer his dramas." Judith addressed only Edmund. To Kate's great annoyance, she no longer existed for the lady.

"Shakespeare's dramas are exceptional," Edmund agreed.

Kate made a great show of clearing her throat as a vocal reminder of her presence.

"I do not understand why he takes this new direction," Judith complained, ignoring her.

Edmund turned up his palms. "Who among us can readily understand an artist?"

"Perhaps Master Shakespeare desired the challenge," Kate put in. " 'Tis far more difficult to make an audience laugh than to make one cry."

She heard a pin drop in the silence.

"But 'tis only my opinion," she added.

Edmund took Lady Judith's hand. "A thousand pardons, but I must hurry Kate back to my aunt, who treasures Mistress Beadle's companionship." His lips grazed the back of the lady's gloved hand.

A stone turned in the pit of Kate's stomach.

"I say, Lady Judith, have you plans for the morrow?"

"Nay, I do not believe so."

"May I prevail upon you to join a small supper party. My aunt wishes to meet you during her stay in London."

"Aye. I should like to meet your aunt, as well."

Kate groaned inwardly before realizing that she could not escape the gathering, which increased with each new person Edmund encountered. She had only just met Lady Witherspoon, and could come to no fair opinion. Kate's *feeling* that the lady was a shrew meant little. And one Edmund most likely did not share.

In Kate's opinion, no woman would ever be fine enough for Edmund. But he did require an heir, and since Kate could neither marry him nor provide him with a son, she should lend her support and encourage him in his romantic pursuits.

Edmund swept to a low bow before the lady. "Until the morrow."

The veiled head bobbed.

* * *

In recalling the unexpected meeting with Lady Judith, Edmund realized he had not drawn a complete breath the entire time. He'd worried what the two women might say to each other. He feared Kate might blurt whatever was on her mind, as she was wont to do. Instead, Edmund found her silence even more disquieting. He dared not ask her what she thought of his intended bride. Some sixth sense warned him against it.

The first time they were alone together, Edmund expected that Lady Judith would question him further about Kate. He must avoid being alone with her. Conversation between him and Judith proved difficult enough, as they had little in common.

When Kate and Judith stood beside each other, even with Kate dressed in common garb, it was plain to all that they were as unlike as a peach and a pit. Kate being the peach, Judith the pit.

Bloody hell! Edmund immediately chastised himself for having such thoughts. 'Twas an unfair comparison and one that should not be made.

Lady Judith had been raised in the accepted manner, her ideas and education influenced by her parents and peers. Further, the lady could hardly be set down for her average appearance. Most women of Edmund's acquaintance did not possess Kate's willowy height, nor her golden eyes and high, regal cheekbones.

He approached his aunt's chamber with resolve. He required the old woman's help, but he was late for his appointment with her. He hoped she hadn't imbibed too much sack while waiting.

Edmund had no trouble filling his time since his Aunt Cordelia and Kate had arrived in London. Once he'd participated in every game, even those he did not particularly enjoy, to fill his time. Now, he had little time to play his favorite sports and hone his skills. Where previously he found himself late for appointments because the play lasted longer than expected, of late, his tardiness resulted from a heavy schedule. The demands of his aunt, sister, and Kate kept a man well occupied. On second thought, Kate made no demands. He offered his services to her.

With arrangements to make for tomorrow's entertainment following dinner, he hardly had a moment to visit with his aunt, but Edmund considered his business urgent. Seated on a bench beneath a window in her solar, Lady Cordelia squinted as she embroidered.

"By your leave—"

"Edmund!" She smiled up a him, blinking her hazel orbs as she adjusted from the light of the window to the dimmer light where he stood. The blinking gave her an expression of profound bewilderment.

Despite Lady Cordelia's endless ills, Edmund was fond of the old woman. He strode to her side. "How do you feel today, Aunt?"

"I am much improved. The physician I visited this morning prescribed saffron and a diet of eggs eaten two at a time, four times a day. I believe I feel better."

"And after only a few hours? I am pleased more than I can say, Aunt."

"You are late. You promised to attend me midmorning."

"Begging your pardon, Aunt Cordelia, but I was detained through no fault of my own."

"You are never at fault."

"Perhaps occasionally," he admitted, with a grin and a wink.

The old woman chuckled and wagged her head. "I shall forgive you. Once more."

"Where is Kate?" he asked, looking around the chamber as if she might pop out from behind a pillar.

"She is in the garden planting something. She said the garden was sorely neglected and she must set it as right as she can before we return to Rose Hall."

"She speaks the truth."

Cordelia raised her hand to her throat, the way she often did in an attempt to cover her three doughy chins. "Why have you let the Stamford House garden go to weed, Edmund?"

"I have no excuse, Aunt," he admitted with a shrug and a sheepish smile, "but an unpardonable lack of interest. Since I have no one to walk with in the garden, I rarely go there. In fact, roses, lilies, ivy, and apple trees are never uppermost in my mind."

"What is uppermost in your mind? Marriage, by chance?"

"In a manner of speaking."

"Pray God!" Her round eyes grew rounder. "Your life will have purpose!"

Not quite the purpose she thought.

"Aunt Cordelia, I wish to find Kate a proper husband."

"Kate?" the old woman repeated, blinking rapidly, leaving no doubt about her confusion.

"Yes. And I believe my task would be less difficult if she were clothed in the first of fashion."

"Methinks Kate needs no help from you, Edmund. She is quite beautiful. I doubt men of her class notice the girl's attire."

Edmund shook his head and took up pacing the small chamber, clasping his hands behind his back. "We cannot take the chance. I shall provide the funds for her wardrobe, but I should like you to take matters in hand at once. We will be having guests on the morrow and Kate must look her best."

Aunt Cordelia inclined her head, and a faded curl escaped her cap, falling askew on her milky-white brow. "Why do you take such an interest, eh?"

"Kate deserves a provident match and a life of ease. What opportunities has she had thus far in life? She was abandoned to be raised by a gardener and his wife."

"But she has been blessed with a fair face and many talents. When Kate strokes my temples, the pain flies a—"

"Dear Aunt, Kate was my childhood friend, and I would arrange a proper marriage for her. The village parson with an overbite will not do."

"I have told her as much."

"With Kate's intelligence and wit she might capture a . . ."

Edmund paused in his pacing, letting his thoughts go. A peer of the realm? A knight? Hardly. He must find her a husband within societal limits. A barrister would do quite nicely. A far better choice than the limner. An experienced matchmaker would have realized at once.

"Go on, Edmund."

"She might catch the eye of my barrister, James Moore, who will be among our guests tomorrow eve."

Cordelia inclined her head, blinking into space. Edmund wondered if the new spectacles he'd heard of might lessen his aunt's incessant blinking.

"Will you help?" he pressed. "You have an eye for color and style much like the queen, herself," he coaxed.

His aunt lifted the silver goblet by her side and

sipped. "Perhaps something of mine could be made over by the morrow, eh? And I shall order additional gowns made especially for Kate."

Edmund strode to his aunt's side and planted a kiss on her forehead. "I shall be eternally grateful."

"Grateful enough to plan a marriage of your own?"

"Aye. The moment Kate is betrothed." He started toward the door but stopped suddenly. "By your leave, Aunt, let this be our secret. I shouldn't want Kate to know that I am arranging a marriage for her. She might not appreciate our efforts. As a girl she possessed a rare and terrible independent streak."

Cordelia held a finger over her lips. "Say no more. But I shall immediately require a seamstress and several of your serving maids who are familiar with a needle. And Kate, of course."

"I shall fetch her myself."

Edmund made his way to the garden with purpose to his stride. Until recently his sole objective had been pursuit of the sporting life. One day he bowled, the next he might play tennis with his friend, the Viscount of Lavingham, Christopher Carew. At least once a week he took up his longbow.

He'd also wiled away the time with visits to his mistress until she married several months ago. He'd been adrift without a woman since then, and reluctant to court Judith Witherspoon.

For most of his youth Edmund had looked forward to becoming master of Rose Hall. He'd become the Earl of Stamford by default.

He met his obligations at court and Parliament, but 'twas not the country life he was born to. Edmund meant to farm, feed the masses, and provide work for the country folks. He dreamed of raising a family and teaching his son to fish in the same stream he had as a boy . . . fishing with Kate.

But an earl did not farm. He left the running of his estate to his steward. An earl counseled the queen and made laws to benefit his country. With Reggie's unexpected demise, Edmund's dream ended.

He found solace in sport.

To make up for the lack of attention during his childhood, Edmund required the approval and love of all those around him. It did not take him long to discover that winning at sports competitions rewarded him with a shower of admiration. Winning became all-important. He could not expect the unconditional love bestowed upon him by his hound, Percy. God's blood, he missed Percy!

Patches of weeds grew in the small garden behind Edmund's town house. The bleak, barren branches of a dying cherry tree reached for the sky. A gravel path wound beneath two apple trees at one end of the garden to a pair of cherry trees at the opposite end—one living, one dying. Amid the neglected flower beds several stone benches provided resting spots. In the center of the garden sat a lovely marble fountain filled with dried leaves.

Although the light had faded and the air held a chill, Kate sat on her heels and continued to dig. She would not be in London long enough to restore the garden, but she could at least rid the area of weeds and plant needed herbs.

Although *Two Gentlemen From Verona* had been delightful, she had not accomplished her purpose. One goldsmith's opinion was not enough. Beacham's ignorance of her ring's origin could not dishearten her. A skilled craftsman had created the intricate ring; she would find him or find someone who knew him. Early on the morrow, she would contrive to embark on an outing to Goldsmith Row by herself. She could not leave London until she had visited each shop.

Engrossed in her thoughts and work she did not hear Edmund until he stood above her.

She started at his voice.

"Mistress Kate, do you garden by moonlight?"

Her heart leaped at his smile.

Oh, fie! No less than a pound of dirt lodged beneath her nails, spattered her dress, and more than likely smudged her face. "I do."

Edmund held out his hand. "You must come in, now. 'Tis growing dark and cold."

She looked down at her hands, caked with dirt. She stared at his outstretched hand, large, smooth, clean, and warm. She knew the warm, sheltering feelings of his handclasp and always took pleasure in it, no matter how fleeting.

Rocking on her heels, Kate turned back to the garden. "I must finish planting the sassafras and comfrey. No home should be without these remedies, Edmund."

"Are you scolding me?"

"Would I be so bold as to scold the Earl of Stamford?"

"Aye."

"Why did you allow your garden to go to ruin? Roses, sweet william, tulips, and pansies would make beautiful beds."

"Beds? Oh, aye." Edmund folded his arms across his broad chest. As he cocked his head, the unruly midnight lock fell across his brow. "The garden is never used, and I know not one rose from another. Except for a professional gardener like your papa, men do not take an interest in discovering a new rosebud. We are happier discovering the fox during a hunt."

"Others might enjoy your garden."

"No *others* come to Stamford House."

"Your sister has been here frequently—"

"Only since you and Aunt Cordelia arrived."

"You have invited Master Moore and Judith Witherspoon to dinner on the morrow."

"James Moore has never asked to see my garden, and I would never jeopardize Lady Judith's health by bringing her out in the cool night air. She might catch her death . . . of something."

"In just a short time, one of your gardeners from Rose Hall could transform this plot of land into a beautiful garden."

"Would that make you happy?"

"Aye, because in the end a lovely garden would bring you joy."

And she would do the largest or smallest thing to make Edmund happy. Behind his disarming grin, the smile that caused her knees to go as limp as runny porridge, Kate detected discontent.

"A fully stocked fish pond would give me greater joy," he chided, giving her the grin that melted all resolve. "Come, Kate."

"Edmund—"

"I shall send for a gardener from Rose Hall on the morrow." His other hand shot out so that he extended both to her. "Now, come."

Kate lowered her eyes. "My hands are dirty."

"It makes no matter. I have no fear of dirty hands."

She put her hands in his, and Edmund pulled her to her feet with ease. "What *do* you fear?"

The corners of his mouth turned up in a wry smile.

He shrugged. Kate's pulse bounded into a racing beat. She truly had no resistance to his charm.

"I fear nothing," he replied after a moment's thought. "What do you fear, Kate . . . besides poor Percy, who adores you?"

"I fear never knowing who I am." Tugging her hands from the encompassing warmth of his, she turned on her heel.

"Stay, Kate."

She stopped.

"I know who you are."

She turned. His green eyes gleamed fiercely as they met hers. "You are the first star."

"What?"

"Look up. Do you see it shining, lighting the night before all the others? 'Tis the loveliest."

Kate's heart pounded wildly, while her mind whispered . . . her papa's warning. Edmund wanted something from her. Else why would he speak to her with a silver tongue?

"Now, go, Kate. My aunt awaits you."

With a slight nod, Kate did as he bid. Slowly, for her knees knocked uncontrollably. She took time to compose herself as she made her way to Lady Cordelia's chamber. But the earl's uncommon compliment was forgotten the moment Kate heard what Edmund's aunt desired of her.

"I am what?" Kate repeated, hoping she had not heard the lady correctly.

"Edmund has given me the task of creating a dinner gown for you."

"Nay."

"Oh, I quite excel at dressmaking, my dear. And we have the finest seamstress to help."

"I meant, I do not need a gown."

"Edmund insists. And I desire you to attend me looking your best."

Edmund again. Did he think he owned her? In his arrogance, did he suppose Kate was just another of his possessions, that he could force her to do as he pleased? Aye. He paid her well to be Lady Cordelia's gentlewoman. In that respect only, did he own her.

Lady Cordelia furnished one of her own gowns of scarlet velvet, merrily babbling about how it could be redesigned for Kate.

The following evening, Kate conceded that Edmund's aunt, with the aid of a talented seamstress and several handmaidens, had accomplished the impossible.

For the first time in her life, Kate was attired in the height of fashion, complete with six yards of an open, stiff, uncomfortable ruff, a dangerously low neckline, and an impossibly awkward Spanish farthingale.

This was her comeuppance for being critical of Judith Witherspoon.

How would she sit with the padded hoop protruding like an unwanted shelf from her hips? How would she stand? For that matter, how would she walk without falling over?

No matter that the crystal-beaded stomacher allowed only the most shallow of breaths. If Kate swooned from lack of air, the evening would end sooner.

'Twas a thought. A contrivance she might feel impelled to call upon.

EIGHT

You will endure constraints with grace

Kate's lungs adjusted to the lack of oxygen soon after she entered the dining chamber for the dreaded petite banquet. But she feared her breasts would spill out of her gown. The beaded stomacher not only deprived her of a single, deep breath; the smothering garment pushed Kate's breasts to hitherto unknown heights.

She was not the only one who worried about an imminent bursting over. Throughout the meal Edmund and James Moore eyed her cleavage surreptitiously. Even Viscount Chumley worried. More than once, Kate caught Alexander's furtive glance.

But the vexing complications of fashionable attire did not end with a flattened stomach and pushed-up breasts.

Unused to wearing a farthingale, Kate very nearly crashed to the floor when it was time to be seated. Too late, she realized she could not recall Cordelia's hurried instructions on how to sit gracefully. Chairs constructed to accommodate farthingales were in short supply in Edmund's home.

Steadied by the barrister, who might have wondered if she'd been sipping sack all afternoon, Kate finally found the hard wooden seat without knocking anything from the table. Once seated, she feared moving. She sat as straight and stiff as a bowstring.

Earlier in the evening, before James Moore and Edmund had concluded their business and entered the dining chamber, Kate was all but ignored. Jane and Viscount Chumley had returned for another evening—which spoke ill of their social life in London. Aunt Cordelia made small talk and blinked at Lady Judith and her mother.

Judith Witherspoon possessed a plain countenance that might have been considered attractive had she smiled. Her blue-gray eyes, more foggy, London-sky gray than country blue, focused over the shoulder of whomever she might be speaking with. A rather disconcerting affectation. Her narrow lips were dyed a deep crimson shade that, unkindly, bled into the corners of her mouth.

Kate suspected Judith's fashionable, ghostlike white complexion had been accomplished with a mixture of ceruse and vinegar. Bedecked with jewels, her silk gown and rather flat chest could barely be seen. However, the lady appeared perfectly at ease in her ruff and farthingale, a feat that Kate now had reason to admire—and envy.

As usual, Jane was resplendent, wearing a dark violet gown, thick ruff, wide farthingale, and deep square neckline. Edmund's sister flicked her fan in a rapid, ceaseless motion.

Kate still had not found her fan, a gift from her papa, and she had forgotten to wear her girdle. It seemed she was always without a necessary item, left behind in haste.

Hopefully, the lovely, ivory-spined fan would be found before the next social engagement—should there be one. Not only did she wish to avoid another petite banquet during her London visit, Kate considered feigning one of Lady Cordelia's headaches shortly, or falling into a swoon to escape the torment of her gown.

"Are you not hungry, Mistress Kate?" James asked. Her dinner partner pointed to her full plate with a greasy fingertip.

"I am overwhelmed by abundance."

The gathering dined on plentiful courses of crab and sturgeon, quail and duck, venison and mutton, bread and cheese, pudding and berries.

Kate ate little, continuing to answer the questions of James Moore, who seemed inordinately fascinated with her life in the country. The handsome barrister brushed against her often; his hand gently touched her forearm with increasing frequency throughout dinner. Having been asked by Edmund to entertain the barrister, she felt bound to give James her complete attention. But she managed to keep an eye on Edmund and Lady Judith as well.

The Earl of Stamford inevitably reacted to whatever Judith said to him with a forced, polite smile. Kate knew Edmund's smile; she had basked in its warmth quite often as a child—and many more times since they'd met again.

Edmund's smile melted her bones, tickled her toes, made her moist in unspeakable places.

What had he called her? The first star of evening.

Kate's heart thumped a quick, merry beat. She cast a glance his way.

Oh, fie! He caught her. Edmund's eyes met hers, held hers.

Time stopped.

Kate ceased to breathe.

Inert, Kate felt her soul departing her body, spiraling toward the dusky green shelter of Edmund's gaze. All at once he seemed the only man in the room.

Pins and needles danced down her spine. 'Twas if she'd been awakened to new life after a long sleep. She held her breath. And then, too soon, the unsettling moment passed.

Edmund's mouth quirked up at the corner. Did he know she'd come undone?

"Do you embroider?" James Moore asked.

"Embroider? Nay, I like to fish, sir," Kate replied. She smiled brightly at her companion, feeling guilty for neglecting him.

"You fish?" Moore repeated.

"Yes."

"Oh."

Kate could not be certain whether his "oh" signaled approval or disapproval. She feared the latter.

"Pray, what do you enjoy, Master Moore?"

"I enjoy games of triumph."

Cards bored Kate. "Do you favor a game of chess, as well?"

"Nay. I never play chess."

Kate hid her disappointment. A part of her hoped to discover that she had a great deal in common with James Moore. Enough to take her mind off the Earl of Stamford.

"Mayhap I can show you the way of it."

"My thanks, Mistress Kate, but I do not care to learn chess."

Forcing a smile, Kate directed her comments to city weather. Perhaps in the course of the evening she would hit upon something the barrister enjoyed.

Following the petite banquet, a madrigal was offered, then a wait played the bagpipe. The haunting sound of the bagpipe pleased Kate, but the musician ended his performance much too soon to suit her.

As the party left the dining chamber for the great hall, James Moore clasped Kate's arm. His gaze fixed on her breasts. "Would you walk with me in the garden?"

Seeing no reason why she should not, Kate agreed. It seemed unlikely they would be missed. Lady Cordelia was in lively conversation with Jane and Viscount Chumley. Edmund appeared well occupied with Judith Witherspoon and her mother.

Kate led the handsome blond barrister to the garden. Several torches had been placed at turns on the path but more at random than with care. The servants of Stamford House did not expect anyone to venture out into the barren garden. No guests in recent memory had done so.

"I fear the garden has been sorely neglected," Kate said.

"Do you enjoy gardening?"

"Aye. A beautiful garden can be achieved within weeks."

" 'Tis true, I am certain." The barrister's gaze had once more drifted to the deep valley of Kate's cleavage.

She stepped out ahead of him. " 'Tis."

With one stride he was beside her again. "I beg you not to fret over the state of Stamford's garden. We are not here to view the flowers, Mistress Kate."

"No?" She splayed a hand over her décolletage.

"We are here to walk in the fresh night air. And to take the opportunity to know each other."

Kate felt suddenly wary of what knowledge Moore required. "The evening air is cool," she replied, laying down a cause for flight.

"Are you cold?"

"No, no." Not yet. " 'Tis a bracing air." Kate felt torn. If the barrister continued to behave as a gentleman she would rather have her teeth chatter from the cold than return to watch Edmund woo Lady Judith.

James slipped his arm around Kate's waist. "Are you enjoying London?"

His forward touch flustered her. "Aye, aye, but I prefer the fresh county air. I have not always to hold a pomander—"

Crushing her ruff, Master Moore moved closer to whisper in Kate's ear. His hot breath tickled. "Only look who joins us on the other side of the garden."

"Edmund and Lady Judith," she pronounced, drawing away.

The barrister chuckled. "Lord Stamford has come to watch over you."

"Nay. Methinks he comes to steal a kiss from Lady Judith."

"You are wrong. I possess an exceptional understanding of human nature, Mistress Kate. Lord Stamford fears I may compromise your honor."

"Lord Stamford has no fears concerning me," she insisted.

"I disagree. Stamford stands ready to protect you from any improper advances I might make."

Kate peered through the flickering torchlight to find Edmund's gaze on her. She could not identify the look in his eyes, nor guess what she might read in them. But he was watching her.

With an indignant puff, she raised her chin and turned away.

What made Edmund believe she required watching? Did he think Kate a simple country miss who could not fend for herself? The arrogance of Edmund's intrusion caused her stomach to burn.

Unfortunately, there was no maze where she and Moore could find privacy in this small garden. James took no further notice of Edmund and Judith. He appeared intrigued by Kate's breasts. His unnatural preoccupation made it seem as if he had never seen a woman's breasts before.

"Do you mind if we sit for a moment, Master Moore? There is a bench beneath the cherry tree."

"I should like that very well."

She moved quickly toward the bench. "I wish to contemplate the stars."

"The stars rule our bile . . . and our destiny," he said, whisking a square of linen over the stone bench to make it clean for her.

"I believe so as well!" Kate declared, delighted to hear James Moore was not skeptical of the science as was Edmund.

She sat down and patted the empty space beside her, urging the barrister to join her. He did, grinning broadly. Kate hoped Edmund witnessed her invitation. Her agitation with the earl emboldened her.

"I oft consult an astrologer on behalf of my clients, as well as myself," James added.

"How wise of you."

"I am a practical man. Without an astrologer I would not always know what course to take in legal matters." He lowered his voice and leaned in to Kate again. "I knew when I met you that you were the beautiful woman predicted for me. A woman from a far place who would capture my heart."

"You flatter me, but the prediction you cite is general in nature and might mean another."

"Mistress Kate would you—" The lawyer halted

midsentence. A terrible frown drew his brows together over the bridge of his nose.

"What it is?" Kate asked.

"I do believe Lord Stamford and Lady Judith are coming to join us."

Kate bristled. Could she not have a word with a man in private without interference from Edmund? What was he about?

In the heat of anger, she reached up to frame James Moore's face between her hands. With no thought other than to give Edmund something to be truly upset about, Kate quickly lowered the startled barrister's lips to hers, kissing Moore hard and full on the mouth.

She heard the gasp, but Kate could not be sure if it came from Edmund or Judith. She withdrew only in time to see the earl hurry his lady from the garden.

"Mistress Kate!" James Moore was plainly stunned.

Wide-eyed in horror for what she'd done, Kate pleaded for the lawyer's forgiveness. "I do not know what came over me."

Moore reached for her. "I do hope you will be overcome in the same manner again."

Leaping up, Kate cried headache and fled to her chamber, leaving the flummoxed barrister alone and dazed in the cool, weedy garden.

Once behind closed doors, Kate flung herself across the feather bed without heed to her farthingale. Her dress flew up in the back. But she did not heed the cold air caressing her bare bottom. She sobbed with wretched abandon. She'd behaved like a hoyden for a reason she did not fully understand.

Kate felt certain of only one thing. She required the counsel of a skillful astrologer. Her stars were askew.

* * *

As soon as he could gracefully excuse himself from Lady Judith, Edmund marched to Kate's small chamber. James Moore had left within seconds of the shocking incident in the garden.

Edmund's blood boiled. His jaw ached from clenching his teeth. Enveloped in red-hot fury, he burst into the room without a knock—and was met by the sight of Kate's bare bottom. And the sound of her sobs.

A beautiful, softly rounded, creamy, inviting bare bottom.

Heart-wrenching sobs.

Transfixed by Kate's captivating bottom, Edmund hardly noticed the sobbing had stopped. Her head snapped around and she tried to set herself straight, rolling over, pushing down on the farthingale, rocking to a sitting position.

Edmund's anger threatened to dissolve in a gale of laughter. Wondering at her tears, spellbound by the mass of honey curls falling like a dazzling golden curtain beyond Kate's shoulders, he was momentarily immobilized. Mesmerized.

In the silence, an astonishing transformation occurred. Eyes brimming with tears a moment before, now flashed golden daggers at him.

"Do you no longer knock on a maiden's door?" she hissed.

Edmund's fury reasserted itself. Glowering, he seized Kate's wrists and brought her to her feet.

"What was the meaning of the scene in the garden?"

"What scene, pray?" She wrenched from his grasp.

"You kissed James Moore like a wench working

in . . . in some bawdy house." Edmund ground the words through his teeth.

She sucked in her breath in a noisy gasp. "Did you not request that I entertain Master Moore?"

"Not in that manner!" he roared. "I did not expect you to entertain my barrister in such a bold, utterly brazen manner!"

Bloody hell! He'd lost control. Beset at once by both anger and desire, he flailed his arms in frustration. Kate's heaving breasts, the intoxicating tangle of her flaxen curls and her lips, full and moist, conspired to ignite an aching in Edmund's loins such as he'd never known.

He fought through the pain, longing to ask Kate if she enjoyed the barrister's kiss. Had Moore's kiss made her heart quicken? Had Moore's kiss held more passion than Edmund's?

Instead, he continued to rage. "Bloody hell! Is this how you entertain in the country?"

"At every opportunity," she bristled.

"In London society, women do not seduce men. Such behavior frightens a man of goodwill and honor. 'Twill be a wonder if James Moore calls upon you again."

"It does not matter."

"And I cannot blame him."

"Why should I care?"

"You must have a husband."

"No, I must find my mother before I marry."

"Find a husband first, and then you will have the means and time to search for a mother . . . who does not want to be found."

Kate's hands balled into fists at her waist. Her eyes narrowed in steely defiance. "You will not dissuade me."

"You are too stubborn."

"And you are far too arrogant."

"If you persist in the behavior you displayed in the garden your reputation will be such that no man will want you," Edmund warned.

Or every man in London would be beating down his door for a chance at Kate.

She folded her arms beneath her breasts. " 'Tis fine with me," she huffed.

Her angry motion drew Edmund's attention once again to her bountiful breasts. His marveling gaze fastened on her left breast. A dusky mole shaped like a heart beckoned the touch of his fingertip, the brush of his lips.

God's blood! He wanted her. He ached for her. He would die for her.

Had he gone mad?

Edmund took hold of himself, raised his eyes to Kate, and breathed deeply. He must overcome this undeniable physical attraction. The gardener's daughter was untouchable to him. But the futility of his feelings only served to stir Edmund's simmering anger.

If this were a game, he would not be winning. He'd never had such a worthy opponent as Kate in any tennis match, bowling game, or game of billiards.

Edmund took another deep breath and swiped the lock of hair back from his forehead. "Have you not heard me, Kate?" he asked in a conciliatory tone. "With your beauty and intelligence you can make a good match that will enhance your future."

"My future is written in the stars, not by you, Lord Stamford."

Damn her, she would not give an inch. Well, he would just have to find Kate a husband without her help.

"We shall be leaving for my bookseller's first thing in the morning. Be ready."

Edmund stormed from her chamber before she could reply. He returned to the great hall slowly. Calming himself for Lady Judith, who remained serene and malleable in all matters. Thank the Lord.

Aside from a clipped, "Good day," greeting the following afternoon, Edmund remained aloof and silent. Tension had been the third passenger in the coach during the ride from Stamford House to Cheapside and the bookseller's shop.

Kate told herself Edmund's disapproval mattered not. The only matter of importance was finding the woman who birthed her. She did not understand a whit why Lord Stamford insisted she purchase a book. But he had been behaving strangely of late.

The bookseller's shop was small, dank, and dark. The musty smell of the rush-covered dirt floor and the acrid odor of tallow candles had Kate holding her pomander extremely close to her nose.

Edmund made the introductions tersely, through compressed lips. "This is Mistress Kate. I have brought her so that she might purchase a book of her choice. Kate, this is Master Webster."

A tall, hulking man, Master Webster bowed deeply. The fabric of the bookseller's garments was worn thin, and one of his unwashed stocks bore holes. In his own unkempt fashion, the bookseller cut quite a remarkable figure.

He possessed a wide mouth and large hooked nose. Streaks of gray ran randomly through his long walnut-colored hair. A flowing moustache and abundant beard covered most of his face, save for his nose and eyes, the shade of dark ale.

"'Tis my pleasure to serve you, Mistress Kate." The giant whistled when he spoke. Every uttered "s" became a whistle.

"My thanks, kind sir." Kate tipped her head and smiled, determined to be pleasant and polite.

"I beg your leave," Edmund said, backing toward the door. "I have an appointment to keep but will return shortly."

"Are you leaving me?" Kate asked.

"Selecting a book is a personal matter," he replied smoothly. "And there is no one I trust more than Webster to assist you. By the time you have selected your purchases, I shall return."

"But I must visit Goldsmith Row. I shall not tarry here."

Edmund's brows drew together in a menacing frown. "Do not leave Webster's shop until I return for you," he warned.

"But—"

"I shall not be long."

Edmund disappeared before Kate could say more. He oft did that. Resigned, she turned to the bookseller. "What books do you suggest?"

"Have you read Chaucer, Mistress Kate?"

"Aye," Kate nodded.

She thought Webster to be at least some fifteen years older than she. Turning away from the bookseller, she moved toward a stack of books. Though she loved books, at present Kate preferred to be in a goldsmith shop.

As she reached out for the book atop the stack, Kate felt Webster's breath upon her neck. He stood so close behind her she could feel the heat of his body and its unpleasant moldy odor. She stepped away.

He followed.

Kate turned. "Sir, you stand too close."

"Mistress, are you a married woman?"

His impertinence astounded her. "Why do you ask such a question?"

Webster grinned. Several bottom teeth were missing, the reason he whistled perhaps. "I am seeking a wife, and you are most pleasing to my eye."

Oh, fie.

"You flatter me, sir, but unlike you, I am not seeking a husband."

"A woman is not complete without a man, and you would make an excellent wife and mother."

"Mother!" Kate exclaimed. "You have made a mighty leap."

"I have six children in need of a mother."

"Six children? God save you!"

"The wee ones have been motherless for more than a month, now."

"A month?" she repeated. "You have been a widower for only thirty days?"

"Thirty-one."

"I do hope you find a mother for your children soon," Kate said as she glided to the door. "My thanks for your help, but I have remembered another appointment." Before departing, she turned and gave him a little wave. "Good day."

She all but slammed the door behind her. Although Kate worried about walking the street by herself, and Edmund had warned her to stay put . . . at the moment Kate could not think of anything more dangerous than being alone with a man who had sired six children!

Surely she could find Goldsmith Row, where she had urgent business. No doubt Edmund would be angry with her for leaving the shop, but when he heard of the bookseller's forward behavior, even he must forgive her.

Securing her pomander close to her nose and breathing deeply of its heavy ambergris, Kate sailed along the dusty road as if she knew exactly where she was headed. She smiled at the beggars, wishing she had a spare shilling to give them, ignored the many vendors who cried out at her to buy meat pies, oysters, and cakes.

In the midst of the melee, with so much to see, she did not notice the man following her as she passed a puppeteer and several print shops and taverns.

Kate had made her way to Fleet Street. Which was not where she wanted to be. She stopped to look for a kindly face to ask directions to Goldsmith Row.

The man who darted up alongside Kate not a moment after she stopped, startled her.

"Are ye lost, little lady?"

Dressed as a beggar, the stranger smelled heavily of ale.

"I am looking for Goldsmith Row."

"Aye, 'tis on my way. Come with me."

Before Kate could refuse, the ruffian clasped her wrist and hurried her toward a narrow, dark alley.

"Prithee, sir. Tell me the directions and I shall be off with no bother to you."

" 'Tis no bother," he replied gruffly, giving her a broad toothless smile. "We're takin' a shortcut."

Kate dug in her heels. "Nay."

Balking did no good. No one on the road took notice or cared about her predicament. Kate knew true fear for the first time. Her stomach tossed and pitched. Soon she would be sick all over the man.

Ignorant of the state of her stomach, the scurrilous rogue yanked her forward. “Aye. You’ll come with Ned one way ’tor the other. Easy or not.”

They had reached the shadows. Her pulse raced like a runaway pony. Kate opened her mouth to scream. A gritty hand clapped hard over her mouth.

Though muffled, Kate raged at the man as he hauled her deeper into the forbidding, foul-smelling alley of rotting vegetables, discarded rags, and waste.

Dear God, was she about to die?

NINE

The conjunction of Pluto assures your safety

Kate struggled, but she could not scream. Neither could she breathe. The rank hand muffling her cries was also smothering her. But the rogue did not appear to notice her distress as he dragged her stumbling body out of sight.

"I'll have yer ring milady," he growled. "And yer girdle."

Thump. Thump. Thump. The hard, heavy beat of fear pounded against the walls of her heart like a battering ram. Her pulse raced like a hare in the wood.

With as much strength as she could summon, Kate kicked her left foot backward toward her abductor, lashing out in the general direction of his private parts. 'Twas an honest effort, but she missed her mark. Her patten caught in her shift, throwing her off balance and flat against the malodorous fellow she wished to distance herself from. As she fought to regain her footing, she heard the unmistakable sound of her only lace-trimmed undergarment ripping.

"Kate!"

Edmund.

At the sound of the Edmund's voice, the thief dropped his foul hand from her mouth. Intending to beat on the maggot, Kate turned and—was sick all over him.

Crying out in disgust or rage—Kate couldn't be certain which—the horrid man ran down the alley into the dark stench.

Coughing and sputtering, unable to stand on legs gone to pottage, Kate braced herself against the brick wall.

Edmund rushed to her side. "God's blood, Kate!"

Head spinning with relief, she mustered a feeble smile.

The earl regarded her through narrowed, shadowed eyes. "Are you hurt? Are you all right?"

"Aye." She pushed away from the wall and wobbled toward the street. "I am fine."

Edmund caught Kate's elbow, steadying her. "Why did you leave the bookseller's shop? Did I not warn you?" he demanded in a soft, raspy voice.

"Aye."

"The streets are dangerous for a woman alone."

"Nothing is more dangerous than a widower with six children."

His jaw tightened. "You are fortunate I saw you pass by the tavern."

"Tavern?"

"Carew met me at the Bird in Hand for an ale."

"You left me in the bookseller's shop alone so that you might drink with a friend?" Kate cried.

" 'Twas an opportunity for you to make the acquaintance of Master Webster, a good and educated man."

"Why should I wish to do that? The man has more children than a hen has chicks!"

The muscles in Edmund's jaw constricted. He gazed straight ahead as he guided her along the street. "I beg your forgiveness, Mistress Kate," he snapped. " 'Twas a mistake. I can see that now. As well, I see that I must watch you every moment."

Kate jerked her elbow from Edmund's grasp. "You are not my keeper, Lord Stamford. I am not a hound like Percy, and I do not bear watching. Last eve I kissed Master Moore out of anger at you for that very thing. Watching."

"Watching?" he repeated.

"You watch me as if I were a child."

"There are certain instances when a woman requires protection," Edmund declared in an extremely annoying self-righteous tone. "You have just experienced such an instance. Had I not been watching—"

"You were not watching! The only time—"

"I thought you safe with Master Webster."

"No woman is safe with Master Webster," Kate declared. Taking a deep breath, in part a sigh, she continued in more mollified tones. "Do not concern yourself with me, Lord Stamford. I beg of you. I promise I shall take more care in the future."

"So be it. I shall not even glance your way at the queen's ball."

Kate stopped in her tracks. "Queen's ball?"

"Aye. You are my Aunt Cordelia's gentlewoman. You shall be attending."

Feeling much aggrieved, Kate attempted to assist Lady Cordelia with her final preparations for the queen's ball.

This eve the lady's flushed cheeks were caused by excitement rather than fever. Her face had been whitened, her coarse hair drawn back, curled, and dressed with sapphires and rubies.

"I have not been to a ball in ever so long, eh?"

"Are you certain you require my services?" Kate asked.

She had neither been to court nor to a ball and had little desire to attend, save for a bit of curiosity.

"Oh, aye." Cordelia blinked her kohl-lined, hazel eyes at Kate. "I shall be meeting my friend Lady Mason, and what should she think if I had not a gentlewoman accompanying me?"

"The lady's thoughts are not mine to know."

"She should weep for me."

"Never fear, Lady Cordelia, I shan't leave your side."

"You will enjoy the ball, Kate. Look how lovely you are in your new gown."

" 'Tis a beautiful gown," Kate agreed.

The folds in the old woman's snow-white brow deepened, suggesting a troublesome thought. "Do you know how to dance?"

"Is there a soul in England who does not know how to dance?"

Touching her fingertip to the corner of her mouth, Lady Cordelia thought a moment before shaking her head. "Nay, methinks not. But the queen especially favors the galliard."

"A dance I know well," Kate assured her. "But should a gentlewoman dance at the ball?"

"You may with my permission, and I should certainly give it whenever I am not in need of your service."

"My thanks, Lady Cordelia."

But who would she dance with? The limner? The bookseller? The barrister? She did not expect them to be at the ball. The men she had met thus far in London held little interest for her. And she expected they felt the same about her. Kate had no desire to meet any man, unless he happened to be a goldsmith.

"After attending Lady Mason's physician this afternoon, I consulted her fortune-teller as well. Both pleased me."

"The city seems to agree with your health," Kate commented.

Contrary to Kate's experience, Lady Cordelia had not been attacked by a villain. *Her* life had not been in danger.

Body-racking shudders still assailed Kate when she thought of how close she had come to being robbed of her ring, of her life.

She preferred the country, felt more grateful than ever to have been raised by a gardener and his wife. Simple, honest people.

" 'Tis the air! The physicians!" the old woman exclaimed with an enthusiastic clap of her hands. "I feel like a babe again."

A babe? Kate chuckled. "It pleases me to see you robust once again," she said, doubting it was the foul air responsible for Cordelia's blooming health. More likely being with friends and family made the difference.

A rap on the chamber door brought Lady Cordelia to her feet. " 'Tis time to leave for the ball!"

In the privacy of her small chamber, Kate had practiced moving her head while wearing a ruff. She had practiced walking and sitting in the steely boned Spanish farthingale. If nothing else, she felt confident that she could remain steady on her feet throughout the eve and be seated without embarrassing herself.

Dancing was another matter. The prospect of hours alone in the company of Jane, Judith, and Lady Cordelia still another.

Nonetheless, Kate and Edmund's sick old aunt were off to the ball.

Donald Cameron, Duke of Laird, kept a London residence on the Strand, near Whitehall Palace. He resided in the well-appointed town house when visiting court on diplomatic business. Donald had long acted as liaison between Queen Elizabeth and her nephew and heir, King James of Scotland. His king.

But Donald was weary of political manipulations and court intrigue. Concerned with Anne's health, he'd left his heart in Scotland, chafed at having to be in England.

His ethereal lover of over twenty years had turned Donald away many times in the past without affording him the opportunity of seeing her. Her latest, capricious rejection troubled him beyond measure.

Dear Lord, had it been twenty-five years? His memory did not serve him as it had when he was younger. Where had the time gone?

Like a lovely, elusive illusion, Anne had lured Donald into her life with an unspoken promise of sharing their lives. A promise that had not come to fruition in the way he'd hoped. But he stayed. No woman he'd met in the past possessed the quick intelligence, humor, and passionate nature of Anne. Her fragile beauty reminded him of one of the faerie creatures who might be found floating above the moors. She was never far from his thoughts.

Still exhausted from his journey, Donald rested on his grand canopied bed before a roaring fire. Where once it took him only a few days to recover from travel, it now took a full week. His gaze fixed on the flames, but his mind was lost in musings; he did not really see the flames at all.

In some inexplicable way he felt tied to Anne's soul, a consequence, he supposed, of the length of their strange relationship. Donald knew all was not well at Downes Castle, just as surely as he knew his name.

Following a sharp rap, his chamber door opened. His valet had come to dress him for the ball. The queen's ball promised to be a lavish event. Although Donald did not enjoy such affairs, attendance was necessary.

As Rob dressed him for the eve, the duke paid little attention. He was a large man, standing six feet and three inches tall, with the solid trunk of an aging soldier. His auburn hair receded a bit more each year, and scars from old battles fought for space within the deepening folds of his face. Donald's brown eyes had seen more battles in his fifty years than he cared to remember. He had oft smelled death. And in his weariness he understood well why Anne had withdrawn from the world. His own faith in humanity waned. His spreading middle girth served as a constant reminder of advancing old age. He silently raged against his loneliness. Too late, Donald had felt the fear of spending his last days alone and forgotten. Anne must marry him upon his return to Scotland. He would not take no for an answer.

Donald's first wife Caragh died in childbirth. The child, a daughter, died as well. Fearing to love again, he chose to devote himself to his country, to improve the lot of his fellow Scotsmen. He had told himself he did not love Anne. 'Twas no more than a fondness he felt for the English lass.

Raising sheep and farming gave him a prosperity he had not thought to have; defending his people at the English court lent him a leadership role he had not sought.

While Donald counted dozens of acquaintances and scores of cousins scattered about the country, he had but one close friend who could be trusted. Only one who would sit by the warmth of the hearth in the evenings. Anne, who might or might not agree to his company depending on her mood.

Up until now, this arrangement with the ungovernable woman had satisfied Donald. No questions asked; no permanent attachment assumed. With each other they had found pleasant companionship and sexual pleasures, trust and respect. In the past, he could not desire, nor ask for, more. But now, with advancing age, loneliness loomed ahead like a dark abyss, ready to swallow him. Unless he made changes in his life, unless he persuaded Lady Anne to marry him.

Confident that he would soon change his life, the Duke of Laird left the stillness of his home for a boisterous eve at the queen's ball.

The great hall at Whitehall Palace was ablaze with torches and candlelight. The queen's most gifted musicians played, and the ladies and their lords danced in a swirl of colorful costumes and glittering jewels.

Queen Elizabeth had not yet made her entrance when Edmund escorted Lady Judith across the hall to where his aunt held her own court.

Lady Cordelia, with a silver goblet of sack in hand, was happily surrounded by a bevy of old friends—and one excessively somber gentlewoman.

But Kate's solemn expression did not hide her beauty.

One look, and she took Edmund's breath away.

He slowed, gawking like a schoolboy at the gardener's daughter. Thankful for his height, that he could see above the heads of the crowd, he could keep her in his line of sight, ravish her with his unseen study.

The slender, proud form of his former fishing companion stood in striking contrast to the women surrounding her. Kate, a graceful willow swaying alone in a copse of buckthorn bushes.

And if her gown was any indication, his aunt had succeeded in selecting a wardrobe beyond compare for her companion. Yards of fabric had been fashioned into the white-on-white brocade gown, stitched through with golden thread and trimmed with pearls. The pointed bodice emphasized Kate's tiny waist, and an open ruff of Italian lace displayed the elegant column of her neck.

'Twould be delightful to slide his fingertips along that exquisite arch . . . stroke the silky texture. To know her.

Edmund's gaze drifted to Kate's porcelain breasts, rising high above the low square neckline. The plunge of deep, sweet décolletage would prove tempting to a saint. He was no saint. 'Twould be heaven to press his lips against her breasts. To taste her softness. To know her.

"Edmund?" The squeaky voice of the woman at his side reminded him he escorted Lady Judith.

But he had not finished his perusal of the loveliest woman at the ball. His were not the only eyes upon her. She was the object of much attention, from lords and ladies alike.

Observing Kate from a distance, once more without her leave, Edmund found he simply could not look elsewhere. Ropes of pearls circled her neck and were woven through her tawny curls.

Edmund's palms grew moist. His mouth dry.

"Edmund?"

"Yes, Judith."

"Why have we stopped?"

He smiled down at her. "Have we?"

"In a matter of steps we shall be at your aunt's side," she pointed out with some asperity.

Feeling the cad, Edmund gave Judith a rueful smile. "Come, I did not mean to tarry."

Aunt Cordelia welcomed them warmly. Kate offered a gracious but distant greeting. When her eyes locked on Edmund's, his heart bolted.

Bloody hell.

Time was running out to find her a husband. Kate and Aunt Cordelia would be returning to the country soon. If he could only turn Kate's mind from searching for her natural mother, she might be more receptive to potential suitors.

Edmund feared Kate would be hurt if she continued in her quest. If he ever laid hands on the stargazer who advised her to find her mother, Edmund swore to run the woman out of the country. Jutta. That was all he knew of her, her name and that she lived in the village. At least, here in the city the astrologer could not influence Kate.

As it was, she was quite unpredictable. From moment to moment, Edmund never knew quite what to expect from her.

"Where are you, Edmund?" his aunt cajoled. "You appear miles away when you should be dancing with Lady Judith."

"Indeed." With a bow to his lady and a sidelong glance at Kate, who looked askance, he reluctantly led Judith to the dance floor.

Although he'd left her company, Kate lingered in

Edmund's mind. Over and over, he searched the throng for her. Later, after the queen had made her entrance and joined the dancing, Edmund caught sight of his aunt's gentlewoman dancing with Christopher Carew. He felt both a sense of relief and satisfaction.

During their interrupted meeting at the tavern, he had asked his friend to dance with Kate at the ball. He wished her to enjoy the only court function she would ever likely attend. He could not condemn his amber-eyed friend to spend the entire eve on the sidelines with Aunt Cordelia and Lady Mason.

Shortly after her dance with Carew, Edmund spotted Kate dancing with Donald Cameron, the Duke of Laird. All eyes were on the couple, who appeared quite striking together. Edmund gave a low grunt of disapproval. The duke was too old to be a spirited husband to Kate. She needed someone young and strong and potent. A masterful man. A man more like . . . himself.

Knowing he risked her wrath, Edmund surreptitiously watched Kate with the duke. She smiled often at Laird. They talked. He laughed. Edmund chafed.

When he discovered them dancing again near the end of the evening, his stomach roiled with displeasure. Was the Scotsman thinking he could take Kate as his mistress?

"Weel na, I am honored a young bonny lass would deign to dance with an old Scot a second time."

"Nay, my lord, 'tis I who am honored that you would ask me."

Kate felt safe in his arms. She had liked the Duke of Laird the moment the side of her farthingale knocked the goblet out of his hand. She hadn't meant to turn so quickly. And he *was* holding his ale too low.

"Ye dance with the lightness of a feather."

Kate felt her cheeks heat. "Pray, you are too kind."

"Ye must attend many balls."

She lowered her voice. "In truth, I am a gardener's daughter."

Donald Cameron frowned, an expression of disbelief that pleased Kate. "Weel na, I wouldna have guessed," he said. "Ye are wise for so young a lass, gardener's daughter or no."

Because she had taken an instant liking to and trusted this sweet man in his glorious kilts, Kate whispered her secret. "I was sent abroad and educated by nuns in an Italian convent."

His warm brown eyes widened in surprise. "An' how did yer mother an' father manage such a feat?"

"I was a foundling," she explained, no longer feeling the shame of it as she had when she was young. "The funds were given with the condition they be used for my education long ago. When I was left at Mama and Papa's door."

The duke shook his head. " 'Tis astonishing."

"I suspect my father to have been a wealthy noble, and my mother . . ." Kate paused to draw breath. "You are familiar with the story, my lord."

"Oh?" His bushy, snow-peppered auburn brows gathered in a downhill slope.

"A nobleman taking advantage of a poor serving girl, or peasant?" she prompted.

"Ah, weel na, aye. I am familiar with that old tale. But you appear weel, lass, an' obviously attached to wellborn acquaintances."

She smiled. "When I was a girl, I fished with Lord Stamford."

"Lord Stamford?" The duke hiked a brow. "A good man."

"He has made me gentlewoman to his aunt."

Laird's expression grew grave. He lowered his voice. "Serving as his aunt's companion is all the earl has asked of ye?"

"Oh, aye, my lord," Kate replied quickly, unwilling to damage Edmund's reputation, no matter how she felt about him at the moment. "Lord Stamford is a fine gentleman. And I shall not repeat the sins of my past, you can be certain."

The duke smiled then, a broad friendly grin that seemed to wipe away the scars settled deeply into the lines of his craggy face. "Aye. Ye have beauty an' grace. Ye shall lead a sweet life, lass."

" 'Tis my fondest wish." Kate felt reassured by Donald Cameron's words and smile. She had confided more than she ought to a stranger.

"Ye shall marry a prosperous merchant an' raise a flock of children."

"Perhaps," she agreed. "After I find my mother."

"An' tell me how do ye hope to do that, lass?"

"With the ring I was sworn to never remove. If I find the goldsmith who created the ring, he in turn will tell me who commissioned it to be fashioned."

"Have ye thought yer ring might have been stolen or—"

"If it were stolen, why would I be forbidden to remove it?"

"Weel, 'tis a proper question. May I see this ring?"

Before Kate could show the duke her ring, she heard a familiar voice at her side.

"By your leave, Laird."

Edmund. He stood so close to Kate he risked a farthingale wound.

One explanation screamed within her head. Lord Stamford had been watching her again! Like a salter, not to be stolen from his table, he'd come to be certain she was safe.

With a pleasant smile, the duke stepped aside. "Lord Stamford. Ye look weel."

"My thanks. I did not know you were in London."

"I have only recently arrived to do business with yer queen."

"You are a loyal and steadfast spokesman for King James and Scotland," Edmund said in a respectful, yet rather terse, tone. "I admire your dedication."

"There is much to accomplish," the Duke of Laird replied modestly.

"I see you have met Kate."

"Aye, bonny Kate." The duke smiled down at her.

She returned his smile, happy in the feeling she had made a friend in London.

"Kate is my Aunt Cordelia's gentlewoman," Edmund said.

Kate stiffened. Not only did she not appreciate being talked of as if she had evaporated from their sight, she feared what Edmund might be about to say next.

"Aye. An' I have no doubt the lady is fortunate, indeed."

Edmund's emerald eyes clouded. "Indeed. By your leave, Lady Cordelia has been asking for Kate. She must return to her duties."

A surge of disappointment mingled with fresh anger in Kate's midsection. She dipped a curtsy to the Duke of Laird. "My thanks, my lord."

"Nay, thanks to ye, lass. Ye have lightened this eve for a lonely old man."

With a firm hand, Edmund hastily guided Kate toward a vacant area near the rear of the great hall.

"How did you happen to dance with an old Scottish duke?" he demanded.

"Were you not watching?"

"Insolence does not become you, Kate."

"If you must know, I bumped into the duke. 'Twas an accident. Being a kind gentleman, he took mercy upon me and asked me to dance. Lady Cordelia was otherwise occupied so I saw no reason not to dance. I like to dance."

"You had already danced with Carew."

"Should I enjoy only one dance?"

"No. I am going to dance with you, as I intended from the start. Come."

But Kate did not budge. "Have you taken pity on me?"

"Nonsense," Edmund scoffed. "Come."

"The Duke of Laird is a kind man," Kate muttered.

"Aye, but he is old and a Scot. Moore has asked to call upon you again. Evidently you did not scare him off."

Kate laughed. "Your barrister is a brave man."

As Edmund's sandalwood scent filled her senses, the male heat of him slid beneath her skin. For the first time since arriving at the ball, Kate felt alive. Her body tingled with anticipation. She and Edmund danced together as if they had done so for years. 'Twas a dance of wits as well.

Edmund did not share her good humor. Though he smiled, the sharp timbre of his voice bespoke a churlish mood. "I explained your bold behavior by telling Moore you were weary and agitated from your recent journey from the country."

"Why does the barrister require an explanation?" she wondered aloud.

"Smile, Kate."

"Smile?"

"For those who watch us, and there are many."

"Why do they watch us?" she asked, turning her head to see if she could detect curious eyes.

"Do not look!"

She rolled her eyes. "Pray pardon, my lord."

"And do not roll your eyes in that way," Edmund admonished her beneath his breath. "I have never danced with any of my aunt's previous gentlewomen. And you . . . you are the fairest woman at the ball."

His strained compliment did not ease Kate's annoyance with him. "How do you expect me to smile when you intrude upon my affairs?"

Smiling broadly, Edmund dipped his head in silent greeting toward another couple. "I am attempting to assist you."

"How?" Kate bristled. "Despite your promise, you do not accompany me to Goldsmith Row. I am forced to go alone—"

"No one forced you," he interrupted, his gaze flitting about the dance floor. "Smile, Kate."

"Explain how you are helping me, *my lord.*"

"I am engaged in finding a prosperous husband who will keep you in fine fashion."

"By your leave?" Shock flashed through her like a bolt of lightning, deadening all feelings left in its wake.

"Smile, Kate."

"I do not desire a husband. I do not seek one. I do not care to meet another limner, bookseller, or barrister. Do I make myself clear?"

"If you do not smile, the queen will take me to task."

"I should like see your head on the tower of London," Kate shot back . . . and smiled.

"You will understand the wisdom of my—"

"Shall we stroll in the garden, my lord?" Though she spoke through her teeth, Kate smiled.

But there was no joy in her smile. 'Twas for the others, for those Edmund thought might be watching. Fearing she could not contain her anger another minute, flight seemed advisable.

Edmund frowned. " 'Tis cold, Kate."

"I shall warm you with the flames from my tongue, Lord Stamford."

TEN

While the moon is in aspect to Venus you will not speak in anger

Kate had seen several couples slip through the side door to the garden, no doubt bent on romantic interludes. She, however, had a tongue-lashing in mind as she marched toward the door.

Once outside she sucked in her breath as an icy breeze stung her cheeks. Having no mind to return for her cloak, Kate could only hope that her teeth would not chatter and undermine the fury of her words. 'Twas unnaturally cold for this late in spring.

Surrounded on two sides by open, columned galleries, the queen's great garden at Whitehall Palace was laid out in knots. An astonishing number of blazing torches shed light on the paths and brightened the night.

Along fine walks of grass, Kate sallied forth, flouncing past raised flower beds planted within low brick walls. Edmund whistled in a nonchalant fashion as he trailed behind her.

Plots of spices scented the quadrangular area with exotic aromas. Overlooking all, high atop posts and columns, heraldic beasts with horns of gilt bore the queen's arms. In the center of the garden stood an elaborate fountain and magnificent sundial. Although she had not come to view the garden, Kate could not help but take note. Her love of gardening triumphed over her fury. But only for a short time.

Upon reaching the far side of the fountain near the brick boundary walls, Kate spun upon Edmund. Bursting with indignation and plagued with goose bumps, she spoke her mind.

"What gives you the right to interfere with my life, Edmund?" Before he could answer she dug her fists into her hips and leaned forward. "Do you th-th-think me to be your slave?"

"You know I do not," he responded. Frowning, he lowered his eyes and rubbed the back of his neck. "On the contrary, you are—"

She could not bear to hear his platitudes. "By your leave, my lord. You do not own me. Ju-ju-just because I am your aunt's gentlewoman, you do not have the—"

"Pray, be still, Kate." Edmund splayed his large hands before him as if he feared she might spring upon his person.

"Are your teeth chattering? Is that why you stammer?"

"Nay!"

"As you will." 'Twas a condescending reply. He went on in a soft, soothing tone, as if he were attempting to calm a madwoman—which further infuriated Kate. "I promise to find you an upstanding fellow."

She scowled and rubbed her arms briskly.

He gave her a lopsided smile.

The kind of smile that tickled Kate's heart and arrested her breathing. Why must he be so charming? Why must he be so tall, dark, and compelling? Why must he have such an appealing cleft in his chin, and shoulders as broad as the Thames?

To her great consternation, Kate felt her anger ebbing away.

Dismissing all the angry words she meant to say, she turned her gaze heavenward. A pale crescent moon and a blanket of glittering stars filled the clear night sky.

"Are you thinking the planets will hand you a husband?" Edmund asked in a soft, droll tone.

"I trust the stars more than my lord," she sniped.

"You wound me."

"Do you know what I seek in a man?"

Edmund shrugged. "What every woman seeks."

Kate advanced upon him so that they were only inches apart. "Which would be?"

"A kind fellow, with great wealth."

"You mistake the matter, Lord Stamford. I seek much more."

"Pray, enlighten me, Mistress Kate."

She whirled around on the path, thinking to return to the ball before she was missed by Lady Cordelia, or worse, by Lady Judith.

Gazing over her shoulder to where Edmund stood beneath the flickering light of a torch, Kate enlightened him quietly. "When the time comes, I shall seek a husband who is fair and just. A man who owns more than sheep. He shall have intelligence and humor and care not a wit what is said of him because he shall be true to himself." She made for the arched entrance. "And he shall want four children."

Edmund followed Kate; she could hear his boots on the path.

"You desire more than one man can promise," he said. A peevish growl laced his tone.

"There is more."

"God save you!" His boots made a skidding sound on a patch of gravel.

Kate turned and met his eyes. Edmund must not mistake her meaning, nor her resolve. Though there was no one visible in the garden to hear them, Kate spoke in a hushed voice. "I desire a husband whom I may love without reservation. I shall not be merely one of his possessions. My husband will love me with his whole heart and soul . . . evermore."

A silence fell between them, and when at last Edmund responded, he did so with a strange hoarseness. "Loving you will not be difficult . . . for any man."

Kate's heart fluttered madly, and sunk. She lowered her eyes for a fleeting moment before meeting his gaze once more. "Your time would be better spent hawking with your friends—"

"I do not hawk."

"I mean to find my own husband, Lord Stamford."

He hiked an imperious brow. "As you will. But never say I did not attempt to help."

"Oh, fie!" Kate blurted, jolted by fresh anger.

"What say you?" Edmund appeared shocked.

"Prithee, do not meddle in my life henceforth," she warned with a wag of a finger, before turning and sailing from the garden.

Bloody hell! It had been such a simple plan. A plan contrived with the best, most noble intent. How could Edmund have guessed Kate would resent his efforts to find her a husband and save her from a life of servitude. Bloody hell!

There was no understanding the woman.

She successfully avoided Edmund for a week, choosing instead to spend her time with his aunt and sister. Although Edmund knew Kate looked upon physicians with a skeptical eye, loathed shopping, and felt uncomfortable in Jane's presence, she nevertheless accompanied his two relatives to every physician, seamstress, and fortune-teller in London—rather than spend time with him.

Each time Edmund stopped by the garden hoping to find Kate alone, he met new evidence she'd been working in the neglected spot, but she was never anywhere to be seen. He decided his impertinent childhood friend gardened by moonlight purposefully to avoid him.

Edmund grew more disgruntled as the days went by with only a passing nod from Kate. While he oft heard the merry peal of her laughter from behind closed doors, the cause of her amusement was not shared with him. While he might inhale her sweet rose fragrance, 'twas only the slightest whiff that lingered in the halls where she had passed.

Day by day his desperation grew until Edmund did what he knew would be the only way to regain Kate's favor. He accompanied her to every goldsmith in London. 'Twas a tiring, futile ordeal, but Kate appeared content once again.

They had reached the last shop.

"No, mistress. I've ne'r seen the like."

"Do you know where I might look next?" she asked the puzzled goldsmith. "We have exhausted our search at the known goldsmith shops."

"You may have to travel outside of London," the craftsman told her, scratching his head.

Master Brown had been their last hope in London. Upon seeing the crestfallen expression on Kate's face, Edmund felt as if the hand of Hercules gripped his heart and squeezed. Her pain had become his. God's blood.

Clasping Kate's hand, Edmund led her from the shop. "Come, we shall not give up."

"Not give up?" Withdrawing her hand, she inclined her head as if he were a great puzzle. "Only days ago you refused to assist in my search."

"Because I feared what has proved to be so. No one has seen a ring similar to yours or recognizes the craftsmanship. I wished to save you heartache, Kate, but you railed against me as if I were the worst villain."

"I had to make the attempt even though I understood disappointment might be my only reward. Nothing is achieved without effort." Kate's shoulders sagged; her voice softened to barely a whisper. "I know 'tis impossible to visit every goldsmith in Britain."

When Kate looked up at him, tears misted her eyes, the gleaming deep gold giving way to the shadowy shade of dark ale. Her lower lip quivered. "Shall I never know, Edmund?"

Edmund felt as if his heart were being torn from his body. "One day you will know," he said, a lie of kindness meant to comfort. "Perhaps the one who bestowed the ring upon you is also searching . . . and will find you."

Her eyes widened. "Do you truly think so?"

The moment of satisfaction Edmund found for his quick thinking gave way. The new hope shining through Kate's tears caused Edmund's throat to close. He choked.

"Aye," he lied, when at last he found his voice again.

She smiled, a small shaky smile. "You are as kind as you were when just a boy."

In an impulsive move to offer further comfort—as any friend would do—Edmund took up her hand and squeezed it. Soft and warm, her long, slender fingers wrapped around his hand as if it were the natural thing to do. His heart pounded in a sequence of off-rhythm beats. He liked the fit and feeling of Kate's hand in his.

By the time his heart returned to a normal beat, Edmund's feeling of contentment vanished. If he and Kate were seen walking hand in hand, Aunt Cordelia's gossiping friends would embellish his innocent, benevolent gesture to something lewd and improper. 'Twas how gossip prospered. Lady Cordelia would take to her bed in a swoon.

Lady Judith would certainly hear of it as well. She likely would not understand that Kate had been his faithful companion in years past. Judith would not understand the bonds of friendship that might exist between a man and a woman. How could Edmund expect Judith's understanding if he did not fully comprehend it himself? Quite.

Edmund stopped in the center of the road and released Kate's hand, holding his index finger across his lips as if he'd just had a thought. He had.

"There is a fair at Charing Cross. Would you like to attend?"

Kate's head snapped up, and her shoulders straightened. "Oh, aye, Edmund!"

He took it as a favorable sign that she called him Edmund. When the gardener's daughter addressed him as Lord Stamford, it usually meant she was vexed with him. At last she had forgiven his bungled matchmaking attempts!

Assailed by a brief but deep stab of disappointment, Edmund put aside his plans to meet Carew for a game of tennis and a tavern visit or two. Kate required cheering.

'Twas midafternoon when Edmund and Kate reached the fairgrounds at Charing Cross. Beneath a hazy sunlit sky, tumblers and acrobats, jesters and musicians roamed the fairgrounds pestering all to perform for a shilling or two.

Dust and noise abounded. Vendors hawked meat pies, ale, old clothes, and candles. An array of goods from lace to cutlery were on display, and the aroma of warm gingerbread and roasting almonds filled the air.

Though she tried, Kate could not take in all of the sights and sounds, the disparate crowd of people at once. "I have never been to such a large fair," she exclaimed in breathless wonder.

Edmund chuckled softly. "You will find something to please every subject in the queen's kingdom."

"Look! A cunning woman!"

But Edmund did not share Kate's excitement. "A fortune-teller who will cozen many a man and woman before the fair is over."

"I must see if she will cozen me."

"Kate, do you intend to consult her? Is not one stargazer enough?" he asked.

But unable to discourage her, Edmund trailed close at Kate's heels as she hurried to the fortune-teller's crude table.

"Jutta read the planets and stars for me before I left Rose Hall—"

"By your leave?" Edmund interrupted, his tone plainly incredulous.

"How else could I wisely determine my actions if I did not know what lay ahead here in London?"

"Kate, you are not a light-minded woman, how come you—"

"But . . . something is awry," she interrupted, before Edmund could mock her unmercifully, as she knew he prepared to do. "What Jutta predicted for me is oddly off the mark. And I wrote down all that she had to say so that I would not forget."

Her handsome escort groaned.

Despite Edmund's evident displeasure, Kate continued to defend her astrologer. "I fear 'twas a conjunction of the planets Jutta could not fathom nor take into account."

"And mayhap your destiny is not written in the stars. Perhaps you alone influence your future," Edmund argued. " 'Tis only for healing purposes that we should turn to the science of astrology. And even then I am not quite certain."

But Kate no longer listened. She had reached the fortune-teller.

"Welcome. I am Madame Loca, at you service."

Madame Loca possessed a dark olive complexion and flashing, raven eyes. Her high cheekbones stood out sharply and her hair fell over her eyes and about her shoulders in an ebony mass of tangles. Though the day was warm, the young fortune-teller wore layers of plum-colored clothing, and scores of silver bangle bracelets tinkled on her arm.

Kate suspected the forbidding woman was a gypsy, people known for their unfathomable powers to see into the future.

Loca peered up at Kate through her veil of dark hair. "Your fortune for a shilling."

"Edmund, would you mind?"

Edmund withdrew a coin and tossed it to the small table. " 'Tis a waste of a shilling," he grumbled.

"I shall repay you," Kate assured him.

"Do not think of it."

Kate took a seat on the wobbling stool across from the fortune-teller. With a quick smile, she encouraged Madame Loca to begin.

"You have a cloud hanging over your head, lady."

Kate slanted Edmund a knowing sideways glance. "You see, Edmund? The fortune-teller speaks truly from the start."

Edmund rolled his eyes. "Which cloud do you speak of?" he asked Madame Loca. "The cloud above us or the one Kate carries in her mind?"

"Hush," Kate hissed beneath her breath.

The fortune-teller gazed into her hazy ball as if she had not heard either Kate or Edmund. "You shall find love at the end of a difficult road."

"I knew it! I could have told you that, Kate. Show me a beautiful woman who will not find love," he crowed.

Although she fixed a sweet smile upon her lips, Kate narrowed her eyes in warning as she gazed up at him and made her request in a decidedly icy tone. "Please leave us for a moment."

"Bloody hell!"

"Edmund!"

"I am merely attempting to save you from disappointment."

"Edmund."

"Pray pardon. I shall stand way off by the tree."

Kate leaned closer to the fortune-teller. "By your leave, my friend is not a believer."

"He is your lover."

Madame Loca's words pricked at Kate's heart. "Oh, nay. Nay. Edmund can never be my lover."

The fortune-teller shrugged. "I see a life of ease. Many children."

An image of the bookseller and his six children flashed through Kate's mind. "Less than half a dozen children?"

"Four."

Kate let out her breath and asked the most important question. "Do you see the clearing of the cloud that hangs over me and darkens my life?"

"Aye."

"Verily?"

"Aye. Verily.

"When?"

"When you open your heart."

"But my heart is open," Kate protested.

"You must open your heart to all possibilities."

"I do not understand," Kate said.

"All will be made clear."

A heavy, melancholy sigh whispered through Kate's body. Edmund had spoken the truth. She had been cozened. The fortune-teller had no insight.

She felt his eyes upon her, watching her yet again. But when she looked over to the tree, he was not there. 'Twas a bullish stout man who leered at her. Kate's gaze fastened on the stranger's startling blue eyes. He hurried away.

Where then was Edmund?

Kate scanned the crowd, an uneasy feeling stirring in the pit of her stomach. She hadn't far to search for Lord Stamford.

He leaned against a post, his arms folded against his chest, head cocked to one side, contemplating her with an enigmatic smile.

With a start, he straightened. Too late, he must have realized he'd been watching her again. His lips quirked in amusement as he cast Kate a roguish wink and strode off toward a vendor.

No matter how she resolved to control her emotions, Edmund's lusty, black-clad form never failed to make her heart jump, her knees weak, and her bones to melt to butter. If the earl were her lover, Kate should most likely die in his arms of bliss, pure, utter bliss.

A theory Kate would enjoy testing, but knew she never could.

"I see fur," Loca said, gazing into her cloudy ball. "You must overcome fear of animals."

Kate feared only dogs. "Percy?"

"The animal will be a loyal ally."

"Percy!" The fortune-teller went too far.

"The name is not clear."

The bullish man passed behind Madame Loca once again, not ten yards away. Was he attempting to hear Kate's fortune? Had an important person heard of her search among the goldsmiths of London? Someone important to her past . . . and future?

Edmund's low whistling brought Kate back to her senses. Her imagination soared while Lord Stamford waited impatiently. He carried two meat pies.

"Do you see naught else in your crystal, Madame Loca?" Kate entreated the stoic fortune-teller rather desperately.

She had learned nothing. She remained incomplete. Adrift. Was there no one who could supply her answers?

"You are like the restless wind swirling through tunnels and forests, over meadows and sweeping the ramparts. Be silent and open your heart. Contentment will come to you."

The bullish man strode passed in the opposite direction.

Kate beckoned the fortune-teller with a crooked finger and whispered low. "Am I in danger?"

Madame Loca consulted her crystal ball, peering at length into the smoky glass. "Aye."

"Aye?" Although she had asked the question, 'twas not the answer Kate had expected.

Gazing into the flawed crystal, the olive-skinned fortune-teller nodded her head in a grave manner.

"Where does the danger lie?" Kate asked with racing heart.

" 'Tis not clear."

Oh, fie!

The fortune-teller raised her head and smiled. She refused to say more. No amount of prodding by Kate moved her. Finally Kate stood, and after bidding the tangled-haired woman a good day, she marched to where Edmund waited.

"Has the future been made clear to you?"

"Prithee, do not mock me."

"Very well. You are not in a sporting mood." He gave her one of the meat pies as he took another large bite of his.

Kate gulped down the pie. "Mmm. My thanks; 'tis tasty."

"Aye. And did Madame Loca tell you anything of import?" he asked, before licking his fingers.

In grave fascination, Kate watched the tip of his tongue slowly swipe each finger. A delicious chill ran through her. *Oh, hey-ho!*

She would give all her earthly possessions—save her ring—if Edmund would lick her fingers clean.

"Kate?"

"The fortune-teller says that I'm in danger."

"Foolishness."

"There is a man watching me, perhaps following me."

"Kate, influenced by the charlatan wench, you have allowed your imagination to run wild."

"I know when I am being watched."

"Describe the man."

"He puts me in mind of a bull. He is of average height, round and solid with a wide face and flaring nostrils. His eyes are a bright blue, but he wears dark clothing."

"Where did you see him?"

"Where you stand now. He passed by twice while Madame Loca read my fortune."

Instead of expressing alarm, Edmund chuckled. "By your leave, the bull is in league with Madame Loca."

"I do not agree."

"Pray, put this incident out of your mind, Kate. Look, I have a gift for you, so that you will always remember our day at the fair."

He reached into his pocket and pulled out two dainty amber earrings.

"Ooooh, Edmund. How lovely."

"The amber is quite like the shade of your eyes, don't you think?"

Kate did not know what to think.

"I thank you, Edmund."

Light-headed with delight and a dash of confusion, she gazed at the delicate jewels. Jewels for the ears were the newest fashion. She would treasure them always, the only jewelry she owned beside her rose-and-crown ring.

All thoughts of the strange man vanished.

'Twas much later in the day that Kate spotted his bull-like figure standing in the shadows on the Strand, directly across from Stamford House. Before she could point him out to Edmund, the stranger slipped deeper into the shadows and disappeared.

Rather than risk Edmund's cynicism, Kate said nothing.

ELEVEN

Good tidings await you

It was dusk by the time Kate and Edmund returned to Stamford House. 'Twas late, but he did not suppose Aunt Cordelia would miss them overmuch. He hadn't planned on visiting the fair.

And he hadn't expected the number of messages awaiting him. His light-hearted mood evaporated within seconds of ushering Kate over the threshold. Although she'd been saddened by the lack of information about her rose-and-crown ring, she'd been happy at the fair.

Edmund paid no mind to her fear that she was being followed. 'Twas Kate's imagination run amuck yet again. Who would follow a gardener's daughter? And for what reason? Absurd.

The marshal of the hall delivered the first bit of news. "Lady Judith Witherspoon is with Lady Cordelia in her solar, my lord."

Edmund tipped his head in acknowledgment and repressed a groan. 'Twas *trying* to be near Judith.

"The Duke of Laird called upon Mistress Kate. He left his card and these roses."

Kate beamed with pleasure as she took up the large

bouquet of scarlet roses from the bench. The sweet fragrance of the flowers caused Edmund to sneeze.

What was the duke thinking? he wondered. The Scot's sense of protocol seemed sorely lacking. A nobleman sending flowers to a gentlewoman? It wasn't done.

"Look, are they not beautiful?" Kate asked. She buried her nose in the flowers and inhaled a noisy breath.

Edmund dutifully regarded the roses. And instantly regretted the small size of his gift to Kate. The amber earrings, that reminded him of the shade and sparkle of her eyes, fit quite comfortably in the palm of her hand—perhaps on the tip of her finger. The duke's gift of roses filled Kate's arms to overflowing.

"Beautiful and extravagant, as well," he replied dryly, and sneezed once more.

Kate inclined her head, her finely arched brows slanted in the slightest of frowns.

The marshal jumped into the thick, rose-scented silence. "Master Moore also called and left his card. He requested to ride with Mistress Kate on the morrow."

Edmund's belly constricted into a tight lead ball. True, he had recently promised not to meddle in Kate's affairs, but he no longer trusted James. Left alone with Kate, the barrister might take liberties. Kissing the barrister the way she had in the garden no doubt had stirred the man to lust. James had cause to believe Kate a brazen woman, one with whom he could have his way without protest.

Kate smiled. "I should like to ride with James."

The hair on the back of Edmund's neck stood on end. "The barrister asked my permission."

Her eyes darkened. "Have you become my—"

"I am your . . . lord and master." He enunciated each word slowly and clearly.

Kate Beadle's sweet mouth dropped open. A hot crimson flush stained her cheeks. Her eyes grew as wide as tennis rackets and flashed like summer lightning. There was no doubt in Edmund's mind. He'd enraged her.

"I engaged you as companion to my aunt," he added hastily. "I cannot release you to ride with Moore on the morrow."

"And I thought you were my friend," she hissed, out of the butler's hearing.

"You have been with me all the day. Aunt Cordelia shall expect you to spend time with her on the morrow."

The butler's stoic expression did not change, but his dark brown eyes darted nervously from Kate to Edmund and back.

"Is that all?" Edmund inquired of his distressed servant.

"A message from Rose Hall," he replied, delivering the folded parchment to the earl.

Edmund tore open the message while Kate purred over the roses. Roses she could easily grow herself, if he were not mistaken.

My Lord Stamford.

The poaching at Rose Hall has increased. I require direction. Mantraps are required at once.

"What is it?" Kate asked.

"The poaching has grown worse at Rose Hall."

"If you would only open the grounds to the villagers for a short time, the poaching would come to an end," she admonished him softly. "They are hungry."

"Edmund, you have returned."

He recognized the distinctive voice at once, but because he had been deep in thought while mulling over the poaching dilemma, the sound of it jolted him.

Forcing a smile, Edmund turned to greet her. "Lady Judith!"

Judith Witherspoon descended the stairs in a measured, regal fashion. "I have just enjoyed a visit with your aunt."

Edmund ignored her questioning glance, the icy smile she cast Kate's way.

"And lightened my dear Aunt Cordelia's day, I am confident." He extended his hand to help her down the final step.

A twitch of Lady Judith's scarlet lips passed for a smile before she turned her gaze to Kate. With a plainly critical eye, the woman he would marry scrutinized his former fishing companion.

But what could the lady find to criticize? Dressed in a new over gown the soft shade of primroses, with piles of petticoats instead of a farthingale, Kate looked like a splash of sunshine on a rainy afternoon. Quite pleasing in Edmund's opinion.

"Edmund, have you been with Kate?" Lady Judith asked in her treble-pitch voice, a pitch that promised to become annoying over time.

"Aye," he replied with what he hoped was a soothing smile, "we have been attending to rather delicate business."

Lady Judith arched her brow. "What type of delicate business leaves a spot of grease on a woman's gown?"

"Oh, my," said Kate lowering her eyes. Upon finding the spot on her skirt, she rubbed it with her thumb. "Meat pie, I fear. From the fair."

Lady Judith was clearly aghast. "You went to the fair, Edmund?"

" 'Twas necessary to my business," Edmund explained, as in a manner of speaking it was. The fair had restored Kate's spirits.

"The servant class cannot seem to eat with grace. You cannot expect much in their company," she said, staring at the telltale spot on Kate's skirt as if the grease might be a gargoyle.

Kate drew herself up. Although she smiled at Judith, Edmund caught the sharp glitter of anger in her eyes. "But fortunately, you may expect respect and courtesy from the servant class, Lady Judith."

" 'Tis fear," the lady declared, white-lipped. For some reason that Edmund could not fathom, she'd taken a dislike of Kate.

"Do I appear fearful?" Kate asked coolly.

A fierce surge of pride swept through Edmund. He could not help but admire the way Kate stood up to Lady Judith, as if she had no regard for class distinctions. Which if Edmund did not miss his guess, she did not. The conversation held promise of becoming unpleasant—rapidly—unless he did something.

But providence stepped in and the door knocker sounded.

A fresh sense of dread fell over Edmund. What more could befall him?

A maiden shivered on the stoop. He recognized her from his sister's household. "Are you not Lady Jane's gentlewoman?" he asked, peering over the butler's shoulder.

"Yes, my lord. She bids you come quickly. Young Frances is ill."

* * *

Lady Jane had not invited Kate to her daughter's bedside. Kate invited herself, persuading Edmund she had learned much about healing in the country and from the nuns who operated the Italian convent where she studied.

"What does the physician say?" Edmund demanded of his sister, not long after he and Kate were shown into a small chamber adjacent to little Frances's bedchamber.

"He fears the pox and recommends bleeding her." Jane's green eyes misted. "Frances is so little, Edmund. I cannot bear such a cure."

"How old is your daughter?" Kate asked.

Lady Chumley glanced at Kate as if belatedly realizing Edmund had not come alone. The stiffly starched ruff of the viscountess's gown forced her chin to a higher angle than normal. She blinked, much like her aunt Cordelia. Jane appeared disturbed and a bit bewildered by Kate's presence.

"Frances is but five years old and my only child."

"May I see her?" Kate asked softly. 'Twas clear that no matter how pretentious Edmund's sister might be, all arrogance fell away in the face of danger to the daughter she clearly doted upon.

"Do you believe you can heal Frances?" Skepticism laced Jane's voice.

"I cannot be certain without examining her."

"If you are what you claim, why have you not healed my aunt?"

"Pray forgiveness, but Lady Cordelia requires no healing."

"Aunt Cordelia has visited every fortune-teller and physician in London," Edmund added. "She has shown the stamina of a Jersey bull."

"She *has* appeared rather stout," Jane said. Still,

she hesitated. "You are seeking a position as a children's nurse, are you not?"

"Aye."

"Mayhap this will test your skill. But be warned. I shall hover over you at all times. Come."

Kate and Edmund followed Jane into her daughter's bedchamber. Green velvet drapes fell from the four corners of the canopy bed, and a gold-threaded tapestry blocked the only window in the chamber. A fire burned in the small fireplace, contributing to the chamber's stifling air.

Frances's nurse, who had been holding a goblet of water to the child's lips, gently settled the little girl back among the down pillows and stepped away.

Jane sat on the bed beside her only child. "Frances, Lord Stamford and Mistress Kate have come to see you."

Frances parted parched lips to smile at Edmund. She possessed the same raven-colored hair and startling green eyes as her uncle, but the resemblance ended there. The little girl's nose turned up daintily, and her cheeks were chubby and flushed.

Edmund bent low to kiss his niece's cheek. "I came as soon as I heard you were unwell, sweeting."

"My brother dotes on Frances," Jane explained unnecessarily.

'Twas plain for Kate to see. She had not thought to be exposed to this side of Edmund's nature. He would be a caring, affectionate father one day.

"Who would not dote on her?" Kate asked as she moved toward the child's bed. "You are a beautiful child, Frances."

As Kate stepped up beside Edmund, Frances eyed her with open suspicion. "Who are you?"

"My name is Mistress Kate Beadle," she said, laying a hand on the child's forehead. "And you are a trifle warm."

The child frowned and pouted simultaneously.

Kate turned to Lady Chumley. "May I look beneath your daughter's shift?"

"I . . . I . . ." Jane turned to Edmund, who nodded.

"Frances, I brought Mistress Kate with me to look after you. She has healed many children," he said, before leaving the child's bedside to give Kate room.

While Edmund had not the least knowledge of her nursing skills, Kate was grateful for his confidence—though slightly exaggerated. But Frances obviously heeded her uncle's counsel. Her plump little body relaxed against the bedclothes.

Jane stood, allowing Kate to take her place on the bed.

"How old are you, Frances?" Kate asked as she sank to the child's side.

Frances held up her hand, spreading her chubby fingers as far apart as they would go.

"Five. My, my what a grown girl." Kate kept up a steady stream of chatter, asking myriad inconsequential questions as she examined the child.

She loved children. She loved their innocence and honesty. If fate and the constellations were kind, someday Kate would be a mother to even more children than the fortune-teller predicted. A half dozen at least. Such a brood would require an understanding husband.

A requirement her matchmaker should be made aware of. Nay. Edmund had promised to do no more matchmaking. Now, if Kate could only cure his arrogance.

He'd dared to claim he was her lord and master!

Before she left London, the Earl of Stamford would discover the truth.

Kate took up Frances's hand in hers. "Do you know how to play draughts?"

"No."

"I will teach you then, and we shall play. 'Tis quite simple and amusing."

Kate left the girl's bed, crossing to the far side of the chamber where Edmund and Jane stood observing her.

"Do you know what ails Frances?" Lady Jane asked.

" 'Tis my belief that she has contracted measles."

"No!"

"The rash has started to appear on her chest."

"God's death!"

Edmund wrapped an arm around his horrified sister.

"There is naught to fear, my lady," Kate soothed. " 'Tis a mild case, I believe."

"What can be done?" Edmund asked.

"We shall keep Frances clean and comfortable. 'Tis all that can be done for the measles until they run their course."

"How long will she be ill?" Jane asked in a shaky voice.

"Ten days, mayhap less. The itching will begin soon, but I have a remedy. Do not worry, Lady Chumley. Your beautiful daughter will not be marked."

"Are you certain?"

"If it pleases you, I shall stay with Frances until the worst has passed."

"It does please me," Jane declared.

"How long shall that be?" Edmund wanted to know.

"Three days, perchance more. She will most certainly be fretful."

"Would you mind?" Jane asked, with an eagerness she did not conceal.

" 'Twould be my pleasure."

"I have not been . . . kind to you in the past," Jane allowed.

Kate gave the worried mother a smile. "Neither have you been mean or wicked, my lady. Your child needs my help, and I am most willing to do what I can."

Jane looked to her brother. "Edmund, under the circumstances Aunt Cordelia can certainly spare Kate, can she not?"

"Aye." He nodded and his deep green gaze met Kate's. "God save you," he said softly.

Kate's heart fluttered like a baby chick's wing beneath the intensity of his gaze. If she were not mistaken 'twas a look of admiration and . . . tenderness. Aye, tenderness reflected in the meadow-green gleam of his eyes.

While her thoughts seemed frozen, Kate's body felt as if it were bathed in warm springwaters. For a moment she lost sight of her purpose.

Until little Frances whined. "Mama . . ."

Kate's training asserted itself. "I should begin at once to make Frances comfortable," she said, becoming a bustling model of efficiency. "Cool compresses and fresh air are in order. Prithee have your cook prepare delicious puddings . . . and sassafras tea."

Edmund drew her aside. "I do not like to leave you."

"But you must. Did you suffer from measles as a child?"

He appeared startled. "Nay."

"Then you must leave at once."

The earl's dark frown deepened, his whisper a low rumble. "Might I contract a child's illness?"

She wore a grave expression as she nodded her head. " 'Tis possible. Measles are as contagious as the plague."

He sucked in his breath. "Oh!"

She had not meant to cause him concern. Kate feared Edmund had been too long hearing his aunt's litany of aches and illnesses.

"Have you had measles?" he asked.

"Aye, as a child. Therefore, I cannot contract the illness again. But I cannot vouchsafe for you."

"By your leave, then," he said. "Fare thee well, Frances. I shall leave my oldest . . . and dearest friend with you in my stead. She will help you more than I ever could."

Kate's heart hummed at hearing Edmund call her his dearest friend. She could not hope for more. The striking Earl of Stamford was Kate's oldest and dearest friend.

He blew the little girl a kiss.

Kate wished for one, too.

Frances acknowledged her uncle's parting with a melancholy wave of a chubby hand. "Fare thee well."

Kate called just as he reached the door. "Lord Stamford, please make my apologies to the Duke of Laird and James Moore,"

"Oh, aye, aye."

"You will not forget?"

"Nay."

"My thanks to you."

"I shall return for you in three days' time, Mistress Kate."

* * *

Edmund stopped every day at his sister's home, hoping to see Kate. He never did. She refused to leave her patient's side, a fact Jane reported to him with newfound respect. While he knew Kate possessed many fine traits, Edmund had been impressed with how quickly she won over his niece.

But 'twas a long three days Edmund spent without Kate. He escorted his aunt to Lady Mason's primero parties and attended Parliament. He played a game of tennis with Christopher and billiards with Robin, losing at both. The worst of it was responding to daily messages directed to Kate from the Duke of Laird and James Moore. Before now, Edmund hadn't realized how persistent his barrister could be.

And the duke! 'Twas not right for a man his age to be dangling after so young a woman as Kate. Donald Cameron renewed Edmund's fears of what might happen to Kate in service of a noble home.

He missed her as well. He missed her bright smile and the swish of her skirts, her laughter and companionship. Stamford House had become the quiet, dull place it had been before Kate and Aunt Cordelia came to London.

But in the garden there was a sign of the magic Kate wrought. The first rose had bloomed.

At last the message that he impatiently awaited arrived. Frances had passed the first agonizing days of her illness without a sign of complications. Kate was ready to return to Stamford House.

Despite the excitement stewing in his belly, Edmund felt weary and a bit out of sorts when his coach pulled up at his sister's town house. He blamed his woebegone state on Kate's absence. But when she came into view, she looked worse than he felt.

She slanted him a wan smile. Slashes of deep purple smudges settled in pockets beneath her eyes. Strands of Kate's silky flaxen hair fell limply askew. Her shoulders sloped and her gait had lost its bounce.

Even so, the sight of her warmed Edmund's heart, his body, his soul. He helped her into the coach and they were away at once. "Kate! How do you fare?"

"Weary, my lord, and grateful that you arrived promptly."

"Along with the rest of my family, you have made too much in the past of my tardiness," he said, peeved. "Do you think I like to keep people waiting?"

"By your leave?"

Edmund groaned. Why had he snapped at Kate when, ever since she'd been away from Stamford House, he'd looked forward to being with her again? "Forgive me."

"Methinks someone rose on the wrong side of the bed this morning."

"Kate, my thanks for having saved my precious niece."

"Frances is a strong child. I did not save her, only nursed her."

"My sister looks upon you in a different light."

"Jane was good to me during Frances's illness," Kate acknowledged, and then yawned.

Although Edmund could not fathom how even the most weary of travelers could fall asleep in the rocking, jarring coach, Kate did. The moment he fell silent, she was asleep. Her head slumped forward. She would end with a stiff neck if he did nothing.

Wrapping one arm about her, Edmund drew her close until her head rested on his shoulder. His heart, or something near to it, swelled, pressed against his chest. The tightness forced him to take shallow breaths. All the way home.

Unaware of Edmund's strange physical state, Kate rested against him like a sleeping doll. In the circle of his arm, she felt light as gossamer, appeared as vulnerable as a child. Indeed, she was but a country girl, a gardener's daughter. Gone were the spit and fire of her spirit, lost to sleep and dreams. As he gazed at her dark eyelashes curling against her cheek, the ribbon of sunlight caressing her moist, barely parted lips, Edmund experienced an epiphany. Kate was a woman to be protected and pampered.

But not by him, of course.

He woke her just before they reached Stamford House.

"I believe you should retire immediately and rest."

"I believe I shall."

And he would as well.

Edmund did something he never did in the afternoon. He took to his bed. What's more, he was asleep before his man had closed the drapes. The next awareness he had was the sound of his bedchamber door opening. He looked up to see Kate standing in the threshold. A vision. She held a candle and wore only a linen shift of fine white lawn. Golden wheat curls tumbled past her creamy shoulders in breathtaking abandon. There was only one explanation. He'd died and passed to heaven.

But the vision spoke. "Are you well, Edmund?"

"Aye." He meant to sound strong and firm. Instead, he croaked.

"I was about to retire for the evening when . . . when I had a feeling you might need me."

Need her? He wanted Kate so badly he'd become

ill with desire. " 'Twas it a feeling, or the stars that guided you to my bedchamber?"

"A feeling. You did not join Lady Cordelia and me for dinner."

"Am I so grounded in my habits, then?"

"Aye."

"Why would I need you, Kate?"

"As . . . as nurse."

"Nay. I do not require a nurse this eve."

She inclined her head. "Are you certain that you are not ill?"

"I shall be fine, if left alone to rest."

"Why is it I do not quite believe you?" She marched toward his bed.

Edmund's feverish body stiffened.

"Go away, Kate. Have you no shame? You are a maiden woman," he railed at her in mounting panic. "You cannot march into a man's bedchamber with no fare-thee-well."

"The nuns at the convent nursed men all the time, and no one thought the worst of them."

"You are not a nun." If she were, Edmund knew for certain he would be struck down dead for his wild thoughts.

"I know that well." She grinned mischievously.

A deeper heat struck his feverish body.

'Twas the fever that made him want her more than life itself. But his pride prevailed over all else. Edmund did not want Kate to see him in this weakened, sickly condition.

She placed a cool, soft hand on his brow.

"Go away," he murmured.

The hazy outline of Kate's magnificent breasts and trim waist showed through the thin fabric of her gown.

The sweet fragrance of roses filled his senses. Why was she torturing him?

"Prithee, go away," he moaned.

The last thing he remembered was Kate's sympathetic smile; the last thing he felt was the gentle touch of her lips upon his brow.

When he awoke the next morning, she sat beneath a window embroidering.

"Ouch! Oh, fie!"

Edmund chuckled. "Tsk, tsk. 'Tis not the language of a lady who sticks herself with the needle."

"Edmund!" Kate jumped up and dashed to his side. After placing her hand on his brow, her eyes danced with joy. " 'Tis over. The fever is broken."

"What are you talking about?" he asked, raising to brace himself on his elbows.

"Take care," she cautioned. "You will be weak for several days more."

"Days?"

"You have the measles, Lord Stamford. You have been in and out of delirium for almost five days."

"Bloody hell!"

She raised her brows. "Tsk, tsk. 'Tis not the language a lord should utter before an innocent girl."

"Have you been my nurse?" Edmund asked, with a sickening dread.

"Nay. 'Twould not be proper. Aunt Cordelia and a hired nurse have been at your side."

"Aunt Cordelia?"

"Your illness has kept her well occupied."

He felt his face, felt small bumps. "I must see my reflection at once."

"I do not—"

"At once, Kate!"

She brought him the polished metal he used to shave. Edmund viewed a pale man with a face dotted with fierce red spots. The bottom fell from his somersaulting stomach. He resembled a spotted owl! Even a mother could not love such an apparition.

"Your rash will disappear soon," Kate said softly.

"Leave me." God's breath, she had seen him like this for days. The humiliation was too much to bear.

Once more, Kate attempted to console him. " 'Tis not as—"

"I shall recover at Rose Hall," Edmund barked. "We shall return to the country at once."

TWELVE

Saturn in the sixth house brings trust and tranquillity

Kate watched over her shoulder for Edmund's bloodhound at all times, fearing the dreadful creature would pounce on her, as he was wont to do. Despite the constant threat of Percy's exuberance, Kate had many reasons to be happy being back in the country. The bullish man could no longer follow her, for one.

She paid her first visit to the stargazer on foot.

"Jutta, nothing has gone according to your predictions. Something is amiss in the heavens." For the first time in Kate's memory, her faith in astrology severely wavered.

But the astrologist did not appear alarmed by the likelihood of a heavenly catastrophe. Although not more than ten years older than Kate, Jutta appeared twice as old. She did not hide her thinning mouse-brown hair beneath a cap. Neither did she cover the gaping space of a missing tooth.

'Twas a mystery to Kate where Jutta had learned to read and write, but she did both well. The baker's wife claimed to have studied under Simon Forman, said to be the queen's favorite astrologer when she was not consulting Dee. True or not, Jutta's unflagging high spirits drew Kate to her.

The astrologer cocked her head. She had no eyebrows to speak of, but what sparse hairs sprouted above her eyes had dipped in a frown. "What has befallen you, Mistress Kate?"

"I visited many goldsmith shops in London and none had ever seen a ring like this before." She twisted the ring on her finger. Reporting her failure served to renew Kate's frustration.

"You missed not one goldsmith?"

"Lord Stamford would not hear of visiting any he suspected of chicanery. However, if another opportunity arises, I should like to visit the charlatans as well. One never knows where the truth lies."

"The earl is guided by a cautious sign."

"Perchance the sign of an overbearing tyrant as well."

Jutta sputtered. "By your leave?"

" 'Tis another matter," Kate declared with a dismissive flick of her wrist. Leaning toward the astrologer, she lowered her voice to a confidential whisper. "Jutta, I fear the stars have been misread and I shall never find my birth mother."

"You fear too soon." Jutta tapped her stubby fingers on the rough-hewn wooden table. "The stars never fail."

"Why did they not predict that Lord Stamford, in his arrogance, would seek to find me a husband?"

"Aye?" Jutta reeled back in astonishment.

"To free me from servitude, he said, expecting my undying gratitude."

" 'Tis decent of Lord Stamford to take an interest in your well-being."

"Lord Stamford is a decent man," Kate agreed with only the slightest reluctance. Decent but misguided.

"But I do not need nor desire his help in such a matter."

"Did Lord Stamford introduce you to a likely husband?"

"Several." Kate gave an exasperated sigh. "James Moore, the earl's barrister is a good man," she allowed. "But—"

"But? . . ."

"I do not love him."

Jutta's mouth turned up in a sly half smile. "Does your heart belong to another?"

Kate could not confide the wayward direction of her heart. Besides, 'twas only infatuation she felt for Edmund, held over from when she was but a child. "Methinks after I find my birth mother 'twill be time enough to seek a husband."

"You are wise."

"Or foolish." Kate could not make up her mind.

"Why have you returned to Rose Hall?"

"Lord Stamford contracted the measles from his young niece and did not wish anyone to see him looking like a leopard with red spots." As Kate recalled Edmund's initial shock, she could not help but grin. His pride suffered sorely to be afflicted with the unattractive rash. "To prevent an accidental encounter, he removed us all to the country where he remains locked within his bedchamber. I have not seen him for days."

"The new head gardener is living in your cottage. Where are you staying?"

"The earl insisted I take up residence in Rose Hall."

A glint of mocking silver light momentarily brightened Jutta's oyster-gray eyes. "Lord Stamford continues to dictate your life?"

"Aye," Kate acknowledged with a sigh. "But 'tis necessary to live in Rose Hall, as I continue to serve as Lady Cordelia's gentlewoman."

"I did not see such a position for you in the stars. How goes it?"

" 'Tis been especially difficult placating the lady this past week. She is verily vexed to be back."

Jutta picked at the dirt beneath her fingernails. "The stars are in the lady's favor."

"Lord Stamford has appeased his aunt by opening Rose Hall for the summer months. He's all but promised Lady Cordelia that when the queen is on progress she will stay at Rose Hall."

"Aye?" Jutta appeared puzzled. Her barely there brows dove into a frown. "Mayhap I should consult the planets once more. I did not see a royal visit."

Kate felt a stirring of annoyance, a prickling in her veins. "Jutta, you have asked me many questions but given me few answers."

"The stars are in flux. Look." Jutta shoved a chart spattered with grease and dirt toward Kate.

The primitive drawings meant nothing to Kate. "Can you tell me what lies ahead?"

"Wait and watch. Trust no one."

Edmund paced his bedchamber by candlelight. Bloody hell! If he had to spend another twenty-four hours alone, he would lose what was left of his mind! He'd ordered Rose Hall into a flurry of activity preparing for summer entertaining, but it would be another day before he could oversee the preparations.

He had designed an outdoor tennis court on parchment. The rose garden would have to be removed, but an outdoor court would be quite the thing. He looked forward to getting on with the construction.

But one bright poppy-red spot remained on the tip of his nose.

The childhood illness bedeviled Edmund. 'Twas a grave injustice. He was not a boy, yet the rash had spread to every inch of his body. He'd itched fiercely for days but heeding Kate's warning had resisted the temptation to scratch. Fortunately, he could not detect any scars in the polished metal he used to study his reflection several times a day.

Judith Witherspoon was not the type of woman who would marry a man with a pocked complexion.

"Come, Percy." For the past several nights after he felt certain the household slept, Edmund ventured out to walk in the garden with his loyal bloodhound.

Percy gave an excited *woof,* and with his long tail swinging at maximum speed, he trotted along beside Edmund. The big dog seemed to have sensed his owner's churlish disposition and had behaved extremely well during Edmund's confinement.

But when they reached the staircase, instead of descending with Edmund, Percy bound straight ahead into the east wing where Lady Cordelia's and Kate's chambers were located.

Edmund gave chase but was no match for the galloping canine.

"Yiiiii!" *Oh, fie! Fie!*

Percy had found Kate.

Edmund reached the open bedchamber door to find Percy hunkered down beside Kate on her bed.

She struggled to remove the bloodhound, pushing at him even as his huge tongue licked her face. "You ill-bred flap-dragon! Off with you. Off!"

Kate's choice of epithets elicited the first chuckle

Edmund had enjoyed in days. Although he had not planned for her to see him until the last spot had faded, he rushed to her bed. The flickering light of one candle cast him in shadow. The Earl of Stamford to the rescue.

"Down!" Edmund commanded in the deepest tone he could manage.

Percy's head snapped around. His big brown eyes regarded Edmund with innocent bewilderment.

Edmund flung out his arm, pointing to the door. "Go."

Kate's feather bed pitched as the bloodhound jumped down. Percy trotted to the doorway, where he sat on his haunches. Droopy eyed, Percy looked pitiful, staring at his master with a pained, soulful expression.

With a rueful wag of his head, Edmund turned his attention to the object of Percy's affection. "I beg your forgiveness, Kate."

Moonlight streamed through the open window, bathing the gardener's daughter in its luscious glow. She sat bolt upright in the bed, clutching her arms against her body, unmindful that her full breasts were visible, straining against her shift, rising and falling in rapid splendor.

Struck speechless, Edmund sucked in a ragged breath.

Slivers of moonbeams showered the mass of spun-gold curls spilling to Kate's shoulders. She breathed heavily through parted lips; alarm danced in her wide, unblinking amber eyes. The lace of her shift caressed the graceful ivory column of her neck.

His heart slammed against his chest.

He wanted her. His loins ached and his body burned for her. It was lust, it was desire, it was overwhelming.

With one small movement he could sink to the bed beside her and make her his.

Her eyes met his. "Pray, Edmund, tell me the meaning of this."

The faint quaver in her voice caused Edmund's heart to roll over. Her body trembled. Did he dare take her into his arms and offer comfort?

He did not dare. Not with the need in him blazing like a thousand and one candles.

"My apologies, Kate."

"I have been in the habit of leaving my door open a crack, the better to hear Lady Cordelia across the hall . . . if she should require my services during the night."

I . . . I thought having a chamber of your own a better arrangement than a small chamber adjacent to my aunt."

" 'Tis most agreeable."

"Pray pardon, Kate. Percy got away from me." Even to his own ears, Edmund's voice sounded peculiar. 'Twas a husky whisper. He locked his gaze on hers, thinking her eyes the only safe place to focus.

But her eyes cast a spell of their own, holding him fast. Like metal to magnet, he was held captive in swirling pools of molten sorrel and gold.

"In the future I shall keep my chamber door bolted," she assured him.

"I had not thought my hound—"

"I had not thought you would be walking the corridors in the eve. . . ."

With every breath he took, the sweet rose scent of Kate invaded Edmund's senses, further stirring his desire for her. 'Twas like dangling a sweet before a starving man. Devouring the beauty seemed the only answer.

"Walking the corridors," she repeated, "with your dog."

"I have been confined too long."

"You appear more handso—" She broke off. Apparently flustered, Kate lowered her head, twisted her ring. "More healthy than before."

Did she think him handsome? Was that what she had been about to say?'

Zounds! A fever twice the strength of that caused by his illness gripped Edmund's body. The fire in him raged. He felt as if he'd been thrown into a blazing hearth, enveloped by its flames.

"I have regained my health." But not his strength.

"Lady Cordelia will welcome your company."

And you? Edmund longed to ask. Would Kate welcome his company once more?

"I shall visit my aunt on the morrow," he promised.

"She will be most delighted."

Edmund could not remember having a strained conversation such as this with Kate before. He wondered at the thick wedge of tension between them. "In the future I shall keep Percy locked up. He has taken a rare liking to you."

"So you insist, but I do not understand why."

But Edmund did. Kate obviously attracted males of every species. He raked a hand through his hair. His bloodhound had licked Kate's cheek, been in bed beside her. *His dog!*

Bloody hell!

" 'Tis your sweet rose scent," Edmund extemporized, having no idea why Percy adored the gardener's daughter.

Blaming the hound's behavior on her perfume seemed as good an explanation as any. In truth, he suspected Percy knew instinctively that Kate possessed a kind and trusting soul and sought her company for those reasons.

Kate chewed at the corner of her lip for a moment before nodding sagely. “Alas. Then I shall use lavender in the future.”

He nodded, implying a change of fragrance might make a difference. But deep in his belly, Edmund realized the womanly essence of Kate that oft made his head spin had little to do with lavender or roses. Sometimes when he stood next to her willowy form, he felt as if he were standing in a field of wildflowers.

A great, silent moan tore at Edmund. He dared not stay longer in Kate's chamber. Dared not allow his gaze to drift to her breasts, to her lips.

He turned on his heel. “Good eve, Mistress Kate.”

In the dark stillness, Kate listened to the click of the door behind Edmund, the tap of Percy's paws fading away.

She thought she would faint. The sharp edge of tension coiled within her still, disallowing all but the most shallow of breaths. She yet felt the heat of Edmund's gaze raking her with undisguised desire. No matter if he'd wanted her for only one fleeting moment, he would never breech the bond of friendship between them. Lord Stamford would never dally with a gardener's daughter. Yet, with one searing look, he'd ignited a powerful, unnamed need within Kate.

Tears of disappointment filled her eyes, a disappointment she did not fully understand.

Rose Hall had been in turmoil preparing for this night. Edmund had chosen Midsummer's Eve, always a night of celebration, to open his country estate for the summer months. Traveling nobles, royalty, and invited merchants would all be welcomed.

One small faded dot still marked his nose, the only remaining sign of the measles. Although Edmund did not like to think of himself as a vain man, the illness had been an assault to his dignity.

With his energy restored, he meant to spend the summer months finding a solution to the poaching at Rose Hall and overseeing the construction of his tennis court. In addition, he would engage himself in a host of summer entertainments at his country estate.

Edmund had not given up on finding a husband for Kate. He had no time to waste. Each moment spent in her company left him wanting her more. Resolved to put an end to such madness, he was determined to see her promised to another quickly, before summer's end.

For the Midsummer's Eve gala he had arranged a masque, musicians for dancing, and a grand feast to be held in the banquet house. Over thirty guests dined on shrimp, cod, oysters, whelks, pheasant, quail, pigeon pie, rabbit, venison, berries, dried figs, and dates. Florentines, filberts, and walnuts were offered along with ale, whisky, cider, and wine.

Edmund could not have arranged the elaborate festivity in such a short time without the help of Aunt Cordelia and her helpmate. Kate. He'd meant to keep Aunt Cordelia occupied. He hadn't meant to keep Kate so busy that he rarely saw her. Tonight she would be at her leisure.

Visitors had been arriving for the past two days. The most important being Lady Mason, who would bend Edmund's aunt's ear all the evening with fresh gossip from London.

Laughter and music filled the great hall and beyond. 'Twas halfway through the feast and Edmund had only caught sight of Kate scurrying hither and yon. She had not sat to sup at any of the long trestle tables.

Christopher Carew had arrived late in the afternoon. Edmund had invited his friend to stay for the week. He sought his opinion of the tennis court, and looked forward to hunting with his friend following the Midsummer's Eve festivities. Carew was not the only special guest he had invited.

After wrestling with his conscience, Edmund invited his barrister, James Moore, to Rose Hall for Midsummer's Eve. He'd been much relieved to hear Judith Witherspoon would not be able to attend. She had made previous plans to accompany her mother to the waters at Bath. Edmund promised himself he would soon make up for his neglect of Judith. He would woo her like a queen as soon as Kate was wed.

When most of the party had finished the meal and was drifting toward the inner courtyard where the masque would soon begin, Edmund excused himself.

"I shall rejoin you soon, Christopher. A matter of importance requires my attention."

"Do not worry over me, friend. A young woman has caught my eye. I believe her to be a friend of your sister's."

"Ah, yes. Lady Mary Thorgenhope arrived with Jane yesterday in Lord Chumley's stead. The viscount could not leave London."

Edmund took leave of his sporting companion, and after searching near the length and breadth of Rose Hall, at last came upon his matter of importance.

Kate sat with little Frances on a stone bench at the entrance to the maze. The intricate maze located on the north side of Rose Hall had been designed by Kate's papa, John Beadle.

"I did not think to get lost," his little niece sniffled. "The hedges are low."

"But higher than your head," Kate pointed out. "Had I not heard you crying, you might still be wandering at dawn."

"You will not tell my nurse . . . or my mama?"

"Nay. 'Twill be our secret. Tomorrow when 'tis light, I shall lead you through the maze and show you how to be certain where you are at all times."

"Thank you, Mistress Kate."

Unwilling to eavesdrop further, Edmund made himself known, striding toward the two. "Have I fallen upon faeries in the garden?"

Frances giggled. " 'Tis Mistress Kate and I."

"I brought Frances to the garden so that she might calm herself before retiring," Kate said. " 'Tis quiet and peaceful here."

Edmund could only admire Kate's swift, smooth fabrication. Frances's eyes shone with gratitude.

"Aye, it is. But it is also time for Frances to be in bed. I shall help you return my niece to her chamber. The masque begins before long, followed by dancing. After traveling to Rose Hall I am certain Master Moore craves at least one dance with you, Kate."

"May I beg off? 'Tis weary I am from the preparations."

"You look well."

Too well. Her sea-green gown dipped to an alluring display of creamy décolletage. He could only imagine the lush contours of her hips beneath the wide farthingale. And he did. Edmund flushed, warm with the imaginings.

"My thanks, Lord Stamford," Kate responded politely to his compliment.

The moments requiring her to be formal with him had begun to annoy Edmund. She was at ease with him only when they were alone.

"Come, Frances." He held out his hand. When the little girl slipped her hand in his, Edmund's heart pitched unexpectedly. The feeling of her small, chubby hand in his was most pleasant. A trusting hand. Innocent eyes gazed up at him; small bowed lips smiled with love.

He wondered what it might be like to have a child of his own. He looked to Kate. "Kate, are you coming?"

"I thought to remain in the garden for a short time."

"But I should like to escort you back to the hall."

Frances screwed up her little lips. "Prithee, Mistress Kate, come to my bedchamber."

"Do you fear your nurse?" she asked the child.

The little girl bobbed her head. "And Uncle Edmund."

"Me? Why?"

"I gave you my measles."

Edmund chuckled. " 'Twas an unintentional gift. I do not seek revenge. You are forgiven, Frances."

After accompanying the child to her bedchamber and nurse, Kate begged off from accompanying Edmund to the courtyard.

"I must return to my own bedchamber. I forgot my fan, but I shall not be long."

He feared she would disappear again. She had been elusive of late. "I shall come with you."

"Your guests must miss their host," she argued. "James Moore has come especially to dance with you."

"Did you invite the barrister because you still seek a husband for me? Edmund, you promised not to interfere—"

"Do you not trust me?"

"No. Not in this matter."

The gardener's daughter was much too candid.

Kate sailed along the corridor. Did she hope he could not keep up with her?

"Why have you avoided me?" Edmund demanded.

"I have done no such thing. Lady Cordelia has given me much to do preparing for Midsummer's Eve."

"Have you thought more about what you will do since no goldsmith in London recognized your ring? Will you abandon the search for your birth mother now?"

Kate slowed, lowering her gaze to the gold band upon her finger. "Jutta said the answer will come to me. I should look no longer."

"The answer will come. Hah!"

"I do not appreciate your scorn," she snapped. And once more, Kate hastened her pace.

"You must look to yourself instead of the stars for answers."

"And pray what can I do?"

"Marry."

Eyes flashing with anger, Kate spun on him. "Why are you so eager for me to take a husband? I am still young. Do you think no man shall want me if I delay? Shall I become as shriveled as a dried fig in mere months instead of years? Do you fear I will be hideous by my twenty-fifth year?"

"Nay. I—"

" 'Tis none of your concern!"

"I wish only for you to be safe and well supported.

You have been my friend since childhood, and I desire more for you than false predictions offered by a foolish stargazer. I wish you to have a good life, Kate."

Kate opened the door to her chamber with admirable vigor. "You cannot enter my bedchamber!"

"I have been here before," he reminded her in a husky tone as he followed.

" 'Twas necessary . . . to call off your beast."

He drew himself up to his full height. He towered over her. "Have you forgotten? I am the Earl of Stamford, Edmund Wydville, master of Rose Hall."

"You do not let me forget." Kate balled her fists and planted them on her hips. "Papa warned me about you."

"By your leave!"

"He warned you might take advantage of me."

"Not I! If I wished to take advantage of you I would not be searching diligently for a man for you to wed."

"Oh, fie! Edmund, you promised that you would do no more matchmaking. You are an arrogant male, to be certain. And untruthful."

Whirling away from him, the fates combined to overcome Kate. She stepped upon the train of her dress and fell forward just as Percy bounded through the open door.

Kate screamed as Edmund caught her, caught her in his arms.

"Percy! Go!"

Percy whined. But he did not move. The tail-wagging bloodhound stared up at Kate's horror-stricken face.

"Your beast is on a mission from the devil," she hissed.

"Percy!"

"He lives to torment me."

"Go!"

At last, objecting with a whimper, Percy turned and strolled away, his tail between his legs. Which is rather how Edmund felt at the moment.

Unwilling to release Kate, he held her fast, reveling in the warm fullness of her breasts pressed against his chest, the scent of lavender in her silky hair. Her new scent. Desire washed over him like soft summer rain. He grew hard and short of breath.

"Do not be angry with me," he murmured in her ear. His heart raced. Could she feel the evidence of his desire? "I will leave off."

He would find another way to provide for her.

"Why should I believe you?"

"It would grieve me to have anything come between us that might end our . . . our friendship."

Wrenching out of his arms with a small cry, Kate wobbled slightly.

Edmund dared not reach out for her again. He ached. His eyes dropped to the bench. To a missive lying there.

Kate answered Edmund's unspoken question. "I received an offer for a position of nurse in Manchester."

Her news was like an iron-fisted blow to his midsection. "No. You cannot go. Aunt Cordelia has come to depend upon you," he protested. "You must reject this offer."

A terse, hot silence enveloped the room. Laughter and music from the Midsummer's celebration drifted through the open window.

"I cannot, Edmund," Kate replied softly. She'd expected him to be angry with her for leaving his aunt. The burden of Aunt Cordelia's aches and pains and endless goblets of sack would fall upon Edmund once again, until another gentlewoman could be found.

"I will raise your wages," he countered.

" 'Tis not the wages."

"Why, then?" he demanded in a timbre at once deep and ominous. His scowl alone would cause a courageous knight to become faint at heart.

Kate stood her ground. Why, then?

She could not say . . . *Because I love you, Earl of Stamford, too much to stay a day longer than necessary.* How foolish he would think her to pine after the most handsome nobleman in all of England!

Straightening her shoulders, Kate inched her chin toward the top of her ruff. " 'Tis precisely the position for which I have longed."

Edmund punched the wall and roared. "You would leave my sickly aunt to take a position as nurse to a stranger's children?"

"I must."

"Bloody hell." He turned to leave.

"Edmund."

He looked over his shoulder.

"I did not . . . do not heed Papa's warning. I know you would never hurt me."

Lord Stamford's only response was a slight dip of his head before stalking away.

She had angered him. But if she stayed he would certainly discover how much Kate cared for him. She could not hide her feelings forever.

Further, she had never traveled as far north as Manchester. 'Twas possible she might find a goldsmith there who would possess knowledge of her ring. In the meantime, there was naught to do but ease Edmund over his anger and make these last days together pleasant. Vowing to do what would please the earl for the remainder of their time together, Kate decided to rejoin the festivities and dance with James Moore as Edmund wished.

Kate found her fan and made her way to the main hall. She was just in time to see the door being opened to yet another traveler. The walls and chambers of Rose Hall were bursting with guests as it was.

"Good e'ven. Donald Cameron, the Duke of Laird to see Lord Stamford."

Upon hearing his voice, Kate flew down the remaining steps to greet the Scotsman. During her stay in London, she had enjoyed his company above all. And despite what Edmund thought, the duke had no untoward designs upon her.

"Weel na, Kate Beadle! How grand you look."

"My lord," she blurted excitedly, "what brings you to Rose Hall?"

THIRTEEN

With the sun in aspect to Jupiter 'twill be a merry month

The whim of an old man had brought Donald Cameron to Rose Hall. A man who'd had little gaiety in his life and whose curiosity had been roused by the enchanting gentlewoman and the taciturn Earl of Stamford.

"Can ye take in this weary traveler?" he asked. "I dinna know ye were celebrating Midsummer's Eve."

"Aye. There will always be room for you at Rose Hall. Lord Stamford will be most happy to see you, as am I." She tucked her arm through his. "You look well."

"For an old Scot?"

Her amber eyes sparkled up at him in genuine pleasure. Perhaps 'twas the lass's lack of pretense that drew him to her. Donald only knew that he'd taken instantly to her natural warmth and blithe spirit. Kate Beadle possessed qualities that were at once familiar to him, yet elusive. He felt she would make a fine companion to his Anne.

"You shall find peace in the country, my lord. No guest of Rose Hall dares offend another, 'else heads roll,' " the young beauty assured him with a teasing roll of her eyes.

"Ye canna be certain Stamford will welcome me. Most Englishmen consider a Scot to be as good as an Irishman. An' that's none too good at all."

"Lord Stamford harbors no such feelings," Kate stated quite simply.

Donald had not the heart to destroy the naïveté of the lass. Scotland was regarded as an uncivilized nation by her countrymen. They regarded the Scottish as little more than barbarians, fighting among themselves and wholly incapable of honoring a treaty. His frequent visits to the English court had done little to affect a different opinion. Nonetheless, he, the barbarian duke, persevered.

Queen Elizabeth respected King James and hoped to unite Scotland and England through him. Many Scots feared their country would be consumed by England. Donald spent his days appeasing either the English court or the Scottish lords. He wished each country might take a lesson from him and Lady Anne. They would then understand it was possible to strike an accord, respect one another, and live in harmony.

"Come with me to the banquet house, my lord," urged Kate. "I am certain some still feast. A hearty tankard of ale and a dozen or more oysters will refresh you after your journey."

"I dinna mean to keep ye—"

"The butler will see that your man settles you in a comfortable chamber. And I promise not to make you dance with me. Tonight."

Like sun on snow, Kate's broad smile melted the tension and troubles that had besieged Donald for the past months.

"Weel na, ye are most persuasive, Mistress Kate.

I should like to steal ye away from Stamford's employ."

A bubble of laughter escaped the young girl, as if Donald had made a jest. But he was serious, as Kate would realize as soon as his questions about her had been answered. Before he left Rose Hall, the Duke of Laird felt certain he would be making Kate a generous offer. She would be good for Anne. The gardener's daughter would bring joy to Downes Castle.

Twenty or more guests yet dined or were deep in conversation in the banquet house, a separate dwelling on the grounds of Rose Hall. Robin and Christopher had joined Edmund for a tankard of ale and excited discussion of the outdoor tennis court.

Edmund listened with one ear, keeping his eye on the door, hoping Kate would return and confess she'd been jesting about accepting the position as nurse in Manchester. He caught sight of her as soon as she sailed through the door.

The amber earrings he'd given her at the fair twinkled on her ears. But she was on the arm of Donald Cameron, Duke of Laird.

All promises not to meddle in Kate's affairs evaporated.

Quickly excusing himself from his friends, Edmund approached Kate and Laird with a forced smile.

The duke dipped his head in greeting. "Lord Stamford, how fare ye?"

"Laird." Edmund reached out and slapped the duke's shoulder in friendly greeting, though he didn't feel friendly at the moment. "What brings you to Rose Hall?"

"I shall not stay long, only a day. The queen has

summoned me to Burghley House where she is in progress."

"Lady Cordelia is disappointed that Queen Elizabeth does not plan to stop at Rose Hall," Kate said.

"She may yet. I advised my aunt not to give up hope." Edmund had issued a rather belated invitation. The queen's presence and the hundreds in her retinue would complicate life at Rose Hall.

"Queen Bess is an inspiration to all Englishwomen," Kate told the duke.

"Not quite," Edmund retorted, raising his eyes heavenward, "praise God."

If all Englishwomen valued their virginity as much as the queen, England would be lost.

The gleam of amusement in the duke's deep brown eyes and the quirk of his lips showed he understood well Edmund's meaning. "Indeed," he said.

Edmund could not totally dislike a man who demonstrated a sense of humor. He escorted Donald Cameron to the chair he had recently vacated. Once the duke was settled and served, Edmund ushered Kate to the inner court where the masque had just finished.

"Do you see James Moore?" he asked, searching the crowd. In his heart he hoped the barrister had been seized with flux and been forced to leave the festivities. 'Twas foolish, for James was the best husband Kate could hope for.

Edmund had no right to hold Kate prisoner. Neither, it seemed, could he let her go with any feeling of relief. Having her marry James would be far preferable than seeing her off to Manchester. He could not visit her in Manchester as he might in London.

"There he is!"

Must she sound delighted? "Where?"

"Mr. Moore is at the far corner of the court. He's

speaking with Christopher and another I cannot make out. His back is turned to me."

"I shall escort you to his side." Edmund walked slowly beside Kate, hands clasped behind his back, the safest place for them to be. "It seems you have two suitors. The Duke of Laird appears smitten with your charms."

"Nay! You jest. Pray, leave off, Edmund."

He would for the time. 'Twas difficult to protect a woman who did not understand she needed protection.

"How soon do you mean to leave for Manchester, Kate?"

"In ten days' time."

"When will you tell my aunt?"

"On the morrow. 'Twill be difficult."

"Then do not tell her. Do not go."

"You knew from the first I must make my own way. You have always known it."

"Aye, but as my aunt's gentlewoman there is no need for you to leave home. Rose Hall is your home. You cannot deny it."

" 'Tis *your* home. I have merely been a . . . visitor."

"Not so. You have ridden Rose Hall's trails and fished in its stream."

"Thanks to you."

Kate and Edmund were within a few feet of the trio of men when Moore spotted them.

"Kate! Lord Stamford, good eve."

Edmund did not like the lecherous light in the barrister's eyes, nor the way James Moore's gaze fixed on Kate.

Carew grinned his greeting. The third man turned and near swept the ground with his low bow.

Edmund felt Kate's hand grasp his arm. He looked

to her in alarm as he felt her weight, heard her soft cry. "What is it?"

"I feel faint of a sudden."

Kate wasn't the sort of woman to faint.

"Pray excuse us, gentlemen." Edmund said, and quickly guided Kate to the nearest stone bench.

Moore followed. The barrister's handsome brow wrinkled in a frown of concern.

"Moore, fetch Kate a goblet of wine," Edmund ordered.

As soon as Moore hastened away, Kate pulled Edmund down toward her. "I must retire to my chamber at once," she whispered.

"Why?" A knot the size of a beehive had begun to form in the pit of Edmund's stomach. His head buzzed a warning as well. "What ails you, Kate?"

"The man with Christopher. Who is he?"

" 'Tis one of the queen's most trusted advisers, Henry Stanton."

"Master Stanton is the man who has been following me."

Edmund could not fathom any circumstance in which the queen would order an investigation of a gardener's daughter. "You are mistaken."

"Nay. I remember him now from the queen's ball, and I saw him again clearly at the fair. Henry Stanton is built like a bull."

"You are overtired from the—"

"Nay." She shook her head, dislodging several silky strands that Edmund ached to set right. "Why won't you believe me?"

"No one could conceive you a threat—"

Daggers were neither as sharp nor as deadly as the glare Kate shot Edmund. She stood, assuming a stance as stiff as the blade of a two-handed sword. "I wish to retire."

"Are you strong enough—"

"I shall not faint." She turned.

His arm shot out to hers. "Stay."

Kate regarded his hand with the disdain she might have shown a slug had it the temerity to land on her arm. Chagrined, and wondering where and when she had learned such toplofty airs, Edmund withdrew his hand.

She gazed up at him, her amber eyes cold and distant. "Where is Percy?"

"Safely locked in the stable."

"My thanks."

Tilting her chin and straightening her shoulders, Kate stepped away in a fine physical display of defiance and stubborn pride. Edmund strode ahead and blocked her path.

"Reconsider, Kate. I do not disbelieve you. 'Tis a simple mistake. More than likely the man you saw resembled Stanton."

"I do not mistake the matter." Her lips did not move as she spoke in clipped tones. "Jutta warned me not to trust *anyone.*"

"Your stargazer includes one of the queen's most valued advisers in her warning? This should prove to you that she is a fraud. You must make your own judgments and decisions, Kate."

"Verily," she sniped, inching her head even higher. "I decide to leave."

She advanced on Edmund, brushing by him, forcing him to stand out of her way. With a rustle of skirts and the enticing scent of lavender in her wake, she was gone.

* * *

The following afternoon Kate strolled through the rose garden. She snapped dead roses and bent to inhale the fragrance of those in bloom. Roses of York and Lancaster, the lovely eglantine, all abounded in brilliant splashes of crimson, cream, and blushing pink. The beauty of a garden always served to calm her. Edmund had been spending time here of late. She hoped he had at last realized the benefits of a rose garden.

'Twas disconcerting to have her mind spinning in circles. Of late, Kate felt like a stable kitten chasing its tail. Her future presented as much of a quandary as her past. Faced with choices she had never expected, her belly churned. Buffeted about on the winds of change, her mind was near to numb.

Although Kate had just received the Manchester position, she felt tempted to press the Duke of Laird. Did he truly require her services as a gentlewoman? Scotland lay as far as one could get from London, from Rose Hall . . . and from Edmund.

Edmund. Unerring. Usually. But in this matter, Kate was uncertain. Could she have mistaken the identity of Stanton as Edmund suggested? Why, indeed, would one of the queen's advisers be interested in her?

Oh, fie! Life had become so complicated.

"Mistress Kate, lovelier than any of the roses in the garden."

"My lord." She dipped in a curtsy to the Duke of Laird.

"Weel na, do ye mind sitting with an old man?"

"You are not old."

"Me bones dinna know that," he said, brown eyes twinkling as he sat upon one of the small stone benches scattered throughout the rose garden. "They tell me differently."

"Did you pass the night well?"

"Aye. Slept like the dead, I did."

" 'Tis the country air," Kate declared, sinking down beside the kindly, unpretentious duke.

"True. I live in the country and dinna like to leave it. 'Tis glad I am to return to me estate each time."

"I like the country better than London as well."

" 'Tis good to know." The duke hunched forward, clasping his hands on his knees. "Lass, I have a friend who lives in the country. She is in ill health, and her companion is old. I seek another, younger companion for Anne."

"My lord—"

He cocked his head and raised a hand. "Hear me out. I know a Scot asking a bonny English lass to serve him is rare. But Anne is English, too, ye see. Ye won't be serving me. Think on it. Would ye be interested in living in beautiful Scotland and never wanting for anything?"

"My lord, you tempt me. But I have just received notice of a long-awaited position in Manchester. I shall be nurse to three young boys."

The creases of the duke's brow deepened to furrows. "Lass, I will double whatever ye have been offered. Me Anne would benefit from yer company. Ye would bring sunshine into her life."

Kate felt flattered and grateful for the duke's confidence. She liked him. She knew him—unlike the family in Manchester. And she had experience serving as companion to an older woman.

Thrown into an unexpected dilemma, she weighed her options. To go to Manchester or Scotland? Which would serve her needs better? Both places would put distance between her and Edmund. Both places would provide fresh searching ground for information about her ring.

"I shall think on it." She would pay a visit to Jutta this very day.

"Thank ye, lass. Ye'll never have reason for regret. I feel it in me bones. Ye'll be happy with me Anne."

Kate twisted her ring. "I have no doubt, my lord."

The duke glanced down at her ring. "Weel na, is that the ring ye mentioned—"

Percy barked.

Kate started and jumped up from the stone bench.

The bloodhound's bark came from nearby.

She looked toward the entrance to the garden. Edmund stood beneath the arbor holding Percy by the collar. The Earl of Stamford glowered at Kate and the duke.

The trembling began in her knees and swept her body. She did not know what had provoked Edmund's obvious ill humor, but if he unleashed his hound upon her, she would scurry behind the Duke of Laird.

She forced a smile. "Good day, Lord Stamford."

He strode toward them. Percy strained to leap forward and pounce upon her. Instead of looking at the beast she feared, Kate chose to keep her gaze on Edmund.

Even with the shimmer of anger rising from his shoulders, he appeared the most dashing of men. Tall and broad, his noble bearing marked him as a man of principle, with the strength of stone and mortar. Like a courageous knight of old, the lustiest of men, Edmund held Kate mesmerized. She fell deeper under his spell with each step he took toward her.

His deep, evergreen eyes locked on hers, sending wave after wave of searing heat throughout her body. In a disturbing state of light-mindedness, Kate became oblivious to Percy. She blocked the Duke of Laird from her vision.

A melting, tingling sensation consumed her. Only Edmund existed. The soft morning breeze feathered his raven hair, which fell in thick, sleek waves to his shoulders. The deep slash of his linen shirt revealed a delicious glimpse of crisp ebony chest curls. A curious burning began within her. Kate was seized by a sudden, fierce longing to meet Edmund's lips with hers, to feel his sensuous mouth against hers. She dared not move.

She could hardly speak for the desire smoking through her.

"Good day," she rasped.

Edmund gavc her a curt nod before turning his attention to the Duke of Laird. "Did you pass a comfortable eve?"

"Aye. I couldna feel more at home. I thank ye, Stamford."

Edmund nodded his head brusquely. He appeared angry with the duke for some reason.

She could not conceive that Edmund was one of those Englishmen who despised the Scots for naught. Perhaps the earl's anger was reserved for her.

Oh, fie! She could not think what she might have done now.

Kate dropped her glance, slyly making certain Edmund kept Percy at bay.

The giant, hairy creature sat on its haunches, drooling. Percy's tongue lolled from the side of his mouth, but his gaze never strayed from Kate.

"I shall be leaving early on the morrow," the duke said to Edmund.

Edmund did not protest. "As you must."

Donald Cameron would expect Kate's answer before leaving. She had hoped for more time to mull over her choices. Forty-eight hours ago she had no prospects of employment other than as gentlewoman to Lady Cordelia. 'Twas a position she could not keep and hope to avoid Edmund. And avoid him Kate must if she were to keep her increasing desire for the dark-haired, green-eyed earl contained.

It was not the weather that had Kate fanning herself. Each offer of employment was tempting in its own way. But she could not make up her mind without a visit to Jutta. Lost in her own thoughts, she had heard little of the men's conversation.

"If ye dinna mind," the duke was now saying to Edmund, "I shall stop again at Rose Hall on me return to Scotland."

"You are always welcome," Edmund responded with rigid formality.

Percy whined and made a leap for Kate, who tripped as she pitched back. The Duke of Laird responded quickly, catching Kate in his arms before she landed ingloriously on her bottom.

"Percy!" Edmund yanked at the beast's collar.

"A handsome bloodhound," Donald Cameron commented.

"He, he likes me," Kate stammered.

"Ye couldn't have a better friend, lass. Ye aren't afraid of him, are ye?"

"Nay . . . Nay," she repeated firmly. Perhaps if she denied her fear enough, it would prove true. She would no longer fear the huge canine.

The earl scowled at Kate as he slipped a folded missive from his shirt pocket. He well knew her pride had prevented her from speaking the truth. At least he hadn't revealed her as a fabricator.

"This message has come for you," he said coolly, as he handed the missive to her.

Puzzled, Kate broke the seal and opened the message under the steady scrutiny of both men. She gasped in surprise, then smiled as warm pleasure bubbled up within her heart.

" 'Tis from Papa. He is to be married."

Although Kate was uncertain she could travel to York in time to see her papa wed, she did not vacillate for a moment. She decided at once to go to his wedding. The man who had been a loving father to her deserved to be happy again. Mama would have wanted that. And Kate did, too.

No matter how he argued, Edmund could not dissuade the headstrong gardener's daughter from embarking on a dangerous journey to York. Several guests still lingered at Rose Hall, making it impossible for him to accompany Kate to protect her.

The following morning he stood in the thick, chilly fog watching the Duke of Laird depart for Burghley House, and Kate in Edmund's finest coach leaving for York.

" 'Tis not a safe journey," he muttered, hoping one last time to force her to change her mind.

"You have lent Robert to ride with me for protection."

He'd ordered a burly guard and a waiting maid to accompany Kate. Still, Edmund felt uneasy. The roads were poor and stalked by highwaymen.

"One man is not enough, and yet I can spare no more. Stay another day, and I will escort you, Kate."

"If I wait another day, Papa's wedding will certainly be over. I must go now. Do not worry, Edmund."

Would that he could cease to worry about Kate on command.

Even Percy appeared to be in a state of despair. Directly following Kate's departure, Edmund's hound had curled up in the corner of Edmund's chamber and had not moved since.

Several hours later Edmund joined his aunt and Lady Mason in the rose garden. They sat on a stone bench near the center of the garden, engaged in gossip, as usual.

"I shall sorely miss her," Cordelia told Lady Mason. "But what could I say? Her papa is to be married. At least the papa who raised her. Poor thing is a foundling you know. Abandoned."

"Abandoned!" Lady Mason clicked her tongue and wagged her head. "Poor child. You did the right thing, Cordelia."

But had he? Edmund wondered. He stepped forward, making his presence known. "Good day, ladies."

Aunt Cordelia greeted him with a smile. Lady Mason dipped her head.

With his hands clasped behind his back, he paced a small area in front of the ladies. "I am worried about Kate traveling alone, Aunt Cordelia."

"Whatever for?" Aunt Cordelia blinked. "She is well taken care of, eh? You set her off as if she were a great lady."

Had he heard a hint of disapproval in his aunt's tone?

"Kate is like one of the family, Aunt."

"The girl has been at Rose Hall since only a babe," Cordelia informed Lady Mason in a hushed aside.

Edmund felt the involuntary constriction of his jaw muscles. He brushed back the pestering lock of hair that had fallen to his forehead. "I do not feel confident that Kate is safe."

Cordelia gave a heavy-hearted sigh. "She *is* a beautiful young woman."

A knot formed in the pit of Edmund's stomach. "The coach might lose a wheel," he chafed. "Anything could happen."

"I do not know how I should get along without Kate," his aunt confided to her friend.

Edmund stopped in his tracks. *Bloody Hell! My aunt cannot get along without her. Without her?* 'Twas all he needed to hear. Guests be damned. He had not a moment to lose.

"I'm going after Kate. I shall escort her to York."

"But . . . we have guests," Aunt Cordelia protested.

"And you are the most famous hostess. I am certain you will care well for those who remain. Make my excuses. You may even claim I have had a relapse of the measles."

" 'Tis highly improper," she exclaimed, blinking as if motes from the wind had got caught in both her eyes.

"The relapse has obviously caused me a degree of madness," Edmund replied with a wry smile. Having made his decision, he felt a great burden lift from his shoulders. Kate was headstrong and stubborn—but if any harm should come to her, he would never forgive himself.

Aunt Cordelia called after him. "How long will you be gone from Rose Hall?"

"I do not know." Edmund waved without stopping as he strode briskly toward the stable. "Farewell."

He started out immediately, riding hard. England's roads were poor, barely more than rutted, overgrown paths that regularly washed out during heavy rain.

Coaches were forced to travel slowly. For that reason, Edmund expected to catch up with his carriage and Kate before nightfall.

Near dusk, when he stopped once more to rest his gelding, Edmund smelled rain in the air. The wind whipped about him, rustling through the trees, biting his face, catching in his hair.

His pulse pounded. Alarm prickled through him, dragging its sharp edge of fear. Edmund berated himself for miscalculating time and distance. His coach was nowhere in sight. He could not explain his apprehension; he only knew he would not rest until he made certain that Kate was safe.

The good-for-naught prospect of idling the night away in an inn roiled in his belly like spoiled sturgeon. He must find Kate. But the narrow, rutted roads made travel after dark impossible.

As he pondered his problem, Edmund heard musket retorts in the distance ahead.

His heart thundered within his chest. A spiking fear struck his gut. Edmund fairly leaped into the saddle. Spurring his mount forward, he galloped at a heretofore unimaginable speed. Finally, he reached an incline where he could see the road below.

'Twas his coach under siege by highwaymen.

Kate was being attacked.

FOURTEEN

Let not spring showers dismay you

Two men, only two men.

Edmund watched, contemplating his next move.

The highwaymen held their muskets on Robert and the coach driver, rendering Edmund's men helpless. One of the thieves dismounted and, with musket pointed, approached the carriage door. Lightning flashed and thunder rolled in the sky as he yanked open the door.

A terrible mixture of fury and fear exploded from Edmund in an earsplitting primal roar. A howling, warrior cry rivaling the rage of the heavens. He thought his lungs might burst.

The highwaymen looked about nervously, and then apparently deciding 'twas only the wind they'd heard, the two villains carried on with their business.

Without thought to his own safety, Edmund spurred his mount and careened down the hill toward the coach. His only thought was saving Kate from harm. Midway down the hill, the deluge of rain began. But it did not slow him.

Galloping through the hard-driving storm, Edmund swiftly drew closer. Mud flew in his face; rain pelted his skin. His heart raced at twice the speed of his horse's hooves.

Through the blur of the downfall, he saw Kate's lady's maid being pulled from the coach. And then Kate, head held high, descended from the carriage with the majesty of an ancient goddess.

Bloody hell! She'd be dead if she defied the rogues. And he knew she would.

Edmund let out another bloodcurdling cry.

This time, highwaymen and travelers alike turned toward him. The thieves froze in a ghostly, rain-swept scene.

Taking advantage of their dead-still reaction, Robert, the guard sent to protect Kate, leaped from his position beside the carriage driver. He landed with a great thud on top of the highwayman who had been standing with his musket trained upon Kate and her maid.

As the burly guard ground the villain into the mud, the second highwayman's horse reared, nearly knocking him to the ground. He looked to Edmund. Racing toward the bandit as if Lucifer and a band of archangels had given chase, Edmund's blood boiled with rage. But before he could close the gap, the cowardly scoundrel galloped away toward the wood, abandoning his comrade to his fate.

More interested in Kate's well-being than capturing a lily-livered thief, Edmund followed for only a short distance.

When he returned to the coach, he found Kate aiming Robert's musket at the captured highwayman as the guard bound the blackguard. Edmund jumped from his gelding.

Kate's eyes went large with surprise. She dropped the musket and ran to Edmund, flinging herself into his arms. She was safe. Safe and trembling against him.

A flash of bright-white lightning bolted across the sky. The heavens rolled with thunder. Edmund reacted instinctively, giving no thought to propriety. He crushed Kate to him, holding her as tightly as he dared without hurting her. He no longer felt the rain, only Kate's slender body pressed against his, her arms wrapped around his neck. Her warmth, her sweet lavender scent . . . the chatter of her teeth.

He stepped back. Rain and tears streamed down her cheeks. There was no way to tell one from the other. Her body slumped from the weight of her rain-soaked clothes, but she gave no sign of being harmed as her lips quavered into a hapless smile.

"They, they wanted our jewelry," she stammered. "They would have taken my ring."

The hell with her ring. "Did they hurt you?"

"No." She shook her head and a hank of wet, tawny hair fell against her face. "You, you came to our rescue before they could do us harm."

Edmund wrapped his arm about Kate's shoulder, holding her close and guiding her back toward the coach. But the wheels of the carriage had already begun to sink into the mud.

He barked instructions to the driver and Robert to unhitch the coach horses and, with Kate's maid, ride to the Red Fox Inn. The inn he had been about to head for when he heard the highwaymen.

Edmund lifted Kate to his horse and mounted behind her.

He had never been this near to her, to any woman he had not paid for the pleasure. A strange excitement tripped his heart.

'Twas slow and wet, and Edmund kept Kate close

to him seeking to warm her. Holding the reins, his arms circled her, grazed the sides of her breasts. Her lithe form swayed against his, brushing to and fro, triggering wild imaginings and deepening desire.

Despite the cold rain, heat shot up within him like the flames of a wildfire. If only he could enjoy the distraction of conversation, but the storm forbade talk.

Edmund ached. He grew hard. The pain intensified. The rain showering his face could not cool his passion. He wanted Kate. Pray God, needed her. Wicked visions of making love to her fixed in his mind. Images he could not erase. Bloody hell, he was no better than a rutting stud. A sense of astounding relief flooded him when at last they reached the inn.

While Kate was glad to be in out of the rain, she felt bereft without the closeness of Edmund. The strength and warmth of him, the steady beat of his heart had soothed her on the ride to the inn.

Upon arriving at the Red Fox Inn, the earl ordered a chamber for Kate and a tub of hot water to be brought to her at once. Mary had laid Kate's clothes to dry beside the fireplace before going downstairs to fetch a tray of food.

Alone in her small chamber, which was ablaze with candles and the roaring cackle of a fire, Kate sat on the edge of the bed and cried.

She had finished her bath, washed her hair, and was wrapped in a horsehair blanket twice the size of the village of Stamford. With the pop of the fire and her own sniffling tears, she almost did not hear the soft rap at her door.

Believing Mary had returned with something to eat, she did not hesitate. "Come in."

"Kate?"

Oh, fie! 'Twas Edmund, not Mary. And he appeared shocked to find her covered by nothing but a blanket.

Pulling the coarse covering tighter, she huddled inward and forced a tenuous smile. Edmund was a gentleman. He would apologize and go away.

But Edmund continued to stare. 'Twas as if he were transfixed. Shadows danced across his tall, dark figure. His damp linen shirt clung to his broad chest and muscular shoulders in a display of breath-stealing maleness. He was a man like no other. His wet, midnight hair gleamed like a starling's back.

Kate grew still. Even her tears were immobilized, ceasing their downward stream.

Obviously, Edmund had not yet been to his chamber. He had removed his stocks, but his breeches were still wet. He stood on the threshold barefoot. Commanding. Virile. The living, breathing form of every woman's dream.

Kate feared her heart had stopped. She stared, unable to look away.

He stared. When would he leave?

"I thought you were Mary with, with food," she explained in a rasp.

Edmund shook his head slowly.

She stated the obvious. "I . . . am not prepared for a visit."

Apparently, Kate's state of undress did not concern him. "I heard you crying. Why were you crying?" he asked.

"For Papa. I will not be at his wedding now, and I did not wish to disappoint him."

"You could not disappoint him, Kate. Nor any man."

The husky timbre of Edmund's voice sent a cascade

of warm shivers along her back, between her thighs. Her heart rolled over and over.

Later, Kate could not say why she did not protest when he closed the door behind him and advanced toward the bed.

"I pray you are right," she murmured.

Edmund brushed away her tears with the soft pad of his thumb. "I am."

His touch ignited a fire deep within her, yet she did not shrink from it. Instead, Kate reached out, laying her hand upon his cheek. The dark stubble of his beard felt rough and warm against her palm. Her thumb dipped to caress the cleft in his chin.

"Why did you come after me, Edmund?"

His gaze never wavered. Sparkling emerald pools edged with silver light locked on Kate's eyes. "I feared for you," he said quietly. "I should never have allowed you to leave Rose Hall alone."

"But I wasn't alone."

"I wasn't with you."

"Thanks be, you came."

His mouth curved up into a melting, seductive smile. "You are a headstrong wench," he teased in a husky timbre.

" 'Tis what happens to a girl when she grows up with a headstrong man."

Edmund closed his eyes and drew a deep breath. 'Twas as if he summoned courage. "I want you, Kate," he whispered. "God's death, I want you."

Kate's heart bolted. *Hey-ho!*

Edmund wanted her!

In less than a bat of an eye, Kate came alive. Alive with the need to laugh and cry at once. She knew the Earl of Stamford could not love the gardener's daughter. He could not love her, but he could make love to her. He *wished* to make love to her.

And Kate wished to make love to him.

There would never be another time like this. The stars had presented an unexpected opportunity. Even Jutta had not seen it, had not predicted such an eve.

Oh, but fie, fie! The queen encouraged a virgin's life.

Alas! What to do?

Kate felt fairly certain the queen could never have felt like this. And this was a decision Kate could not ponder: to remain a virgin, or make a gift of her virginity to Edmund?

The queen and virginity lost.

Tonight Kate would love Edmund with all the love for him she'd stored and hidden away in her heart through endless years. He'd captured her child's heart and won the heart of the woman. She must be his. She was born to be his—if only for this night.

For this one night, she would go wherever fate led. It mattered not if she became the companion to a sick old woman in Scotland or three robust young boys in Manchester. Kate would have memories of her love, her only love, for the rest of her life. Memories that would offer far more comfort than her virginity would ever give her.

Mistaking her silence, Edmund apologized. "Kate, I did not mean to offend you."

"No. You have flattered me, Lord Stamford."

This time she knew who knocked when there was a rap on the chamber door.

"Go away, Mary," she said.

Edmund dipped his head. "Do you mean—?"

Kate could no more prevent the smile that spread

across her face than she could stop a rainbow unfolding across the sky after a rain.

Edmund chuckled. The corners of his eyes crinkled as his mouth turned up into a knee-melting grin.

After a few moments of listening only to the pop and crackle of the fire, she heard Mary leave.

Kate rose, moving regally. The blanket, once wrapped around her, fell to deep folds at her feet. She moved toward Edmund.

His smoldering gaze raked her body.

She shuddered.

"Are you cold, Kate?"

"No, my lord."

In the silence, she could hear each thudding beat of her heart.

Without a word, Edmund gathered her in his arms, lifting her, cradling her. He gently laid her down on the bed.

His gentleness was in contrast to the tumult Kate felt. The fire in her, the need for Edmund licked at her like flames at a wooden gate. She could not wait a moment longer to feel his body against hers. She had waited all her life.

"Edmund, quickly," she whispered, as he stood over her, regarding her with an expression she'd never seen on his face before. An awed reverence.

Tears filled her eyes, happiness bounced like a silken ball against the walls of her heart.

Edmund Wydville, the Earl of Stamford, had never been so thunderstruck in his life. Kate's reaction astonished him, rendered him dazed. Was it another man's loins that burned? Another man's heart that slammed against his chest again and again? His breathing had been reduced to labored gasps.

Edmund wanted Kate more than anything in his

life—a realization that unnerved him, set his limbs to quaking. What if he should fail her? God's blood! He could never forgive himself.

Determined he should be the best of lovers, Edmund refused to respond to Kate's urgent entreaty by taking her quickly. He would make slow, gentle love to her, as she deserved. Devouring her body with his gaze, he silently vowed to give her a night of loving she would never forget. She was like the magnificent statue of a Roman goddess, molded by a genius to be perfect in all aspects.

Edmund's heart-pounding study drifted from the long, elegant column of Kate's neck to her full, high breasts. A translucent, delicate ivory, her breasts rose and fell in a promise of satin and passion. Edmund's gaze fell, lingering on Kate's small waist and well-rounded hips, and down to the soft curves of her legs. His mouth felt as dry as an old, brittle rush.

Feeling a peculiar unsteadiness in his knees, he sank to the bed beside the eager beauty. Summoning the strength to proceed slowly and with care, he closed his eyes for a moment. When he opened them again, Edmund found Kate's gaze on his. She regarded him with a steady intensity. Her golden eyes shone with a luminous quality that stoked the building fire within him to uncontrollable heights.

Bloody hell! He couldn't do this! He couldn't take an innocent girl . . . his oldest and dearest friend . . . He could not take Kate's virginity!

With a moan, Edmund started to roll off the bed, but Kate clutched his shirt.

"Prithee, Edmund, do not leave me now."

"You are an innocent, I cannot—"

"If anyone is to show me the ways of love, it must be you. Can you not see that?"

"Kate, you don't know how it pains me, I mean *pains* me, to—" He broke off, uncertain how to explain. "A man in the heat of desire experiences a great deal of pain."

"Then allow me to ease your pain, Edmund," she purred. "I know nothing can come of this night. Only that the one man I trust will initiate me in the ways of love."

"Kate, Kate . . ."

"You taught me to fish. You taught me to arch a bow—"

" 'Tis not the same! Not the same at all!"

Her hands slipped beneath his shirt. She splayed them softly against him and toyed with the hairs on his chest. God's blood, he could better resist an Irish army than Kate.

Edmund groaned. The fires of a passion he could not deny consumed him. His need for the gardener's daughter defeated his honorable intentions. He was lost. He surrendered.

A candle sputtered and died. Rain sprinkled against the windowpane.

Kate knew when Edmund's resistance died. She felt the corded muscles of his chest relax against her palms.

She tugged at his shirt, whispered urgently in the dimness. "Remove your shirt. Remove it, Edmund."

"Aye." His voice was hoarse and low, more a rumble. "Aye."

She heard the linen rip. Driven by instinct and unbridled desire, Kate nibbled his ear, his neck. *Mmmmhmmm.* She only hoped she would prove a satisfactory lover. She had no experience.

Grappling with his breeches, Edmund cursed under his breath.

Kate's heart pounded hard and fast. Her body moved to a strange new rhythm in her head. Any inhibitions she might have harbored were overcome in a flood of heat and the need to be one with Edmund.

Verily, he *was* her lord and master. He was the love of her life, the man who haunted her dreams ever since she could remember. *Mmmmhmmm.*

Freed from his garments, Edmund at last turned and took Kate into his arms once more. She felt the hard strength of his desire against her thighs. As if in answer, a silky wetness flowed from deep within Kate.

She marveled at the sweet sensation.

Edmund's mouth came down on hers in a fierce, heart-searing kiss. Her breasts, crushed against his chest, swelled. The tips of her nipples grew taut. Alive and afire with exquisite passion, Kate thought she must cry out.

But just as she thought it, Edmund's tongue plunged into her mouth, withdrawing and plunging deeply again and again, until her body arched in astonishing pleasure and aching pain. His hands slid over her hips; his palms cupped her bottom.

She was going to die in Edmund's arms!

But then, when she accepted the inevitable, his lips left hers. He burned a trail of tingling, soft caresses down her neck and—*hey-ho!*—to her breasts. Edmund's mouth covered her nipples. His tongue brushed softly against them, first one and then the other. The raging fire inside Kate reached new heights.

She gasped in pleasure.

He suckled her breasts.

The pleasure Edmund gave was such that Kate silently prayed she would live until the end of this eve.

And then, while he continued to suckle, his hand reached down between her legs.

Kate groaned.

"We can stop, Kate," Edmund whispered. "I can still stop."

"I will kill you, if you stop," she whispered back.

"You are a virgin—"

"Much much adooo . . ." she crooned, "about naught."

Before she swooned from the astonishing sensations, Edmund withdrew his hand and entered her with a gentle thrust, filling Kate with a wondrous, throbbing heat.

They were one!

"Pray God, don't take me now," Kate pleaded breathlessly.

Edmund thrust again, and Kate was lost. Each thrust became stronger, more insistent. Each movement lifted her higher. The moment of pain passed before she could cry out. Edmund's magnificent manhood bestowed Kate with the power to fly to the heavens, gave her the wings to meet whatever fate awaited her in the stars.

Her hips undulated wantonly, wildly. She reveled in Edmund, taking him deeper, ever deeper, inside of her. Moving as one, 'twas as if their bodies were made for each other.

A single shattering thrust of fire transported Kate soaring to the stars. At almost the same moment, in a final plunge, Edmund cried out and spilled his seed.

In a hazy state of pure rapture, she floated back to earth.

"Ooooh, Edmund. Hey-ho!"

FIFTEEN

Your trusting nature will not fail you

Kate fished. She loved with wicked abandon. She owned a spirit of adventure and was the merriest of companions. What more could a man desire?

Edmund thought Kate would make the ideal companion if she would only make peace with Percy—and learn to play tennis.

Somewhat chastened by her experience with the highwaymen, the golden-eyed beauty had returned with him to Rose Hall over a week ago. He'd won her back, the fairest prize of any game he played.

With his hands folded beneath his head, Edmund reclined on a blanket spread in his tree-house castle. What the devil was keeping her? She'd promised to meet him in an hour's time.

Whistling softly, he regarded the thick emerald foliage above him, the hazy strip of sunlight slipping through a gap in the leaves. A patch of mottled blue-gray sky peeked through the minuscule opening.

Yesterday Edmund had allowed Kate to defeat him at archery; the night before she had won a game of chess without his help. In her company, he felt like a young man again, bursting with life and dreams, certain he could right all the ills of the world.

But how was he to make Kate his for all time? Marriage to a gardener's daughter was out of the question; yet he had taken her virtue, rendering her unsuitable for marriage to a man of means. Even the gentry expected a virgin bride. Besides, Edmund could not fathom the thought of giving up Kate, letting her go. She was his.

The only answer was to make her his mistress. But he could not contemplate offering such a proposition to the proud, independent creature. Bloody hell, she'd have his head!

Somehow, he must find a way to be with her.

Where was she? Tardiness annoyed him mightily. As he supposed he had annoyed others in the past.

While Kate believed the highwaymen who attacked her coach on her way to her Papa's wedding were part of a larger conspiracy, Edmund did not. He blamed the stargazer for planting outrageous thoughts in Kate's head. Nevertheless, he'd experienced a numbing terror as the blackguards assaulted his coach. The blood had frozen in his veins. He could still taste the fear. Until that moment, Edmund had not realized just how much Kate meant to him.

Since their return to Rose Hall, she had shown no signs of becoming ill from the ordeal. She might have taken her death traveling in the pouring rain, soaked to the skin until they reached the inn. Ah, the Red Fox Inn.

"Edmund!"

Memories of making love at the inn vanished at the sound of Kate's voice, the crunch of leaves and earth as she hurried toward his tree.

Edmund rose to his knees; any higher and his head would be knocked by a limb. "Up here."

For a woman, Kate climbed with great alacrity and

grace. She also showed a great deal of trim ankle during the ascent. He could not envision Judith Witherspoon scaling an old oak. Without a chuckle.

Ah, Lady Judith. Another matter he must broach with Kate today.

"Good day, my lord." Kate's eyes sparkled with unrestrained joy.

Edmund's heart made a great vaulting leap against his chest. No one had ever looked at him so, with such a loving light. She made him truly feel like a man of legend, as if he were King Arthur incarnate. Edmund would do anything to ensure that Kate always regarded him with the same shining light of admiration.

Leaning over one of the remaining rails, he gave her his hand and pulled her up and into his arms.

"Oh, aye," he said, enfolding her into his arms. "I can see this will be a good day."

The faint, sensuous fragrance of lavender fired his ever-present desire for her. It did not matter they were on their knees; Edmund dipped his head and covered his mouth with hers.

She gently pushed back, gazing up at him, her extraordinary eyes glimmering with amusement. "You asked me to come fishing."

"Aye, and we shall drop our lines soon."

Edmund's murmured promise was lost as he met her parted lips. The world spun away as his tongue slipped into her mouth and he savored the warm cinnamon flavor of her. She purred, a soft, low mewing sound from deep in her throat.

Edmund's heart raced. He warmed. He was hot.

Uncommon need for her overtook good sense.

He kissed Kate fiercely. She responded with a passion matching his own.

Bloody hell! Could he make love to a woman in a tree? Was it physically possible?

His loins ached. His lips, locked against Kate's, sparked as if they were on fire.

A trembling he could not control took hold of Edmund. He swayed. Unable to regain his balance, and with Kate still in his arms—he fell. Sideways. Breaking apart from her.

Kate rolled. Holding her sides, she laughed until tears streamed down her cheeks.

"Are you hurt?" Edmund asked. Or merely a victim of hysteria? he wondered.

"Ah, Edmund. Your kiss is powerful. It knocked me right over, it did!" With that, Kate gave herself up to a fresh gale of laughter.

There was naught for him to do but acknowledge the humor in his spill and the infectious sound of her laughter. Throwing his head back, he laughed with Kate.

Birds perched innocently on neighboring branches squawked and flew from the old oak tree, screeching in protest. Leaves rustled and floated to the ground.

Pushing herself to a sitting position, Kate wiped her tears of mirth away. " 'Tis true, my lord. Your kiss stirs many wondrous sensations within me."

"As yours do mine," he confessed, transfixed by the creamy mounds of her breasts rising above the dark indigo of her gown.

It had been too long since Edmund had made love to Kate at the inn. The longing to feel her body against his, warm and soft and wanting him, overwhelmed Edmund. Smoky desire curled through him, blocking his lungs, his throat.

Kate peered at him with concern. "Edmund?"

"Aye."

"What is it?"

"I want you, Kate."

The smile began at the corner of her lips and curved upward into the most enchanting, seductive grin Edmund had ever known.

"Shall we discover what this old tree castle is made of?" she asked in a hushed, bantering tone.

He knew. "Rotting wood, I fear."

" 'Tis certain to make the experience exciting."

"If we fell to the ground—"

"We shall be each other's cushions." Kate tilted her head. Challenge glimmered in her eyes. Slowly moistening her lips with the tip of her tongue, she slanted him another sultry smile. "Where is your courage, my lord?" she teased

Nonexistent at the time. Just as was his resistance.

More than an hour later, after much creaking and groaning of the tree castle's floor planks, Edmund cradled Kate in his arms, safe and sound. They had not fallen, but they had been to paradise and back. Kate made little sounds of pleasure.

At least he'd had the foresight to bring a blanket, else they would be covered with painful splinters. But Kate deserved better, a bed of roses, a thick cushion of velvety petals.

Edmund felt guilty . . . and content. "I wish I could stay at Rose Hall forever."

"Then why don't you?" Kate asked.

"Because the Earl of Stamford is expected to take his place in London society. And I must lend my voice at court and Parliament."

"Edmund, you do not have to be dictated in all you do by society."

"I fear I haven't the courage to be thought of as an eccentric."

"You have much courage, Edmund. You proved it by running off the highwaymen," she said, smoothing and straightening her skirts. "And was it not you who opened his grounds to the villagers just days ago?"

He did feel good about that, even though he knew he would be the object of anger from his peers. "The forest will be open to all for one week in each season."

"The men of the village will hunt and be able to feed their families. And there will be no more poaching to concern you."

"I trust you are right."

"You are a good and wise man," Kate declared, tucking lose strands of honey silk beneath her caul. "Your happiness should not be hurt by a title."

She made it sound so simple to give up the games, his friends, gambling.

"Kate, methinks you would like to play tennis."

"Aye?"

" 'Tis played with rackets on indoor courts," he explained, working up to his announcement.

Wrapping her arms about her knees, Kate smiled up at him, a trusting, loving smile. "I'll try tennis if you think I would like it."

"Aye, I do. And I am certain that you will play the game well."

"Do women play?"

"I have not seen any, but they will in time."

"You are always ahead of your time."

"Aye?" He paused for courage.

"Aye."

"Then you may be glad to know that I plan to construct an outdoor court, right here at Rose Hall. 'Twill be one of the first of its kind."

Kate's face glowed with pleasure. "How thrilling!"

"The court shall be located where the rose garden is now."

Kate's face paled. The lifeblood drained from it before his very eyes. Her silence felt worse than her rage. Far worse.

"The light there is quite—" Edmund's explanation was interrupted by the sound of a horse and rider.

Edmund rose to his knees to peer down through the branches of summer leaves. 'Twas his man.

"My lord, Lady Cordelia bade me fetch you. Lady Witherspoon has arrived."

The news could not be more ill timed.

Edmund's entire body felt as if it were in the grips of a steel nipper. The life was being squeezed from him.

"I shall return straightaway," he called down.

He turned to Kate.

Anger flashed in her eyes, murderous lightning melded of silver and gold. Her sweet mouth set against him in tight-lipped fury. There would be no farewell kiss.

Edmund was guilty as silently charged, of vile chicanery. He was no better than a malt worm.

"Come. We must go, Kate. We shall discuss the tennis court, the rose garden, at another time."

Kate's spirits were lower than the roots of an ancient birch. The cloud she'd been floating on for days evaporated in the afternoon mist. The glorious days with Edmund were over, and she was angry with herself for believing their romance could continue.

An outdoor tennis court replacing the rose garden! She snapped the heads off dead rose blossoms.

Edmund spent much of his time overseeing affairs

of the estate and the comfort of his guests. Kate supposed he spent time making plans for his tennis court, and with Judith, as well. But she had not seen the two together. Rose Hall had rapidly filled with guests again in the past few days, although the queen had halted her progress and was said to be heading back to Whitehall.

The queen's change in plans threw Lady Cordelia into a fit of vapors. Kate spent hours rubbing Cordelia's temples, fetching her sack, and playing the lady's favorite melodies. Alas, three days had passed and still Edmund's aunt moaned.

The only peace Kate found was in the garden. A garden soon to be gone.

"Kate."

The Duke of Laird strode toward her. "I knew I would find ye here . . . putting the roses to shame with yer beautiful smile."

Kate jumped up and dipped into a deep curtsy. A visit from the twinkling-eyed duke would surely raise her spirits. She was always happy to see him. "Good day, my lord."

"Weel na, how does it happen ye are yet at Rose Hall?"

She brushed the dirt from her skirts. "Alas, a series of calamities."

"Aye? How so?" The aging duke sat on the near stone bench and patted the empty space beside him. "And tell me how yer papa fares. Did ye arrive in time for his wedding?"

Kate sank down beside the duke. "Papa Beadle fares well, but I did not reach York."

"What happened, lass?"

"I was overset by highwaymen."

"Och! England!" The duke slapped a hand to his

forehead. "The country is not even safe for the English."

"Lord Stamford came to my rescue," Kate continued as if she had not heard the slight upon her country.

"The gods be praised."

"They almost stole my ring from me."

Frowning deeply, the duke made a *tsk*ing sound as he shook his head. "Let me see this ring, lass. Seems to me, 'tis bringing ye nothing but grief."

Kate held out her hand. "Nay. 'Tis not the ring. 'Tis me bringing the grief upon myself. Lord Stamford doubts the highwaymen were after my ring. And if I give up my quest to find its origin, I should not feel dismayed."

Donald Cameron's frown deepened as he studied Kate's golden band. Was he perplexed, or did he see something in the ring he recognized?

Disappointed too often, Kate dared not hope.

"Ye say ye've always worn this ring?"

"Pledged to wear it."

The duke's brown eyes met hers. "It puts me in mind of a ring me friend wears. 'Tis similar."

Kate's heart leaped against her chest. "Your friend?"

"Aye. Anne. Dinna ye remember? I asked ye if ye would come to Scotland and be her companion. But ye were already spoken for."

The duke knew of a similar ring. Pins and needles scraped along Kate's skin. Her mind whirled with possibilities. "When I could not travel immediately to the Manchester family, because of Papa . . . they passed me over."

"Then ye are free to go with me? 'Tis the only reason I stopped at Rose Hall, to see if ye might be here. Circumstances change. And I'm on me way home to Scotland."

Circumstances change. Indeed.

The duke patted the thinning auburn strands atop his head. "Me Anne may be able to help you. She may know the goldsmith who fashioned your ring."

Beside herself with excitement, Kate could hardly catch a breath. Did the duke hold out true hope? Or was he attempting to lure her to his ill friend's side?

"What do ye say, lass?"

What to do? What to do? She had no reason not to trust the duke. Yet this was no small decision he was asking Kate to make. "Scotland is so far from Rose Hall," she said, lacing her hands together on her lap.

"Is Rose Hall yer home?"

" 'Tis the only one I've known."

The duke's eyes warmed, and he laid a big, rough hand over hers. "I dinna ask for a hasty answer. Think me offer over well, lass."

"How is your Anne's ring fashioned?" Kate asked.

" 'Tis gold with a ruby rose wrapped round it, a crown of diamonds, and a coat of arms that canna be distinguished, hidden, like yers, by the rose."

"She is of royal birth?"

He shrugged. "Me Anne is a private person and forbids me to pry. Whatever her background, she doesna care for anyone to know it."

"Curious."

"Aye."

"And still you love this woman of mystery." Kate sensed Anne was more than a friend to the Scottish duke. He was deeply in love with his Anne.

"Aye, there is much about her to love," he confessed with a sheepish smile. Taking Kate's hands in his, the duke beseeched her once again. "Kate, lass. Come with me. Talk with Anne, and spend a fortnight. If ye dinna like me Scotland or me woman, I shall return ye safe to Rose Hall."

"My lord, you make it difficult to refuse."

"Think it over and let me know on the morrow." Releasing Kate's hands, Donald Cameron stood, unfolding himself slowly as if all his joints ached. He cast an apologetic smile. "This old man is weary and must rest."

Kate suppressed the urge to reach out and take his hand. Instead, she offered a smile of sympathy for his trials. "You will have my answer early on the morrow."

"Me thanks, lass."

With a nod of his head, the duke straightened himself and strode from the garden.

What to do? What to do? Thoughts tumbled one upon the other through Kate's mind. If she traveled to Scotland with the kindly duke, she might discover her origins. At the end of the journey she might learn the answers to qucstions she'd been asking all of her life.

But if she left with the duke, she might never see Edmund again.

Though he'd vowed to never give his heart to a woman, he would soon marry. The Earl of Stamford would take Judith Witherspoon to be his bride and the mother of his children. He must.

He'd never said he loved Kate. He'd threatened to uproot her rose garden for an outdoor tennis court. Still . . .

To stay or to leave? 'Twas too difficult a choice. 'Twas impossible to decide on her own. Kate meant to visit Jutta right away. Her fate lay in the stars; the stargazer would tell her what to do.

Kate made haste to her bedchamber to get the necessary funds for Jutta's consultation. But as soon as she opened her door, she knew something was amiss.

"Oh, fie!"

Her small bedchamber was in disarray. Her feather bed had been slashed open and the contents spewed about. Her cedar chest had been opened and obviously rifled through. The cupboard was in disarray. Someone had entered her bedchamber and searched it thoroughly. Yet the velvet pouch containing her coins had not been touched. Who had done this? And why?

Intending to report the intrusion and make certain Edmund's aunt was content before heading to the village, Kate hurried to Lady Cordelia's solar.

She found the door to the lady's chamber ajar. Far from missing Kate, Edmund's aunt was deep in gossip with Judith Witherspoon.

'Twas quite improper to eavesdrop. A lady simply did not. Kate stepped closer, inching her head, her ear, toward the open door. The better to hear.

"Aye, Kate is beautiful," Lady Cordelia said, apparently agreeing with a statement made by Judith. "But beauty plays no part when it comes to making a match. The girl is a gardener's daughter."

"But I see the way Lord Stamford regards her," Judith whined in her child's voice. "There is something in his gaze, an affection not there when he looks at me. He appears to, to adore her."

Kate could not help but smile. Her heart skipped a beat.

"Goose! My nephew has known Kate since he was a boy. He could not possibly adore her. She is too familiar, like an old, worn glove."

The wind seeped from Kate's sail.

"I wish he would look at me as if I were an old glove," Lady Judith declared petulantly.

"Edmund plans to marry you as soon as Kate is safely wed. He told me himself—"

"Verily? As soon as Kate is married?"

Lady Cordelia's pronouncement was like an arrow to Kate's heart. Pain rocked her.

"Aye. And if I may confide, he has worked diligently to find her a suitable husband. But it seems no one will do for Kate. She is a sweet girl but far too choosy."

Too choosy? Kate's emotions shot from high to low to somewhere in the middle. 'Twas all she could do at the moment to suppress her indignation. The need to burst through the door and defend herself was almost too great to bear.

Lady Judith's tone took on an edge of excitement. "Obviously 'tis in my best interests for Kate to marry at once. I must find a husband for her! I will join in the search."

Oh, fie! 'Twas all Kate needed. To wed a man of Judith's choice! Hah! Not if she were the last unwed woman in England. She would rather be a toothless spinster begging for alms at Charring Cross.

In the end, Kate knew Lady Judith could do no better than Edmund, presenting her with his limp-wristed limner and disheveled widower with six children.

"Mayhap a woman's touch is what's needed," Lady Cordelia allowed.

"I am certain of it," Judith replied with what could only be described as relish.

"I pray you have better fortune than poor Edmund," his aunt said, releasing a heartfelt sigh before continuing in a softer, confidential manner. "I believe the Duke of Laird has a fondness for Kate. But, of course, he more than likely wishes to make her his mistress."

The Duke of Laird wished Kate to be his mistress! A thimble could have knocked her over, so astonished was she at the news. Certainly, Lady Cordelia's mind had become addled. The duke had never suggested anything improper, had never looked at Kate with the light she expected was lust, that she'd seen in other men's eyes. James Moore's eyes.

"How could Kate live better than to be a mistress to a duke?" Lady Judith wondered aloud. "Have you encouraged her to seek his protection?"

"Edmund would never hear of Kate becoming any man's mistress," the older woman replied with some aspersion. "He has said only a wealthy husband will do for her. He seeks a member of the gentry."

"My barber surgeon is a single man."

Kate fumed. Only Judith would propose a man who pulled teeth to be a suitable mate.

"Send for him."

"Kate will never suspect me of being a matchmaker," Judith said with a sly edge to her high-pitched voice.

The women conspired against her. The injustice of it all made Kate want to weep. How wise she had chosen to eavesdrop on their conversation.

"To be candid, Lady Judith, I wish to see you married to my nephew as soon as possible. Edmund spends far too much thought and time with Kate, when he should be spending it providing a Wydville heir."

"Perhaps you should consider replacing Kate as your gentlewoman," Lady Judith suggested. "She is not suitable. And if she were not constantly about, Edmund might more quickly forget her."

Oh, fie! Judith Witherspoon was a wicked woman! Fie on her! Kate's fists dug into her hips; dismay and outrage rumbled in her the pit of her stomach.

"Aye," Lady Cordelia agreed.

She agreed! Edmund's aunt, the woman Kate thought to be her friend, agreed.

"Do it soonest," Judith urged.

"While 'tis true Kate has not the rank to be a gentlewoman, I am fond of the girl."

Thank goodness for that much, Kate thought. She'd never have believed Lady Cordelia would betray her. Not if she had not heard it with her own ears.

Edmund's aunt went on unhappily. "Mayhap I am to blame for dangling the gardener's daughter before Edmund. But no one has ever soothed my headaches as she does. Kate's gentle massage works like magic."

"I shall learn to massage your headaches away," Lady Judith quickly assured Cordelia. "I will soothe you in her stead."

"Would you?"

She will never be as good as I, Kate declared silently.

"Aye," Judith responded firmly. "Pray dismiss Kate at once."

"She is a sweet girl." Lady Cordelia sounded as if she might be waffling.

"But as long as she remains at Rose Hall, Kate stands between Edmund and me," Judith argued.

"I had hoped she would find a position as nurse. If her papa hadn't wed so suddenly, she would be employed elsewhere by now."

And Kate would not have been loved to bliss by Edmund. Thinking of it even now warmed her.

"If you dismiss Kate, she may be eager to marry my barber surgeon," Lady Judith insisted. "Single women with no means look more favorably on marriage."

" 'Twill be difficult to let her go."

"But it is best for all. Kate will have a husband, and Edmund will marry me and have his heir. I am six-and-twenty. 'Tis time I married and bore children."

"Aye. 'Tis the proper thing to do."

"I do not have time to dangle after Edmund. If he does not offer for me soon, I shall look elsewhere for a husband."

"Oh?" Cordelia was obviously startled by Judith's declaration.

"I must."

"Do nothing in haste, Judith. I will dismiss Kate on the morrow."

Oh, fie!

SIXTEEN

Moon rising brings great joy

Kate had never felt so unhappy. She fled to the rose garden to collect herself. The need to see Jutta was greater than ever. With one look at Kate's chart the baker's wife would know just what must be done. Not that Kate believed she had much choice.

But her garden refuge had been invaded. She watched in dismay as Edmund hastily attempted to conceal the evidence with what appeared to be a strange little jig. He pushed the dirt, dug up by Percy, back in place with his boot as the big dog barked and pranced. The scurrilous beast had escaped from his master's side and had been digging in the garden. It was not the first time. The hound seemed especially to like uprooting the eglantine bushes.

Kate contemplated the pile of dirt. 'Twas a symbol of what her life had become. A pile of dirt. Her heart sank. She whimpered.

Percy looked up—and bounded toward her.

"Sit!" Edmund roared.

The dog skidded to a halt.

Tears rolled down Kate's cheeks. Wounded moments ago by Lady Cordelia, Kate was pushed over the edge by this fresh injustice. No matter if it was a small thing, digging up the rosebushes. It was just one more lowering event. Was Percy helping Edmund prepare for the tennis court he wished to build here?

Kate could no longer hold back her feelings. The anger, the sorrow, caught in her throat, tossed in her belly, and spilled from her eyes. She'd had enough.

"I'm leaving," she blurted . . . and sniffled.

" 'Tis only dirt, Kate. I shall have it repaired in moments. Look." To emphasize the insignificance of his hound's misbehavior, Edmund whistled as he worked with greater speed. Dirt flew.

"Never you mind. I have accepted another position." She sucked up an oncoming sob, wiped her tears with the back of her hand.

Edmund stopped his foot flailing. He appeared transfixed, a lusty man turned to cold stone by an out-of-sorts cunning woman. The earl regarded Kate with a dark, suspicious frown. "Nooo."

"Yes."

"But you cannot—"

She spun on her heel. "Watch me."

"But I have plans . . ."

Her heart jumped up, alive once more. Hope never strayed far from Kate's heart. She spun back. "What plans?"

"I shall build you a cottage of your own beside the tennis court. It will have as many rooms as you wish. . . ." Edmund's voice trailed off. The corners of his mouth turned up in a soft, triumphant smile. "You will remain at Rose Hall for the rest of your life, as gentlewoman to Aunt Cordelia."

Oh, fie the man!

Kate stomped her foot impatiently. "But I desire a husband and family of my own one day."

Edmund opened his arms, his hands palms up. "To

that end, have I not presented you with any number of eligible men?"

"I desire a husband of my own choosing," she snapped. "At the proper time."

The garden went still except for Percy's heavy panting.

Edmund folded his arms across his chest. "And just when will that be?"

"When I grow weary of the search for my birth mother."

"God's blood, woman!"

"The time may be close at hand."

His eyes narrowed. "What say you?"

"The Duke of Laird knows of a ring similar to mine."

He hiked a dark brow. "Aye?"

Kate twisted her ring. She lifted her chin defiantly, met Edmund's skeptical gaze, and quickly lowered her eyes. "The duke's friend Anne, for whom he seeks a companion, wears a similar ring," she explained.

" 'Tis a ruse!" Edmund exploded. "Are you so gullible to believe such a tale?"

"Aye. I am." Kate raised her chin an inch higher. "I believe Donald Cameron. The duke is a good, kind man."

"A man who covets you." Edmund kicked the ground with disgust.

"Is every man who shows me kindness not to be trusted, Edmund?" She did not wait for his reply. "For you have shown me great kindness."

"You cannot compare. I have known you and had your best interests at heart since you were a child. Donald Cameron wishes only to separate you from your friends."

"Why should he wish to do so?"

"The better to seduce you."

"Nay! For shame, Edmund! To even think such a thing—"

"And shame upon you for *not* thinking of it."

"I shall never be mistress to any man." And then a thought occurred. Kate inclined her head, studying the warrior athlete who had become crimson with distress. "Are you jealous of Donald Cameron?"

"Not I!"

"Methinks you are green with envy!"

Percy, reacting to Edmund's and Kate's raised voices, began to bark.

"Go!" he shouted at the dog.

The bloodhound turned his big sorrowful eyes from Edmund to Kate and back again before he slowly loped from the garden, looking back at his master frequently, as if he expected a reprieve at any moment.

In Edmund's churlish state, Kate hesitated to disclose that her bedchamber had been ransacked, or that she was about to be dismissed. He would not believe her, just as he refused to believe her about the Duke of Laird.

She did not believe the arrogant earl could be jealous of the old duke. Kate's foolish accusation was merely the flapping of an angry tongue.

Edmund ran a hand through his hair. He responded in measured tones. "I am not jealous, Kate. But I do fear that in the light of your innocence you do not always see the darkness in the heart of others."

"My thanks for your concern," she replied quietly. Kate did not wish to argue with Edmund. "I promise to keep my eyes open to the darkness."

He growled. Kate knew he meant to intimidate her, but the low, throaty rumbling was lost on her. She thought Edmund magnificent when he growled. With his mane of midnight-black hair and his broad, muscled chest, he was like a wild jungle cat—untamed and exciting.

Turning a deaf ear to the earl's guttural warnings, Kate asked a question that had long been on her mind. "Edmund, when we were young, did you allow me to be your childhood companion because there was no one else to provide company for you?"

He scowled. "Nay." With his hands locked behind his back and his eyes on the ground, Edmund circled the recently uprooted rosebush. "You learned to fish eagerly. You grasped the longbow as if you were born with one in hand. You still ride like the wind. If you played tennis you would be a worthy opponent in that sport as well, I am certain."

His eyes met hers, challenging Kate to deny what he'd said.

She could not deny the truth, but it was only half-truth. He'd needed Kate's company when he was a boy. He had needed her approval and admiration. He could not bear life alone and unloved.

"Lord Lavingham plays tennis, and he is a far better gamester than I."

"Among women, you have no match."

Kate gave him a wistful smile. Likely, 'twas the highest compliment the Earl of Stamford could pay a woman. She should be grateful, yet she was not.

Kate drew a deep breath, steeling herself. "I will leave Rose Hall on the morrow with the Duke of Laird. I will serve as his lady's companion in Scotland."

"Kate, you cannot."

"Aye. I can."

"Are you not happy at Rose Hall?"

"Aye, but—"

"I shall raise your wages."

"Lady Cordelia—"

"My aunt is difficult, I understand. I shall appoint you the rose gardener and grant you a generous pension."

Kate shook her head. Tears gathered behind her eyes. "I must go. Can you not see?"

"Nay. I do not see." His voice was steely.

Kate had to tell him. "Lady Judith has convinced Lady Cordelia to dismiss me. 'Tis a sign." She raised her eyes to the heavens as if the stars might be shining in the overcast sky, twinkling l-e-a-v-e across the heavens.

Edmund spoke through a clamped jaw. "Neither Judith nor my aunt has a say who will stay at Rose Hall and who will not," he said.

Struggling to suppress a well of tears, Kate shook her head again. It felt as if wild thistles scraped at the walls of her heart. "Edmund, 'tis better this way. The planets have contrived to give us special moments together—"

"Is your stargazer at the bottom of this?" he demanded.

"Nay, Edmund. 'Tis obvious even to one who is not an astrologer. The stars brought us together for a short time, and now they send us on our separate ways. . . ."

"Bloody hell!"

Determined to say her farewell, Kate ignored Edmund's angry protest. Her throat felt as dry as garden dirt in a drought. But she pressed on, hoarsely.

"The memories of our moments together will be with me always, in my mind and in my heart. But tonight I shall advise Lady Cordelia that I am leaving."

"Is there nothing I can say?"

"Nay."

The Earl of Stamford marched off, grinding several fallen rose blossoms beneath his boots.

Whack.

Edmund's archery competition with Stanton did not go well later that afternoon. He could not concentrate on his game.

The family had gathered beneath a massive white tent to watch the event. His aunt, who never appeared at sports events, sat on the sidelines with Lady Judith. Tears streamed down Cordelia's plump, lily-white cheeks. Apparently, even her frequent blinking could not hold them back.

Whack.

Although he missed the bull's-eye this afternoon, Edmund's arrows hit the butt. His game was not putting his aunt to shame, so he knew she wasn't crying for him. Kate must have told her that she was leaving. His aunt was fond of Kate. No matter what Judith Witherspoon advised, Edmund did not believe the old woman would have actually dismissed Kate.

On the other hand, Lady Judith appeared quite content. She applauded each time one of his arrows hit the butt. The pleasant but thin smile never left her rouged lips.

Whack. The arrow shaft quivered.

His sister, Jane, with her husband, Viscount Chumley, in tow, had arrived earlier in the day, along with Frances and her nurse. Jane and Alexander's glazed eyes gave way their boredom with the competition.

Kate appeared halfway through the final set. She

strolled to the sidelines on the arm of the Duke of Laird.

Bloody hell!

Edmund longed to take Donald Cameron in a duel. But 'twouldn't be fair. The man was old. Too old to be taking a young innocent like Kate.

Whack.

Stanton hit the bull's-eye again. Edmund had lost. He was unused to losing and was surprised it did not disturb him as much as he had imagined it would. Perhaps it was because he was already tormented, had been since he'd failed to convince Kate to stay at Rose Hall.

With the back of his hand, Edmund swiped the sweat from his brow as Stanton approached him.

The queen's adviser did not bother to mask his self-complacent smile. "I say, I believe I have won."

"Indeed, Henry. Congratulations."

"Your mind was elsewhere, I suspect."

"Not at all."

Stanton's bovine eyes fixed on Edmund. "Lady Cordelia's gentlewoman once again converses with the Scotsman. Is she in league with Laird?"

Edmund stiffened. Henry's remark triggered a whispered alarm in his mind. 'Twas ominous that one of the queen's most trusted counselors should consider for a moment that Kate could be a threat to England.

"Never fear," he replied. "Kate is but a gullible young woman taken in by Laird's fawning. She does not plot against the crown."

As he spoke the words, a vision of Kate's ring appeared in Edmund's head. A crown partly concealed by a rose. Bloody hell, such a design could be misconstrued by one sworn to protect the queen from enemies both abroad and at home. To some, the hidden crown might mean royalty in hiding. Nay! Preposterous!

Still, Henry might have seen Kate's ring and jumped to an erroneous conclusion. Nay. Nay. He put too much on a silly supposition. Kate's news of leaving had disturbed Edmund to the point where he could not think straight.

"You would be surprised at those who have plotted against the crown in the past," Stanton said. "The queen has a legion of envious relatives both legitimate and illegitimate. Men and women, plain and beautiful."

Edmund's alarm deepened. Fresh beads of sweat broke out on his brow and palms. He must ease Stanton's foolish fears. The tic at the adviser's mouth pulled, giving him an evil sneer.

"I have known Kate since she was a small child. She is the gardener's daughter." Edmund paused and chuckled. "You have naught to fear from her. She knows not one end of a musket from the other."

Henry Stanton nodded solemnly. He ran his tongue around his full lips, wetting them.

"Kate is harmless," Edmund added for good measure.

"You obviously hold the young woman in high regard. Let us hope she does not disappoint."

With a perfunctory dip of the head, Stanton turned on his heel and lumbered toward Rose Hall. The queen's adviser did resemble a bull. Just as Kate said.

Edmund released a sigh. He doubted the Duke of Laird was attempting to enlist Kate in any conspiracy against the crown. He was a simply a lecherous old man—which was terrible enough. Edmund's thoughts turned to Kate's ring once more.

Was it indeed possible the concealed crown held

portentous implications? Bah! Henry Stanton's suspicious nature overrode Edmund's good sense. Edmund would wager his new tennis court that the ring was merely a design hammered by a village goldsmith.

With some relief, he watched the duke take leave of Kate. She turned to Edmund then. Her gaze met his across the grassy space. She started toward him, as elegant as any woman in the queen's court. Edmund envisioned Kate's luscious hips swaying provocatively beneath her farthingale. Ah, to slip a hand . . . Ah, but, no.

The soft pink shade of her silk gown reminded him of a maiden's blush. Kate's blush. A stiff lace ruff cradled the length of her slender neck, and a tantalizing measure of her exquisite breasts rose proudly from the deep square neckline of her gown. Ah, to cup her generous breasts in his palms, press his lips against the small heart just above—ah . . . But, no.

Creamy braid trimmed the long sleeves, stomacher, and hem of Kate's simple dress. Ropes of pearls draped around her neck and adorned the full skirt of her gown. As usual, several strands of tawny silk hair had escaped from her pearl-trimmed caul. She brushed away the runaway wisps that flew in her face as she strolled toward him.

Ah . . . but to be the one to sweep away her untamed locks. Ah . . . But, no.

Edmund wondered if all the male guests gathered around regarded Kate as he did . . . a beautiful goddess moving among mortals. A goddess favoring the peers of the realm with her radiant smile, her musical laughter.

Specks of dust danced in the last hazy rays of sun. The scent of garden roses drifted on the summer breeze.

Edmund's heartbeat quickened with anticipation.

Kate had changed her mind. She meant to stay at Rose Hall. She was coming to tell him so.

"My lord." She dipped her head in the submissive form of courtesy she regularly displayed to him in the presence of others. "My condolences on your loss."

"I thank you, Mistress Kate."

She lowered her voice in a conspiratorial fashion. "You allowed Stanton to win, did you not?"

"Nay. Sadly."

Her amber eyes widened in surprise. The shining golden pools reflecting Kate's wit and intelligence now regarded him with astonishment. "But how could you lose? No one is a better archer than you."

"My mind may have been elsewhere," Edmund allowed.

Elsewhere, in the warm glow of her smile, engulfed by the fragrance of lavender fields that caressed her, clung to her.

Kate's softly curved brows dipped in a slight frown. Her voice dropped to a whisper. "Did you lose a great deal wagering?"

"Stanton refused to wager. Thinking he would lose, I expect."

" 'Tis fortunate for you that he refused."

"Aye. For . . . for my mind was on you," Edmund confessed in a rush of words.

She gasped. "Pray, say it is not so."

"I cannot fathom that you will no longer be at Rose Hall."

Kate chewed on her bottom lip, sweet, pink, and tasty. "But my absence may prove a boon to your archer's skills," she said. "I shall not be about to distract you."

"I shall, shall . . . miss your distraction."

God's blood. The feelings were difficult enough for Edmund to manage; the words were almost impossible to speak aloud.

Unaware of his turmoil, Kate gave him a brilliant smile, warming him in places that should not be warmed in public. "And I shall miss you, Edmund."

"I cannot dissuade you."

"Nay."

"Has the stargazer advised you to leave?"

He should have run the astrologer out of the village long ago.

"I have not had time to consult Jutta."

"Kate, I beg you. Look at my aunt. She has tears in her eyes."

" 'Tis because she longs to be back in London. My advice to you is to take Lady Cordelia to London where she is happiest."

"I shall. What else can I do to please you?" Edmund felt the angst of a desperate man.

She bit down on her lip. "There is nothing."

"The rose garden. If it pleases you, I shall construct my tennis court on the east side of Rose Hall and leave the garden."

" 'Twould please me."

"You will stay, then?"

Kate shook her head. The sadness in her eyes sent a wave of melancholy through him.

"I shall be leaving early on the morrow," she said quietly. "The duke is anxious to return to his Anne."

"No."

"Farewell, Edmund." Kate's voice was but a whisper caught on the wind. She lowered her eyes and turned on her heel.

"Kate, stay."

But she did not hear, or did not choose to stay.

Gazing after her hastily departing figure, Edmund watched as his sister hurried to Kate's side. Kate stopped to greet Jane, and then the two women huddled together as they repaired to Rose Hall.

What did they have to say to each other? He knew only that Jane had overcome her dislike of Kate when she had nursed Frances back to health.

Damn. He could do nothing short of locking Kate up to make her stay. Damn Judith Witherspoon's evil tongue. And pray, what had his aunt been thinking?

Edmund had hardly finished the thought before finding his aunt at his side.

"You must make Kate stay," she said.

"Did you not wish to dismiss her?" Edmund asked tersely.

"Aye. I considered dismissing the girl, but only for an hour." Cordelia held a silk fan in one hand and a goblet in the other. "And then I had a change of heart. With Kate gone, who would soothe my temples during a headache, or play for me?"

"Lady Judith?" he suggested dryly.

"Nay, though she promised she could."

"Perhaps you should have thought of Kate's talents before releasing her," Edmund barked, out of patience.

His aunt blinked. "I never said a word to Kate about my thoughts."

"And why did you have such thoughts?"

Lady Cordelia raised troubled—and slightly glazed—hazel eyes to his. "I am worried Kate holds a *tendre* for you."

A roiling in his belly caused Edmund to be harsher with his aunt than he was wont to be. He fairly growled his explanation. " 'Tis but the affection old friends have for one another."

"Can you not make her stay?"

"I fear not. Kate is stubborn. And she has made up her mind."

She had made up her mind rather quickly and for once without any vacillation that he could see. She was so eager to be gone that she had not even consulted the stargazer.

"I wish you would make another attempt to make Kate stay," Cordelia urged, blinking in her rapid, annoying fashion.

"I have!"

"You do not have to snap at me."

With a groan of frustration, Edmund turned away from his wounded aunt to find Henry Stanton standing in the shade of the tent, nearly concealed in the shadows. With his hands laced together against his portly chest, the queen's trusted adviser was watching Kate, observing her closely as she and Jane entered Rose Hall.

The faint alarm Edmund had felt earlier, now clamored noisily in his head. Did Stanton's inexplicable interest mean danger for Kate?

SEVENTEEN

You will find happiness at your hearth

A light fog blanketed the morning and settled in Kate's soul. Hovering by the door of Rose Hall, she watched the preparations for departure. The scurrying servants, the lifting and loading of heavy wooden chests. She heard the grunts and mumbled oaths, neighing horses and barking dogs.

And she felt an odd sense of detachment from the activity, as if all were being made ready for someone else's journey. Certainly not hers. Kate could hardly believe she was about to leave Rose Hall . . . and Edmund Wydville, Earl of Stamford.

She watched in numbed disbelief as her sole cedar chest was loaded into the oxcart carrying Laird's possessions.

She watched as the coach Donald Cameron had hired for her journey to Scotland pulled up. The duke would ride his horse alongside.

A deep melancholy rolled through her body like thick, steely gray fog. A blur of color and hurried movement jarred Kate from her trancelike state.

Whistling softly, Edmund strode from the direction of the stables. 'Twas a flat tune, he whistled. Percy trotted at his side.

A wrenching ache tore at Kate's heart. Edmund's towering figure stood out among all of the others gathered in this business of leaving.

He drew closer. Kate did not need to stare as she was. She knew she would never forget Edmund. She knew every line, color, and texture of him. She knew his every mood and expression. The Earl of Stamford was forever etched in her mind and heart.

A sudden gust of wind swept back Edmund's dark hair. Thick and loose, the sloe-black strands fell to his shoulders, massive shoulders squared like a soldier's about to surrender to the foe. Despite a strong gait, the earl's muscular body moved rigidly as might a man who walked in his sleep.

Kate saw beyond the grim, tight set of Edmund's mouth to his usual mischievous grin, to sensuous lips that had caressed hers with heart-melting sensitivity and fierce passion. She would never know a more magnificent man than Edmund.

He headed toward the duke to take his leave. The parting was brief as Kate expected it to be. Donald Cameron turned to oversee the last of the preparations, and Edmund strode toward Kate, a tail-wagging Percy close at his heels.

Kate could not take in a full breath. But it was not fear of Percy. She hardly noticed the hound. Her lungs felt tight and full, as if they might burst. At the same time, a flood of tears threatened to unleash itself. She dared not move.

Edmund bounded up the stairs to where she waited.

His expression was solemn. "Good morn, Mistress Kate."

"Good morn, Lord Stamford."

"I see you are prepared to depart."

She nodded, unable to speak. A thick knot blocked her throat.

Edmund dipped his head. There were no words for this parting. Even Edmund had no words. Each thumping beat of Kate's heart roared in her ears as she waited for him to speak.

At last, he did. "I want you to take Percy."

"Percy?" She must have misunderstood.

"He will provide excellent protection for you."

"I need no protection."

Edmund planted his feet apart and folded his arms across the broad expanse of his chest. "Do you not recall being besieged by highwaymen on your last journey?"

"I do," she assured him. "But on this journey the duke and his man will be there to protect me."

"And Percy."

Kate forced the sweetest smile she could muster. "My lord, 'tis an extraordinary gift"—she paused to insert a bit of regret into her tone—"but alas, I cannot accept."

"But I insist, Mistress Kate. Just observe how my hound regards you. See his tail wag. Percy adores you."

"He believes I am game he has not yet captured."

Edmund's soothing smile belied the edge to his voice. "On the contrary. Percy would rather be with you than me."

Kate loathed to argue with Edmund on their final meeting. She would never see him again. But the earl's stubbornness left her no choice. She would rather take an adder for a pet than Percy.

"I beg to disagree, Lord Stamford. Percy's loyalty is to his master. And I know how much your bloodhound means to you. I cannot allow you to make such a sacrifice."

"For you, 'tis not a sacrifice but a pleasure."

"Please, keep your hound." Kate could feel the panic rising in her chest.

"He will ride on the coach beside the driver."

" 'Tis a high perch for a hound," Kate objected. "Are you certain the height and movement will not make him sick?"

"He's a sturdy animal."

Kate started down the steps toward the coach, eager now to be off. Without the hound. "If Percy could talk, I feel he would protest being sent to cold, cold Scotland."

"He should be happy anywhere with you," Edmund declared.

"I fear in a short time he will be in despair from missing you."

Edmund continued as if he had not heard her. "He will obey you on command. There are only three words you need to remember. Sit. Stay. Go."

"Sit. Stay. Go."

"Go, means attack, as well as remove yourself from my sight."

"How does Percy know which to obey?"

"By the tone of your voice . . . and the circumstances. Should you find yourself accosted by highwaymen, Percy will understand and attack."

"I hardly know what to say." Kate felt distinctly faint.

"Words are not needed." Edmund smiled broadly.

"I am overwhelmed by your kindness." She forced what could only be a pathetic smile.

Edmund took a step closer, brushing against her, sending sparks flying from all directions straight to her heart. His voice dropped to but a whisper. "Kate, if you find this new position not to your liking, you need only to send word. I will come for you."

The tears that had all but been forgotten as she and Edmund argued over Percy, began to build once again behind her eyes. She did not trust her shaky voice. "My thanks . . . for all that you have done. I will never forget you, Lord Stamford."

Edmund's dark brows came together in a deep frown. "And I you . . ."

"I wish you good fortune with your outdoor tennis court."

"Are you certain you cannot stay? The first match on the completed court will make an exciting end to the summer." Edmund was at his most charming. He coaxed Kate with promises that shone in his eyes and soothed in his silky tone. "Lords and ladies will come to Rose Hall from miles around. You should not miss it, Kate. I shall be happy to ask the duke to delay his journey." He turned as if he would speak to Donald Cameron at once.

"Stay, Edmund." Kate reached out, laying a gentle hand on his arm. " 'Tis difficult to leave once. I should not like to go through this again. The time has come. Farewell, Edmund."

"Godspeed, Kate." His voice broke.

Lowering her head, Kate dipped into a curtsy so he would not see her tears. With head still down she spun around toward the coach, suppressing the sobs that threatened to overwhelm her. The waiting coachman helped her into the carriage with polished deference, as he might exercise to a member of the gentry rather than the serving class.

When she had discreetly wiped away her tears and steeled herself, Kate looked out.

Edmund scratched behind his hound's ears, setting Percy's tail into brisk motion. After a bit of this, Edmund ordered the animal in a gruff voice, "Go."

Percy bounded forward.

Oh, fie!

Kate had held out hope that at the last the beast would refuse to leave Edmund. But then, having Percy at her side meant keeping a connection to Edmund. Mayhap the hound was better than naught. Perhaps in time she would come to love Percy. Although she rather doubted it.

Edmund turned his gaze from his hound to the coach. His eyes met hers, filled with a sorrow that dulled the usual sparkling green valley depths. Kate longed to jump from the coach and into his arms.

But 'twould be in vain.

A searing pain shot through her. The last thing she saw before closing her eyes and laying her head back on the padded bench was Henry Stanton sidling up to Edmund.

The queen's trusted adviser led his big bay.

Swamped in misery, the Earl of Stamford looked after Kate's departing coach, unaware of Stanton's presence. Edmund's gaze fixed on the carriage as it rumbled down the tree-lined road. His heart constricted in a painful spasm. Had he known Kate's leaving would cause physical distress, he would have forbidden it. Bloody hell, he would have locked her up!

"Is the gentlewoman leaving?"

Startled by the sound of Stanton's voice, Edmund spun on the man at his side. "Aye," he snapped, and instantly regretted his rudeness.

"Where does Mistress Kate journey?"

"She has taken another position . . . with the Duke of Laird."

"I expect you will miss her fair face."

"I expect I will."

But as soon as he spoke the words aloud, Edmund reminded himself he had been abandoned before and had survived. This emptiness he felt would not last. He was popular among his peers; he'd gained many friends and need not feel alone or unwanted.

Thankfully, Stanton kept his counsel as the traveling party of coaches approached the bend in the road. Donald Cameron, the Duke of Laird, was the only one who looked back to wave before the coaches and wagons that carried their belongings disappeared from view.

Edmund's stomach sank when he heard Percy's farewell bark.

Henry Stanton cleared his throat. "My thanks for a most pleasant stay at Rose Hall, Lord Stamford."

"Are you leaving as well?"

"Aye. I can never be away from court for long."

"You have been a worthy opponent," Edmund said. "I look forward to another match with you."

The adviser's mouth twitched. "As do I."

Edmund placed a hand on the bullish man's shoulder. "I wish you a safe journey. Give my best wishes to the queen."

With a nod, Stanton mounted his bay and was joined by two personal assistants who'd been waiting near the gate. Edmund watched the trio ride out. But he did not truly see them.

The sadness in Kate's eyes haunted him. At least he could take comfort knowing that Percy would protect her. She did not seem to fear the Scottish duke or marauding highwaymen. She had only expressed fear of one man . . . Henry Stanton.

Stanton. He had ridden out within minutes of Kate's and the Duke of Laird's departure. For a moment Edmund experienced a prickly feeling in his gut. What if Kate was correct in her mistrust of Stanton? For some unfathomable reason, could the queen's adviser be bent on harming the gardener's daughter?

Nay, nay. Such thoughts were foolish. He must rid Kate from his mind. She'd left Rose Hall. She'd left him.

Edmund stewed for days. He missed Kate. Aunt Cordelia had returned to drinking more sack than was good for a woman of her advanced years. She'd also reverted to reciting a litany of physical ailments at every opportunity. And complaints.

Judith Witherspoon had not the knack of rubbing her temples in the same soothing manner as Kate. Neither could the lady play the lute near as well. Worse, his aunt had confided to Edmund, Lady Judith did not seem inclined to leave Rose Hall before summer's end, and Cordelia was becoming bored with her company.

Edmund commiserated but could not offer real comfort. He felt poorly himself. He forced himself to rise from his bed in the morning. He'd lost his appetite.

"You should not have given Percy away," his friend Christopher admonished. "You would not feel churlish if he were by your side."

Edmund nodded. He missed Percy, too.

He struggled to complete the outdoor tennis court that at the onset had given him such excitement. He practiced for the tournament he'd proposed. Each player contributed to the winning prize. Lord Cheltham had just added one of his Irish-bred horses to the stakes.

After a morning spent at tennis with Christopher, Edmund went off to the stream. He sought solitude, not fish. He sought the spirit of Kate, which might still linger there in the flowers, in the tumbling laughter of the stream.

Whistling softly to keep himself company, he climbed to his castle in the tree. He could see clearly now 'twas but a small ruin of rotting planks. He should not come here again. It was the place of daydreaming, and he wasn't a child any longer. Reality had long ago replaced a boy's daydreams. He laced his hands behind his head and leaned back against the broadest, sturdiest board.

Gazing up at the sky, he wondered if the planets indeed held his fate in their motion as Kate believed.

A soft breeze rustled through the leaves. Edmund could almost smell Kate's crisp, lavender scent as he conjured visions of her. Kate's eyes danced before him, teasing him, adoring him, promising him heaven in her arms. The memory of her laughter brought a smile to his face, tugged at his heart.

Lost in reverie, Edmund did not hear the sound of horse hooves until they were upon him. His body tensed.

"Edmund! Are you here?"

Zounds! 'Twas Judith Witherspoon. No other woman had been here with him but Kate. Judith's trespassing seemed somehow unfaithful to Kate. But as Edmund pushed to his feet, he feared for his aunt. He could think of no other reason that would bring Judith into the woods but Aunt Cordelia. Some actual illness had at last befallen his aunt.

"Edmund!" Judith's high-pitched child's voice struck him as doubly irritating.

He peered over the rail. "I shall be down directly."

"Are you up a tree?"

"I shall be down directly," he repeated firmly.

When Edmund jumped to the ground, Judith gawked at him as if he were a monkey in man's clothing. She had dismounted and was tying her mare.

"What brings you here, Judith? And how did you find me?"

"The yeoman of your stable told me where I might find you."

Barnes would do or say anything for a shilling. 'Twas time to replace the man.

"Is something amiss with Aunt Cordelia?"

"No." Judith's blue-gray eyes fixed on his. " 'Tis I who am facing a dilemma."

A bad feeling settled in Edmund's stomach. "Pray, enlighten me."

"I know not how to say this but plainly." Judith plucked a wild daisy, and as she strolled along the stream, she ripped the petals from the flower, one by one.

Edmund followed a step behind.

" 'Tis time for me to wed. I am past twenty-one. . . ."

Well past twenty-one years, Edmund thought.

"As it is, it will take months in order for the banns to be read and the ceremony due me to be arranged."

"I see," he said, knowing he should say something.

Lady Witherspoon was a scarlet woman. Auburn hair and kohl-rimmed, bloodshot eyes gave way to reddened cheeks and lips. Red leather slippers peeked from beneath the layers of her red silk gown. Slippers instead of riding boots!

Edmund feared the lady could not hold her own in a race with him across the meadows.

"I should like your pledge now, Edmund, or I will seek another eligible man to be my husband."

An ultimatum. He felt the blood draining from his face. Damn, it drained from his entire body, leaving him cold. The mushrooms at his feet possessed more vigor than he did at the moment.

"Edmund?"

Judith's crimson lips were drawn tight. Her eyes narrowed on him.

"I cannot talk of this until my tennis court is completed and the tournament ended."

"A tennis game delays the announcement of our marriage?" she squealed on a note that would have certainly caused Percy to howl.

" 'Tis extremely important," Edmund replied with equanimity, though he was swiftly losing patience.

Being a petite, rather square woman, the top of Judith's head just reached Edmund's chest. He was forced to look down, and she to stretch her neck looking up.

"Methinks your thoughts yet linger on Kate, my lord. I have seen how you look at her. I am not stupid."

Edmund knew dangerous ground when he walked upon it. He stood on quicksand. "My interest in Kate is entirely virtuous."

"Since when does an earl take interest in a gardener's daughter?"

How could he explain the feelings he could not wholly understand himself? "My . . . dealings, er . . . friendship with Kate began before I gained the title of earl."

A friendship. Although he recognized it was unusual for a man to enjoy a friendship with a woman, nonetheless, there it was. Edmund grinned.

Judith raised a disbelieving eyebrow. "Edmund, I will make you a good wife. One who will look the other way should you care to dally. But I refuse to wait any longer to be wed. Need I remind you of my dowry and friends at court?"

"Verily, the world knows I am no less than a cad to ask you to—"

"Queen Elizabeth has given her approval of our match, and as you well know, there is not a better one to be found for you in all of Britain."

Pray God, 'twas true. This little plump red ball before him was the best match in terms of title and wealth. "We shall make our final arrangements following the match," he assured her. "Until then, I must devote my energies to the tennis court and winning the tournament."

Lady Judith leveled a narrowed gaze at Edmund. "If you persist in this foolishness, you may win your tennis tournament, Lord Stamford, but you shall certainly lose me."

'Twas late in the afternoon. With her elbows braced against the damp, cold ledge of the window, Kate cupped her cheeks in her palms. Caught in a cloud of lethargy, she gazed out onto the unfamiliar landscape. The moors beyond Downes Castle were shrouded in mist, the earth and sky muted in shades of brown and baked clay.

She doubted roses of any kind could grow here.

Although the Duke of Laird made every effort to make the journey to Scotland as comfortable as possible, it had been wrought with pain for Kate.

The dull ache in her heart would not leave, had become a permanent part of her. Her limbs felt leaden. Even making light conversation seemed a formidable task. And for the first time in her life, she had no appetite. She could sleep night and day.

Downes Castle was a disappointment. Cold and crumbling, she could not imagine finding happiness or peace within the damp stone walls. The kindly duke apologized for the state of the castle and promised her he would begin repairs immediately. He apologized for Anne.

Although they had arrived three days ago, the mysterious lady of the castle had been feeling too ill to see thcm. Her old retainer Sally repeatedly assured Donald Cameron and Kate that her mistress was anxious to see them and begged for their understanding.

Kate turned from her window. Percy lay in her line of sight, curled in a corner of the adjacent chamber.

"Percy?"

The hound did not move.

"If you do not eat soon, you will die."

Percy opened one eye.

"I cannot have your death on my hands."

The beast made a whimpering sound and rested his large head on his two front paws.

"You are the only tie I have with Edmund now." Kate rose and advanced slowly toward where Percy lay. His mournful eyes followed her. "As I suppose I am your only link to your master."

Kate had never talked to a dog before. She felt foolish doing so, did not expect him to understand her. She spoke in a soft, calming tone. While Edmund claimed Percy adored Kate, she had a difficult time believing an animal, whose appearance alone frightened her, could possibly hold her in affection.

"I wish to be friends with you," she told the bloodhound.

Percy sat up on his haunches. His tail slapped from side to side, whipping the rushes spread on the floor.

Kate stopped. She had reached the arched doorway. He was only three feet away. "We both love Edmund."

Percy barked.

Startled, she jumped.

The dog whined.

Kate reached for the purse on her girdle and withdrew several of the raisins she kept there to feed the birds. She held her hand flat as she offered the raisins to Percy. He had wanted to be friends all along; it was she who had been frightened. She was frightened now. The big brown beast might take a bite of her hand.

"Come, Percy."

Percy bounded forward. He did not seem to notice Kate's trembling smile or her shaking hand. He slobbered the raisins up with his thick rough tongue. They disappeared in seconds.

Kate reached out and gingerly patted the top of his large knobby head. "Perhaps we shall ride together one day. We shall play ball to pass the time as well. I know you like to fetch Edmund's tennis balls."

Percy barked up at her several times as if he were replying, or asking for more raisins. As Kate pondered what the homely beast was trying to convey, Sally rushed into the chamber.

Mistress Anne has asked to see you and the Duke of Laird."

Kate's heart pounded heavily against her chest as she hurried down the cold, barren corridor to the west wing where Anne's suite was located. If she did not meet with the lady's approval, where could she go? What would become of her?

The duke waited.

"Dinna worry, Kate. Me Anne will love ye on sight," he said as he opened the door.

"I pray so, my lord." Her mouth was so dry, she rasped.

Donald Cameron nudged her into the room.

The first thing Kate noticed about Lady Anne was her golden, amber eyes.

EIGHTEEN

Do nothing while Venus and Neptune are in opposition

The aroma of fresh-baked bread permeated the small cluttered room where Edmund found the stargazer known as Jutta. He'd ridden to town especially to see her, and had used all his charm when introducing himself—to no avail. The hard edges of the astrologer's mouth did not soften; neither did her narrowed granite eyes. The baker's wife regarded him with undisguised suspicion. What had Kate been saying about him?

There was naught to do but throw himself on the astrologer's mercy—not that she appeared to possess such a quality. "By your leave, Mistress Jutta, I must ask you to prepare a chart that will show Kate Beadle belongs at Rose Hall."

Jutta brushed away strands of coarse, mousy brown hair from her face. "Mistress Kate does indeed belong at Rose Hall. The stars have spoken."

Edmund was momentarily taken aback. "Does Mistress Kate know this?"

Jutta shrugged. "I cannot be certain, milord. She's not been in the shop regular, of late. I am used to reading her chart every week. But 'tis been over a week since I saw her last."

"However has she made any decisions?" Edmund wondered aloud.

The baker's wife scowled at him.

"Never mind."

"Is Mistress Kate ill?"

"No, she has gone to Scotland."

Jutta's sparse brows met above the bridge of her crooked nose. The frowning astrologer obviously considered a sojourn in Scotland worse than a fatal illness.

"The planets did not predict such a journey," she mumbled.

Edmund allowed himself a sigh. "Would that for once Kate had sought counsel from the constellations."

"Aye."

"Jutta, I am leaving for Scotland to fetch Mistress Kate. If I am to bring her back I must have a chart proving what you say. My word alone will not convince her to leave with me, I fear."

"She does not trust you?"

Unused to such insolence—except from Kate—Edmund stiffened. "Foolish as it may seem, she believes I seek to possess her."

"And do ye?"

"I gave her my bloodhound. If I were a possessive man, I should not have given Kate my best hunter. I should have kept him for myself," he explained righteously.

Giving Percy to Kate had been difficult in one respect. The hound afforded Edmund the only unconditional love he'd ever known.

"Instead, your dog is with Mistress Kate?"

"To protect her and provide companionship. She will not be lonely with Percy."

Jutta cocked her head. She regarded him as she might a Bedlam inmate. "But you want the hunter and Kate Beadle back?"

Edmund did not care for Jutta's tone, nor her implication. "Only because Kate and Percy belong at Rose Hall."

The baker's wife pushed herself up from the table and moved toward a cupboard. After poking through the papers with a floured hand, she turned and handed him a rolled parchment. " 'Tis already done. I expected Mistress Kate to come for a reading."

"God reward you," Edmund said with genuine enthusiasm and a grin he could not suppress. "This will make it far less difficult to persuade Kate to return with me."

The stargazer's flat expression did not change. "Mayhap."

Undaunted, he pulled out a crown and pressed the coin into Jutta's hand as an expression of his appreciation.

Edmund had no curiosity in a chart showing the position of the planets. He did not believe in astrology, except as it pertained to health, and therefore only glimpsed at the chart before shoving it into the leather sack on his saddle.

He galloped back to Rose Hall where he ordered his gelding made ready for a long journey on the morrow. Next, tamping down his excitement, Edmund hurried to bid farewell to his aunt.

Standing at the door to Cordelia's chamber, Edmund took a deep breath and swiped a hand through his hair before knocking. He never knew what to expect from his aging aunt, who once again claimed to be on the brink of death. One of these days he feared she truly would be. Pray God it wasn't today.

An unfamiliar lady-in-waiting opened the door. Middle-aged, gaunt and deeply wrinkled, she curtsied low and led Edmund into the darkened bedchamber.

Cordelia lay upon her bed fully clothed. Her eyes were closed and the back of one hand rested upon her forehead. A physician Edmund had never seen before held her other hand.

"Aunt Cordelia?"

"Edmund?" She opened her eyes.

"Yes, 'tis I."

She turned her head toward him and offered a feeble smile. "You are just in time to meet Oliver Davys, my new physician."

Yet another, in Aunt Cordelia's growing retinue. Edmund had hoped to find his aunt alone.

"Welcome to Rose Hall, Master Davys."

Dressed in traditional flat cap and long black robe, the healer was a striking man in a swarthy sort of way. More than likely, he was a wealthy man as well.

The physician bowed his head. "My lord."

"I met Doctor Davys while we were in London, and he helped me more than any other physician," Cordelia said, rising up in bed and resting on her elbows. "I invited him to Rose Hall so that he might attend me. I hope you do not mind, Edmund."

"Not at all." He dipped his head toward the physician. "My thanks to you for assisting my aunt."

Davys bowed deeply. "To heal is my purpose, my pleasure."

Aunt Cordelia beamed and blinked.

Edmund frowned.

In his opinion, albeit hastily formed, the physician healed with honeyed words and flattering attention. But he evidently prospered . . . and appeared to be not much older than Kate.

"Did you bring your wife to Rose Hall?" Edmund asked with feigned nonchalance.

"I am not married, my lord. I have been too busy to form an attachment."

" 'Tis a shame," Edmund replied, working quickly to a frown. "Married life is to be desired, so my aunt tells me."

Davys's admission was too good to be true. Within weeks Kate might be safely married to a physician! Although he had promised not to meddle in her affairs, Edmund rationalized that he'd made the vow before she had gone off to Scotland.

Nay. Nay. He'd promised. In truth, he could not find Kate a mate or he would not have failed in his attempts thus far. Perchance, in his heart, he did not wish to find her a husband.

"A man without a wife has not a life," Aunt Cordelia pronounced, rising from her bed.

"Quite right," Davys agreed, with a rueful twist of his lips.

Edmund could not agree. A man must have the proper wife or he was better off without. But he had no time to argue his point. Armed with the stargazer's chart and another candidate, well, a potential candidate, to be Kate's husband, Edmund was convinced he planned the proper course of action. He must not delay in rescuing Kate from Scotland and the old duke.

Edmund strode to his aunt's side. "I am leaving for Scotland on the morrow, at first light."

"Eh?"

"I intend to fetch Kate and return her to Rose Hall where she belongs."

"But Edmund, your tennis court will be finished on the morrow," Cordelia protested. "Your tournament will begin the day after."

'Twas true. Disappointment stabbed at his gut. "I cannot delay. Too much time has already passed."

"But you have been eagerly awaiting—"

"Aye, but I fear for Kate's well-being. Her life means more than an outdoor court or the winning of a tournament."

There would be another tournament. He would see to it.

But there would never be another Kate.

Kate stood closely beside the Duke of Laird, resolved not to show her nervousness.

Lady Anne's spacious bedchamber was warmed by a roaring fire. Flames crackled in the massive stone fireplace flanked on either side of the hearth by imaginary beasts carved from stone and deepened by age to a dark honey shade.

Her knees went to whey as Kate's gaze fixed on the bedridden woman. Anne lay motionless like a child's marionette in a giant's bed.

Rich, black velvet fabric fell from each corner of the intricately carved French walnut bed. Tied back with gold tassels, the fabric once unbound served to curtain the occupant of the bed with privacy.

The last rays of light slid hazily through the old casement windows. Kate was only dimly aware of the Turkish carpets scattered over the rushes and rosemary. The gold-threaded tapestries, carved oak chairs, and cupboards adorning the room barely registered upon her mind.

The woman reclining on feather pillows and swathed in sable blankets appeared small and fragile. In contrast was her oversized retainer, Sally, who stood by the head of the bed as if on guard. The old woman patted her hands against her stomach.

"Me dear lass, how are ye?" Donald Cameron asked in a cheering tone as he approached the bed.

At a closer vantage his smile faded, replaced by a deepening frown, crevices etched in concern. His brown eyes darkened.

Kate's heart raced. Her mouth tasted as if she had been eating straw. Uncommonly anxious, she twisted her ring to and fro.

Anne gave the duke a wry half smile. "I am feeling curious. Who is the lovely young woman at your side?"

"Weel na, 'tis Mistress Kate. She has journeyed with me from England just to meet ye."

"You know I do not receive visitors, Donald."

"Aye . . . but Kate is not a visitor. The lass will make a fine companion for ye—"

"Kate?" Anne interrupted in a stronger voice than Kate thought possible from a woman so obviously ill. "Kate, what is it about your ring that distresses you, girl?"

Kate stopped twisting her ring. Her hands dropped to her sides. She could only shake her head to signal she was not distressed. But she was; she'd become an airling in Lady Anne's presence. Inching her chin a defensive notch higher, Kate offered a silent prayer that she would not faint on the spot and completely disgrace herself.

Apparently sensing Kate's dilemma, the Duke of Laird intervened. "Can ye see Kate's ring?" he asked. " 'Tis similar to yers, me lass."

Anne beckoned with a flick of her wrist. "Come closer, girl."

But Kate could not move. At last she'd come upon

someone who might have information concerning her ring and she'd become mute and immobile.

"You may approach me, Mistress Kate."

'Twas clearly a command from Lady Anne.

But nay, Kate could neither approach, nor retreat for that matter. Her knees were knocking. Could the sick woman not hear the rattling? But to lose courage now was not the thing.

"Come." Donald Cameron took Kate's hand and led her to the bedside.

"You are a beautiful young woman," Anne said with a new gentleness. Her golden eyes glittered as her gaze swept the length of Kate in a lingering, careful scrutiny.

Kate lowered her eyes and dipped her head. "My thanks."

"Now, let me see your ring."

Kate held out her hand. "I have sworn never to remove it."

Lady Anne took Kate's hand in hers, and Kate could feel the woman's fever. Her hands were warm and trembled slightly as if beset by spasms.

Peering from beneath lowered eyes, Kate held her breath as she watched the duke's good friend slowly examine the ring.

Lady Anne's blond hair was matted from being confined to bed. She possessed high cheekbones, but her complexion was yellowed and flushed from fever. Twig thin, she might just as readily be broken. No lines of laughter fanned the corner of her eyes, nor framed her mouth.

A sweet, deep compassion flooded Kate.

Lady Anne looked up at her; a tender smile parted her parched lips. "Kate," she stated softly. "Katherine."

"Do you recognize my ring? Have you seen one like it?" Kate asked with a thudding heart.

"Aye." Anne splayed her left hand out before her.

Kate gasped. Anne wore a like ring on her middle finger. The only difference between the two rings that Kate could see was that the crown was not hidden by the rose in Anne's ring. In contrast to Kate's ring, the rose was a small detail and the crown dominated.

Kate held her breath. Her gaze shifted to Lady Anne as she silently beseeched an explanation.

Lady Anne issued a soft order. "Sally, bring the duke and Kate stools. The time has come to tell my story."

"If it will be too much for ye, Anne, we shall come back at another time. You shouldna overtax yerself."

"Dear Donald, do not worry over me. I must say what is on my mind now that you have—"

A fit of coughing brought Sally scurrying to the bedside. She held a silver goblet to Lady Anne's lips.

"Milady, you are not well. Mayhap another time," the retainer cautioned sternly.

Anne gave her a weak smile. "But this may be the only time."

Kate sank to the chair. Anne still held her hand.

Donald Cameron chewed on his lip as he sat in the chair beside Kate. She glimpsed his struggle to suppress the tears in his eyes.

"I have lived in this castle all of my life," Anne told them quietly. "I was born here. Born to Mary, the eldest daughter of King Henry and Katherine of Aragon."

"Dear God." The duke's oath issued from beneath his breath.

Kate's breath stuck in her throat. Was Lady Anne claiming to be the daughter of Queen Mary? The half sister to Elizabeth, who attempted to restore Catholicism to England?

"Aye, 'tis true," Anne said. "They called my mother Bloody Mary, though she did not deserve such a name, nor blame."

The duke leaned forward in his chair. "Anne, me love, how do ye know this?"

"The entire kingdom knew my mother was with child. But when she did not produce me, she was accused of having a false pregnancy. She hid me here with the only woman she trusted, Sally Pickering."

" 'Tis true, my lord," Sally added. "While she was with child, Mary's husband, King Philip, left her to return to Spain. 'Twas a blow, for she loved him."

Anne continued. "For many years my mother was kept occupied thwarting conspiracies that would have given Elizabeth the throne. The constant struggle took its toll. Alone and weary, she feared for my life. My mother came here to give birth to me in secrecy. She left Sally to raise me. 'Twas for my own protection."

"Dear God," the duke exclaimed.

Kate could not speak.

Anne went on in a strained voice. "Without husband or babe, whatever remained of my mother's heart was broken."

"I am so sorry for her, for you," Kate murmured.

Anne attempted to nod. "They say my mother died of influenza, but 'twas a broken heart."

"You are a princess and have lived as a prisoner," Donald Cameron said in disbelief.

"A prisoner of my birth."

"And you never left this castle?" Kate asked, unable to believe such a wicked fate for one who should have lived a life of wealth and privilege.

"I dared not, cared not. I was happy. My solitude

was the only thing I knew. But I was not convinced my children would be happy with such a life."

"Children?" Donald Cameron repeated.

"Aye. My children . . . and yours."

The duke leaped from his chair.

Princess Anne raised her eyes to his. "I should have told you . . . but I dared not."

"I have fathered children? Kate is . . ." His voice trailed away as he met Kate's eyes. The duke's shock ran deep and clear.

"I feared their lives might be at risk. Elizabeth conspired against my mother; why would she not conspire against my children, no matter who their father?"

A tingling had started deep inside Kate. A tingling and a trembling. She stared at the princess, unable to look away.

The duke's questions came with furious intensity. "Who are they? How many are there? What in God's name have ye done with our children?"

Kate awaited the answers breathlessly.

"I instructed Sally to deliver each child to a deserving childless couple."

"Do ye know their names? Do ye know where they are?"

"Aye, Donald, I do know their names."

Kate did not feel surprise when Anne's eyes met hers, but a startling numbness crept over her.

At last the duke broke the heavy silence. "Kate Beadle?"

Princess Anne weakly squeezed Kate's hand. "You are named after my grandmother, Katherine of Aragon."

Stunned, Kate gasped. She stared in disbelief at the amber-eyed woman clinging to life.

"God's death," Donald blurted.

"You, you are my, my mother?" Kate asked in the merest whisper.

"Aye, and you are more beautiful than I ever dreamed."

Tears streamed down Kate's cheeks. She did not remember the start of them, could not imagine they would ever end. 'Twas a steady flow. At last she knew the truth. She knew who she was. She was not the daughter of a strumpet, nor the unwanted child of a poor servant girl. She was a princess, born of royalty.

But she could never reveal the truth. Her birthright was clear . . . and forever must remain secret.

Princess Anne continued, struggling to finish her story in labored breaths. "Sally made regular unannounced visits to you and your brother and sister in the beginning. I wished to make certain you were all placed in loving homes, living normal lives . . . ones I could not give you."

"I canna believe this," the duke exclaimed, lowering his head, clasping his face in his hands.

"If the couples who raised our children did not abide by my stipulations, Sally would have removed them from their homes."

"What stipulations?" he demanded.

Kate gazed at the man who was her father. A duke, a good, kind man. Her heart went out to him, for his pained expression plainly revealed his turmoil, a man caught in a tempest of anger and grief.

"The families were given funds to educate the children and a ring to be worn by each child at all times." Anne paused, drawing a ragged, hoarse breath. "You will be able to identify the others by their rings. A daughter and a son."

Laird's bushy brows dove into a confused frown. "How could ye hide the pregnancies from me?"

"By voluminous skirts. Sometimes you did not come to me for months. And occasionally, I was forced to send you away without seeing you. Those were difficult times. You have come to mean much to me through the years."

"We will be married now, this eve. You have oft refused me, but now I must insist."

Slanting the father of her children a faint smile, Anne closed her eyes. "On the morrow."

Tears stung at Kate's eyes. "Princess Anne, may I . . . May I call you 'Mother'?"

Anne opened her eyes again. "Aye, my sweeting. Say the word I have dreamed so often. Only in my dreams have my children called me 'Mother.' I never thought to hear . . ." Her voice trailed off; her smile died.

"Oh, Mother . . ." Kate fell to her knees at Princess Anne's bed.

"You are a fine young woman. I love you. You have made me proud . . . Princess Katherine."

"Princess?"

"Princess."

A princess!

Had she been alone, Kate would have pinched herself to make certain she wasn't dreaming.

Anne raised her eyes to the duke and signaled him closer. "Donald, you must find the others," she entreated him in a thin rasp. "Each was pledged to wear the same ring as Katherine's. They may be in danger, too."

"Hush now, lass. Save your strength," he crooned.

But Anne refused to be silenced. "Sally will help you find them. You must find them and have them remove their rings."

The duke swallowed hard as tears slipped down his

cheeks. "To discover I have children, but to lose ye at the same time, weel na, 'tis too much for an old Scot to bear."

"You are strong, Donald. You must take care of Kate now . . . and Cameron and Lucy."

"I will nurse you, Mother, and you will grow stronger," Kate promised over the din of her drumming heart. She spoke urgently, as if haste and determination could triumph over her mother's illness. "We shall find my brother and sister and live together as happily as a family can be."

Princess Anne closed her eyes. "My fondest wish is for you to be safe from the royals and create your own family."

"You must go now," Sally insisted quietly, shepherding Kate and the duke from the chamber. "My princess needs her rest."

Kate took Donald Cameron's hand. In heavy, sorrowful silence, they waited together in the adjacent chamber for Anne to call them to her side once more.

Princess Katherine. Kate rolled the words silently on her tongue. The kindly auburn-haired duke was her father. The ill, recluse princess was her mother. Of all the dire scenarios Kate had imagined in the past, none had been near to the truth.

Would she have been a different person had she known from birth who her natural parents were?

When Donald fell asleep, Kate slipped back into Princess Anne's chamber. She perched on the bed and gathered the sleeping woman's hand in hers.

Kate held her mother's hand through the night, until the dawn, until the small, frail hand she held grew cold.

NINETEEN

Happiness lies just ahead

Kate wandered the cold, misty moors with her father, the Duke of Laird, taking comfort in the close companionship they'd found.

The end of summer in Scotland felt more like early winter weather at Rose Hall. For as far as the eye could see, shades of brown layered the rocky angles of the landscape, fading hazily into an iron-gray horizon.

Chilled to the marrow, Kate hugged her cloak closer to her body. Traces of her breath bleared before her like faint smoke.

Princess Anne had been buried just over a week ago. The grief-stricken duke, her devoted servant, Sally Pickering, and Kate had gathered around the grave marked only with an iron cross. Death had freed Anne to rest beneath the boughs of a sheltering elm just outside Downes Castle.

Kate had wept for the mother she had never known. A woman banished by fear and distrust to another country. A woman raised in a solitude and anonymity that she eventually had come to cherish because it was all she'd ever known.

At last Kate had found her mother, but only hours

before she died. Even as Kate offered comfort to the duke—in faith, her father—the blow reached achingly deep within her.

Donald Cameron's emotions shifted. One day he stormed about the castle in anger, the next, he plunged into a grief-stricken stupor. Walking together helped.

The bleak moors surrounding them rather matched Kate's mood. She felt as one with the sullen highlands. She felt the need to wander where her mother had walked not long ago, to follow in Anne's footsteps for a time.

Kate looped her arm through her father's as they ambled over the cold, hard ground.

Edmund's hound, Percy, bounded ahead, then doubled back again sniffing his way along. Begging to play, he pranced about Kate's feet. She reached down and gave a dutiful pat to his head.

The duke came to a stop. Placing his big, rough hand over hers, his gentle brown gaze met hers. "I canna think what I would have done without ye during this time, lass."

Before Kate could answer, he turned away, fixing his gaze on the horizon. "But now we must look to the future."

"It seems too soon to think beyond this day."

But her father would not be deterred. "We canna tarry. We must return to London."

"Why?"

" 'Tis necessary that I recognize ye as me daughter at once."

"But why? In time it will be known."

He shook his head. "We havna time. I shall claim to have found ye after searching for many years. Ye are the daughter stolen from me mistress—who shall remain unnamed—and left as a foundling on the doorstep of John Beadle."

Kate gave a small shrug of compliance. " 'Tis close to the truth. But who would steal a babe?"

"The MacAllisters, a rival clan and a terrible enemy. Aye, an' what glee the heathen MacAllisters would feel in taking revenge by placing a Scot's baby with an English family."

"The English do believe the Scottish fight too much among themselves, Father. Your tale will be believed."

"It must be. Ye have stirred interest at court. I overheard Henry Stanton puzzle over yer ring some weeks ago. At the time I thought nothing of it, but now his interest troubles me."

Kate felt an unpleasant twinge in the pit of her stomach. "The queen's adviser has followed me."

" 'Tis worse than I feared. We must make haste. If Stanton recognizes ye as the daughter of a Scottish duke and his dead mistress, ye will no' be regarded as a threat to the crown." The duke paused for a moment. "Ye are not a threat, are ye?"

"God save me, no!"

The duke chuckled, but quickly grew serious again. "An' Daughter, although it might be grand being addressed as the princess ye know ye are, yer life will be safer if ye are known to all as Lady Katherine—daughter of the Duke of Laird."

Kate smiled. "Princess Katherine. I do like the sound of it," she admitted.

Better yet, she would be delighted to have the Earl of Stamford address her so and pay homage to her royalty. 'Twould serve him right for attempting to marry her off to a widowed bookseller with six children!

" 'Tis a dangerous title," Kate's father reminded her.

"Aye, and I have no desire to take part in court intrigue. I am proud to be your daughter."

A gust of wind blew wisps of graying auburn hair from the top of his bare head. "An' ye are a beautiful daughter. I will have documents drawn to show ye are mine."

" 'Tis evident in my height."

"Aye, ye do take after me there."

"Father, I . . . I would like to see Papa Beadle and talk with him before you proclaim me as your daughter. I should tell him."

"Aye, lass. We'll visit him on the way to London. I have much to thank him for."

"My thanks to you." Kate kissed her father on the cheek.

The tip of his nose was red from the cold, but the corners of his mouth turned up in a broad smile. "I can see that ye'll be having whatever ye ask for."

"I shall not take advantage of you, Father. Never fear," Kate promised with a laugh. Once more she had forgotten her gloves, and rubbed her icy hands together for warmth. "Must we remain in London long?"

"No, but are ye certain ye will be happy living here at Downes? Ye are a young girl, used to dancing and fishing. And if I am not mistaken the Earl of Stamford is besotted with ye."

"He has been husband hunting for me among the gentry."

The duke hiked a bushy brow. "Aye? Well, now he can marry ye himself, Lady Katherine."

She shook her head. "Edmund has sworn never to marry for love, and I will marry *only* for love."

"Why has the lad taken such a vow?"

"Love brought nothing but misery and death to his father and brother. Lord Stamford therefore wishes to avoid such a fate, and so has decided to marry only to provide an heir."

"Lass, I have loved and lost two bonny women, and I dinna regret a moment. The joy I've known far outweighs the sorrow."

" 'Tis the Earl of Stamford who requires your wisdom."

Her father nodded in solemn agreement. "And I shall share it with the lad at me first opportunity."

"I would like to be there when you do!"

"Come na, lass. Ye'll catch your death in the cold. An' we have much to do if we are to leave for London by week's end."

"I shall come in soon, but first I must play with Percy. He needs to run." She pulled a ball out of her pocket, a toy she'd fashioned stuffed with horsehair and stitched by Sally.

"Dinna stay long." The Duke of Laird bent and kissed her forehead before heading back to the castle.

Donald Cameron was all that Kate could ask for in a father. She would always love Papa Beadle, but rejoiced that the planets had blessed her two times over.

When the duke strode out of sight, Kate turned her attention to the panting dog at her heels.

In the days since Princess Anne's passing, Percy had proved a comfort. Through some sixth sense, Edmund's large, slobbering bloodhound felt Kate's sadness. She was never alone. Percy sat at her feet when she played the lute in her bedchamber, licked her face whenever she sat on her heels to feed or tug at his ears the way she had seen Edmund do. Percy even slept on her bed.

Kate threw the ball as far as she could, and with a frenzied bark, Percy gave chase.

Kate threw the ball several more times to the hound before giving in to the cold. A biting wind from the north slapped at her skirts and stung her cheeks. "Come, boy! Come."

Lowering her head into the wind, she hurried toward the castle, Percy barking at her heels. She had not gone far when she heard the horses, and she turned to see who it was.

Henry Stanton approached with two bodyguards and a riderless chestnut mare.

Oh, fie.

An ominous chill swept through Kate, but she stood her ground as the small group circled her before coming to a halt.

"Sir Henry! 'Tis an unexpected pleasure to see you so far from England." Kate eyed him with renewed interest. Stanton was one of her aunt's—Queen Elizabeth's—most trusted advisers.

His bovine eyes locked on hers. "I have been to the Duke of Laird's manor, but he was not in residence. His servants told me that he might be here."

"He is, indeed."

A smug smile set on Stanton's thick lips. "But now that I have found you, I do not require a meeting with Laird."

Kate felt as if she had swallowed a rock. "How, how may I help you?" she stammered.

In reply, Stanton growled an order to his men. "Take her."

"No!"

Kate spun on her heel and ran. Hampered by full

skirts, heavy cloak, and foolishly delicate leather slippers, she was easy prey. Within a heartbeat, one of Sir Henry's henchmen leaped from his mount and snagged her. Crushing her forearm, he dragged her back toward the queen's scowling adviser.

Percy jumped and barked at her side.

The guard kicked out but missed the bloodhound.

"Stop!" she cried. "He is but a poor, dumb animal."

But Edmund had sent Percy in his stead to guard and protect her. Kate felt like an airling. Percy was not so dumb. He urged her, by his insistent barking, to give the command that would set him upon her captor.

Summoning all of her strength, she wrenched free from the blackguard holding her. She stumbled but quickly righted herself. Pointing at the muttering man, Kate issued the order Percy awaited. "Go!"

Edmund's oversized bloodhound launched a snarling, growling attack, pushing the villain to the ground. From the corner of her eye, Kate caught a glint of metal. Stanton leveled a musket at Percy. As soon as the dog subdued the guard and stilled, he would be shot.

She marched toward her canine protector. "Percy, come!"

The bloodhound looked around at Kate in confusion. He had her attacker pinned to the ground. Success was at hand.

"Come," she repeated, sharply.

Timing meant everything. Kate refused to be responsible for the death of Edmund's beloved hound. She could not live with herself if even one hair on the silly beast's head was harmed.

Percy whined his objection, but obeyed. As he turned, Kate threw herself to the ground and wrapped her arms around the panting bloodhound, blocking him from Stanton's line of sight.

"You are a foolish shrew," Sir Henry spat between his teeth.

"Why are you looking for me?" she demanded with false bravado. Every bone and muscle within her trembled.

"The queen desires to speak with you in private."

Kate could not believe him. Threats to the crown were disposed with promptly. No meeting with the queen was required. " 'Tis my father's decision. I beg you to speak with him."

"And who might your father be?" Stanton asked in a mocking tone. "The gardener?"

Kate rose, straightening her shoulders, her head high and the hound behind her. "The Duke of Laird."

"Nay!"

"He has been searching for me all these years. I was stolen by a warring clan and given to the Beadles."

Sir Henry shifted in his saddle. He swiped a clump of dark hair from his face. "Are you telling me that Laird's journeys to London in the name of King James were also to discover the whereabouts of his abducted babe?"

"Aye. I am." Kate rubbed her bare hands together in a vain attempt to warm them.

"It must have been disheartening to learn you came from a Scot's womb, when you thought yourself English, Mistress Kate."

"My heart is English."

Stanton's penetrating gaze fell to her hands. He jerked his head. "Where is the ring you always wear?"

He knew too much of her.

"I have misplaced it," Kate lied. She had a reputation for misplacing or forgetting necessary items. Perchance Stanton had heard.

"A shame, to be sure." His tone was sharp.

" 'Twas only a trifle."

"But you sought to discover its origins," he countered, ignoring the tic that pulled at his mouth.

Kate found the tic strangely fascinating. "I did, but only because I thought the band might be valuable. No goldsmith I consulted could agree."

"You have no need to sell your baubles any longer. 'Tis well-known that the Duke of Laird is a wealthy man."

She dipped her head in acknowledgment. "I am certain my father would like to welcome you himself if you will but come to the castle, where it is warm."

"What place is this?"

"Downes Castle, Sir Henry. My home."

With a sigh of defeat, or resignation, the queen's adviser dismounted. "Take me to the Duke of Laird."

After leaving Stanton and his men with the Duke of Laird, Kate took refuge in her bedchamber. She had no doubt her father would put any remaining suspicions to rest. In turn, Sir Henry would placate the queen. A new life could begin for the duke and his daughter, Lady Katherine.

Lady Katherine. Kate laughed aloud to herself.

Percy cocked his head.

She could hardly wait to begin preparations for the return journey to England. A return held promise of a meeting not only with Papa Beadle but with Edmund as well.

The prospect brought a joyous hum to her body. As

recognized daughter of the Duke of Laird, Kate was eligible to be Edmund's bride.

Hey-ho!

Owing to her new status, the Earl of Stamford could marry the Duke of Laird's daughter instead of Judith Witherspoon. In truth, since Kate was of royal blood, Edmund was a touch beneath her.

Kate could not celebrate the astounding discovery that royal blood flowed through her veins, nor did she wish to. She'd made an important discovery in the past few days.

It mattered little whether she was a princess or a gardener's daughter; she could only be Kate. A young woman who had been blessed with the love of two mothers and two fathers. A girl who enjoyed rose gardening, playing the lute, and who looked forward to having her own family one day. She was a bit of a hoyden who thrilled to the challenge of fishing and the longbow, and who had a hankering to learn tennis. Lastly, Kate was a woman who had lost her heart years ago to a man she would love for the rest of her life. She would never, could never, love another.

The privilege and fortune she had gained as Donald Cameron's daughter meant Kate would no longer be at the whim of others. She no longer had to earn her way. Although she regretted not having had time with Anne, at least in those final moments questions had been answered and fears put to rest. She knew her natural mother loved her and had made a great sacrifice.

Kate opened her chest to begin packing when Mary, her lady's maid bustled into her chamber. "Lady Katherine, a guest awaits you in the great hall."

"A guest?" She knew no one in Scotland. "How could that be?"

" 'Tis the Earl of Stamford, milady."

* * *

Kate flew along the corridor and down the stairs, with Percy at her heels. She reached the great hall out of breath. She stopped short at the sight of him. And sucked in her breath.

Tall, leathered, and muscular, he exuded virility. He paced the hall with his hands clasped behind his back, a man more magnificent than any knight in armor. It was all Kate could do not to throw her arms around Edmund's neck and cling to him like warm honey to a spoon.

"Edmund!"

"Kate!" He strode toward her, holding out both hands.

She clasped his hands, warm and engulfing. Her gaze poured over him, drinking in his tall, striking form, his sparkling eyes. Could there ever be a man as compelling and dear as Edmund Wydville, Earl of Stamford?

Dressed almost entirely in black, he might have presented a menacing appearance if it was not for his dazzling smile. A smile that warmed Kate like a blazing hearth on a winter day. A smile that made her feel alive again. In the light of Edmund's wondrous smile, the pain of the recent past evaporated.

With the rapid *pit-a-pat* of her heart, Kate skimmed the familiar, rugged angles of his body. She fancied the dark, mayhap dangerous look, of his finely tailored black costume. Dressed in black broadcloth venetians, a black sleeveless jerkin worn over a linen doublet, boots, and a black cloak, the earl might have been mistaken for a highwayman—of some wealth.

In the cold stone vestibule, the heat of his magnetism reached out and ignited a warmth within Kate such as she had never known. Her heart pitched every which way, thundering like a runaway mare. Edmund's hands squeezed hers, his gaze held her locked in the sparkling depths of jewel-green seas.

" 'Tis happy I am to find you safe and sound, Kate." He frowned, leaned close, and lowered his voice. "You are safe and sound?"

"Aye, Edmund," she assured him softly, inhaling deeply of his seductive sandalwood scent.

"I am relieved."

Kate struggled to maintain her composure and suppress her excitement. "What brings you all the way to Scotland? How did you find me?"

"I stopped to ask directions to Laird's estate—"

"The stars led you to me," she cried. "And I have wonderful news for you."

"As do I!" He dropped her hands and opened the leather purse attached to his low-slung silver chain girdle.

"Edmund, you will never believe what I have discovered."

"But I shall. Only first listen. I have traveled far to bring you news of great import."

At last! He realized he loved her. He was about to tell her he loved her, words she'd waited a lifetime to hear. And when he did, she would announce they could be married.

The tension took away her breath. Pins and needles spilled down her spine.

With a most satisfied smile, Edmund withdrew a small parchment from the leather purse. "This chart from Jutta shows clearly that you belong back in England, at Rose Hall."

Her heart swelled against her chest.

"There is more, Kate."

Oh, fie! Why did men have such a difficult time saying what was in their hearts?

On the verge of laughing and crying, Kate could only bob her head vigorously, encouraging Edmund to say the words. His lips parted; his mouth turned up into a wry, devastating grin. Kate's heart pounded wildly.

"I have found you the perfect husband."

Stunned, Kate squeaked a feeble protest as the lifeblood drained from her body.

"Oliver Davys."

"Oliver Davys," she repeated dully.

"My aunt's physician. I can think of nothing finer for you than marriage to a young, wealthy physician. I will build you the cottage I promised where you and Davys can—"

"Oh, fie!" Balling her fists on her hips, Kate stomped her foot. "Fie on you, Edmund!"

"I beg pardon?"

"You arrogant, beef-witted barnacle!"

"Kate! Mind your tongue."

"You are a fool-born miscreant!" she raged.

Percy barked at her and then at Edmund.

Edmund's dark brows bunched into a bewildered frown. "What have I said?"

"Have you forgotten your promise not to meddle in my affairs?"

"I have not." Drawing himself up and straightening his shoulders, Edmund glowered at her. "But when I did not meddle, only look what happened. Here you are, living in a cold, cruel country with a foolish old man who desires to make you his mistress."

"By your leave!" she gasped.

"I only hope that I am not too late," Edmund pronounced indignantly, before lowering his voice. "Donald Cameron has not . . . taken you, has he?"

Kate shrieked. She let out a scream that deafened her own ears and rocked Edmund back on his heels. He backed toward the door.

Percy followed, tail curled between his legs.

"You cur. You bloody fool!"

"Do you forget who you are talking to?"

"Oh, aye." She swore under her breath, advancing upon him. "I know very well."

Percy scampered to the door, the nails of his paws clicking on the stone floor. All else was quiet except for the echo of angry words.

Edmund could not fathom where Kate had learned such language. He dared not speak, for fear of saying the wrong thing. He could not understand her fury with him. He had given up his tournament and risked his life to rescue her, and she reacted like a madwoman. He should not have mentioned Davys. That had been a mistake.

If Kate would be his mistress, he would not be forced to go to such great lengths to keep her. But he knew she would refuse, just as she had refused all of the men he had offered to be her husband. Her pride would never allow her to become his mistress. The mere suggestion would throw her into more of a temper than she currently displayed. If that were possible.

God's blood! Had he fallen victim to the same fate as his father and brother? Was it love?

"Leave! Leave at once!" Kate shouted, pointing at the door.

Percy barked and leaped in the air.

Edmund backed up slowly. Could she be serious? Throwing him out after he'd traveled hundreds of miles over horrid roads?

Kate threw the astrological chart at him.

She was serious.

"Take your hound and go. I never wish to see you again, Edmund!"

He was shocked. "You cannot mean that. 'Tis the Scottish air that has put you in ill humor. This foul weather has that effect upon—"

"Methinks it is *you* who have put me out of sorts. You have vexed me to the point where I should banish you to the Tower of London, were it not for my lack of power."

"Kate!"

"I will live my own life! I shall love whomever I choose. I shall marry whenever I choose."

"Perchance when you are calm we can discuss—"

"Go." She ground the word between her teeth.

"You have not yet told me your good news," Edmund reminded her.

"Be gone! Be gone from my life."

Before Edmund could say more, she spun on her heel and marched up the stairs.

Bloody hell. What had he done? Would he never see Kate again?

TWENTY

The grand trine promises a season of peace and love

Summer had slipped into autumn when Kate and the Duke of Laird arrived at his London town house. Sally Pickering had come along with them to aid in the search for Kate's siblings. A search both Kate and Donald Cameron were eager to begin.

But first the duke made plans to present Kate at court. He insisted that no time be wasted in securing her safety with the public acknowledgment of her parentage. A half-truth he meant to present as the whole truth.

Kate sat next to her father in the lavish town coach he'd hired for the event. On what should have been the most exciting eve of her life, she remained mired in the lethargy that had marked her since her last meeting with Edmund. She even missed his dreadful hound, Percy.

In the heat of anger she had called the earl terrible names, banished him from her life. And she suffered for it, despaired without him. Except for the prospect of seeing the Earl of Stamford at the palace, Kate took no pleasure in this grand night when she would be presented to Queen Elizabeth.

During the long days since she had traveled to visit

Papa Beadle and then to London, she had had much time to think. Kate concluded 'twas better to have Edmund in her life as a friend than not at all.

The carriage pulled up before the palace, which was ablaze with the lights of an untold number of torches and candles. The liveryman helped Kate from the coach, and she tucked her hand under her father's arm.

"Weel na, here we are."

She smiled at his understatement.

His brown eyes shone with love as he looked down upon her. "Are ye fearful, lass?"

"Nay, Father."

Giving her a sly, encouraging wink, the duke turned and escorted Kate into Whitehall Palace. Her father doted on her, lavished her with gifts and love.

Their arrival was announced in sonorous tones. "The Duke of Laird and his daughter, Lady Katherine."

Tears welled up in Kate's eyes as she cast what she hoped to be a radiant smile. She meant to make her father and Princess Anne proud of her this eve. As she stood with the duke at the top of the stairs looking down into the ballroom, Kate imagined Edmund's surprise if he was standing among the many resplendent guests already gathered below.

Holding her head high, Kate felt quite regal for the first time, mayhap the only time in her life.

A London seamstress had created her gown of Italian damask woven with gold thread and studded with diamonds and pearls. The square neckline dipped low, displaying more décolletage than Kate preferred. Where the stiff, pointed bodice ended, a wheel farthingale that spread her voluminous silken skirts emerged. And she at last had learned to walk quite gracefully in the contraption.

The sleeves of her gown were padded, and a wide band of gold metallic lace dripped from the narrow wrists. An elegant ruff set off the ropes of gold and pearls wrapped around her neck. For once, Kate had not misplaced or forgotten any part of her wardrobe. She wore a small pair of amber earrings in her ears.

Parliament had reconvened, and those who had fled London's sweltering summer for the country breezes had returned, as well. Nobles, esteemed gentry, knights and their ladies, in a mass of opulent costumes, convened in the gleaming ballroom to be welcomed by the aging queen.

Kate searched the spangled throng for Edmund but did not see him. Within the hour she learned he was not there, would not be attending. And it was all she could do to conceal her disappointment.

"Edmund has been at Rose Hall since the summer," Christopher Carew, the Viscount of Lavingham, told her as they danced the pavane. Edmund's closest friend had been first to ask Kate to dance. "He has fallen into a strange melancholy. Nothing I say cheers him."

Edmund in melancholy? Kate could not credit it. "I am sorry to hear Lord Stamford is . . . is unwell."

"Knowing your good fortune might lift his spirits. 'Tis not every day one discovers the gardener's daughter is in faith a duke's daughter. I am certain he would chuckle."

Kate was not as certain. "And Lady Judith? What has become of the lady?"

"She recently became betrothed to the Baron of Drakesmore. She will be at the ball this eve, as will Lady and Lord Chumley."

"Lady Judith is betrothed to Drakesmore?" Kate repeated, uncertain she had heard correctly.

"Aye."

"I must offer my congratulations to the lady," she said, wondering if the excited flutter of her heart could be heard. In the end, Edmund had not sought, or had not won, Lady Judith's hand. Although Kate burned to know the reasons, she could not ask the viscount. She must speak with Lady Jane before the night ended.

Christopher's mouth turned up in a wry grin. "Lady Judith will be astounded at your rise in society."

"Aye, I expect she will be," Kate agreed, returning his smile.

"As will Stamford. You know he disappeared before the tennis tournament on his outdoor court at Rose Hall."

"Lord Stamford missed the match?"

"Aye."

For the moment, the astonishing news that Edmund had missed the match put an end to Kate's distress over the placement of the court. Though she doubted she ever would forgive him for constructing a tennis court on the site of the rose garden.

"Pray, when was the tournament held?"

"Late in August. Not long after you left Rose Hall."

"Ah, yes." Kate remembered it well. 'Twas the time Edmund had come to Scotland to rescue her from what he imagined to be the diabolical clutches of Donald Cameron—her father. Edmund still did not know her true relation to the Duke of Laird.

"Stamford sunk into melancholy. He has not been entertaining for the longest time, since his return. He has refrained from all sport and refuses to say where he disappeared to."

"Alas, poor Edmund." Kate commiserated. She understood, for she had been suffering as well since their quarrel.

"Several of his friends have despaired that Stamford will ever be on the town with us again. But not me. Edmund shall recover in time . . . from whatever it is that ails him."

" 'Tis a long time to be prostrate," Kate said softly.

"Lady Katherine, if you would but speak to Stamford, I believe he might listen to you."

"What makes you think that?"

"He has always spoken of you with respect," the viscount assured her. "Even when you were naught but the gardener's daughter."

Kate glared at Christopher.

Oh, fie! She should not have done so. 'Twas improper at court. 'Twas improper any time for a lady.

"A most extraordinary gardener's daughter, to be sure," Edmund's friend added quickly. "Stamford will be delighted to learn you are in truth the daughter of Laird."

"Perhaps." If only Kate were as certain.

"Will you see Stamford?" her dance partner pressed.

"I, I will consider it."

But Kate felt a tightening in her chest. What if Edmund rebuked her, or worse, refused to see her? Her heart cringed from further pain. And she feared seeing Edmund again might bring more pain. What to do?

She looked about the glistening ballroom and found the jewel-bedecked queen. She would never address Elizabeth as dear Aunt Bess. And she felt grateful.

She watched the dancers, a jumble of whirling, sparkling extravagance. During her life as the gardener's daughter, Kate knew with certainty, she had not missed this pomp and circumstance. She felt out of place here. Court was not where she belonged.

Later, when she was introduced to the queen, with her father standing proudly at her side, Kate did not waver under the keen scrutiny of her aunt.

"You have eyes like my sister, Mary."

"I have the eyes of my mother."

The alabaster-faced queen nodded, obviously convinced by Kate's bold reply that sister and mother could not be the same person. "You are welcome at my court as the daughter of the Duke of Laird, friend of King James."

"My thanks, Your Majesty."

The moment was over almost before it had begun. She had passed muster. She felt the tension drain from her father's shoulders. Grinning broadly, he led her to the dance floor.

Kate danced until her feet were sore. But without Edmund, her shining eve of passage paled. What to do? What to do?

Edmund remained in the isolation he had imposed upon himself. Since he disliked solitude the most, 'twas the only fitting punishment. He'd driven Kate away from Rose Hall and lost any esteem she might have held for him.

It had not taken him long to discover that it mattered little who kept him company or applauded his sporting achievements. Without Kate to share the victory, winning no longer brought a sense of triumph. He felt no elation.

The world Edmund had known before Kate no longer satisfied him.

He often wiled away time in the rose garden, where

he'd first discovered her again after their years of separation. In the end, Edmund had not the heart to plow over her rose garden to make way for the outdoor tennis court. He'd had it constructed near the east wing, not as favorable a spot. But he was glad for it, for memories abounded in the rose garden.

As plainly as if it happened yesterday, he could see Kate's wide-eyed apprehension when Percy hurtled toward her, just before knocking her over into the dirt and manure. He remembered her indignation when she recovered herself. The memory still brought a chuckle.

Amid the pink and crimson blossoms, he closed his eyes and inhaled the fragrance Kate used to wear. And he could pretend for a moment she strolled close by. When he brushed a velvet rose petal, he imagined he was touching her cheek. Being among the roses made Edmund feel closer to Kate.

Times, happy times with Kate, popped into his mind when he least expected. Her excitement when the arrow she aimed hit the bull's-eye, or when she caught a fish only a bit bigger than her little finger.

Edmund's spirits lifted when he recalled her laughter, the smile that made his heart pump faster. But then he remembered making love to her, and the silky softness of her skin. And when he remembered lying with her, the ache in him grew fierce.

If it were possible to marry the gardener's daughter himself, he would do it. He would make a far better husband for Kate than any of the candidates he'd introduced her to.

But at the present, he was in for another of his aunt's lectures. She had summoned Edmund to her chamber.

Rather than lying prone in bed as was customary since returning to Rose Hall, Cordelia stood at the window sipping from a silver goblet. Sack, he supposed. Relieved to see she did not appear to be ailing, he greeted his aunt with a kiss on her forehead.

"Good day, Aunt Cordelia."

She blinked up at him. It might have been her eyes adjusting from the bright light of day to the dark room that caused the old woman to blink, but he knew better. 'Twas habit.

"I was taking a last look at the gardens," she said.

"A last look?"

"Edmund, I am leaving for London with or without you, eh? It has become clear to me 'tis the country air that is the cause of my indisposition. Even my physician admits he cannot cure me if I continue at Rose Hall."

What new rub was this?

"How long will you be away, Aunt Cordelia?"

"I will not be returning . . . except for the occasional visit." She blinked again.

"By your leave. Is it something I've done . . . or said?"

"Nay. " 'Tis my disposition. I am more suited to the city than I am to country living."

"I see." Once Edmund had thought the same. But the longer he resided at Rose Hall the less inclined he was to return to London.

"Jane has invited me to stay with her while I make suitable, permanent arrangements. I believe I could afford a town house."

" 'Tis likely," he agreed. Despite Cordelia's presence, Edmund had thought of himself as being alone in the country. Now he truly would be, and the thought did not send him into a tailspin as it once might have. "I will miss you, Aunt Cordelia."

"Nay. Nay. You must come with me, eh? Parliament is in session. Bull baiting is—"

"That's bearbaiting, Aunt. A sport I do not relish."

"You do not relish any sport of late."

"I have lost my youth. My vigor is gone," he confessed.

"Nonsense."

"In truth, I have been stricken with a strange malaise ever since returning from Scotland. Methinks I contracted green sickness in that forbidding country."

" 'Tis only unrequited love."

"Love?" he repeated, attempting to sound surprised.

"If you wish to feel yourself again—"

Ah, here comes the lecture, he thought.

"You must see Kate and tell her how you feel," his aunt told him.

Kate? What could Aunt Cordelia possibly know about his feelings for Kate?

Edmund assumed an air of indifference. "What good would that do? Even if it should be love I feel for Kate—and I am not saying it is."

But he knew it to be true. He distinctly remembered the misery of his father and brother when they were in love. Edmund felt their pain now.

Bloody hell, he'd been felled by the very thing he'd struggled to avoid.

"Edmund, 'tis plain to see that Kate has formed an affection for you."

"She does not wish to speak to or see me again."

"Poof." Aunt Cordelia sank to her bed. "You cannot believe what a woman says in anger."

" 'Twas more than anger. 'Twas a tempest. Even Percy cowered before her rage."

His aunt stroked the gold pendant at her neck. "Jane's message carried news of Kate."

"Aye?" Edmund's deadened nerves came alive. Still, he masked his curiosity with a feigned casual air. "How so?"

"Kate was presented at court by her father."

"Impossible," he scoffed. "John Beadle has no entry to court."

"John Beadle is not Kate's father. She was a foundling, eh? Do you not remember?"

"Aye." He remembered everything about Kate. Far more than his aunt would ever know.

"Donald Cameron has claimed Kate as his daughter. One of three children taken from him by a rival Scot clan when they were but babes. 'Tis the talk of London."

"God's blood!"

His aunt shot him a withering look. "Pray pardon, Edmund."

"Forgive me. But that must be what Kate meant when she said she had good news to tell me."

"But she did not tell you the news?"

"I fear I did not give her the opportunity."

"Edmund, if you love Kate, go to her and grovel. As the duke's recognized daughter she is quite eligible to marry."

"If I love her . . ."

"A woman delights in a man going down on bended knee to beg forgiveness. A gift of jewels would be suitable, as well."

"I don't know." He feared Kate would refuse to see him.

"According to Jane, the duke's daughter has many suitors."

Edmund's heart roared in protest. Nay! He would go to her, ride through the night, run off the other suitors with his fists if necessary. And if Kate refused to see him he would break down her door.

What-ho? Edmund slammed his fist into the flat of his other hand. 'Twas the very sort of thinking that put him in this fix.

Kate did not belong to him. She belonged to no man. Unless she came to him, Edmund could not claim her.

"Edmund?" Cordelia prompted.

"Aye, I am certain Kate is much sought after," he said. No woman he'd ever met could offer as much to a man.

"Come with me to London and speak with her."

"I am the last person in the world she wants to see."

Cordelia blinked at him as if he were a blinding light. "I leave at dawn tomorrow. I hope you have the good sense to travel with me."

Kate dismounted and walked her mare into the wooded copse. She could find her way blindfolded. The fallen leaves, varying shades of crimson and gold, crunched beneath her feet. Her heart thudded heavily against her chest.

She caught sight of Edmund's gelding first, tethered by the stream. His fishing pole leaned against a tree trunk. She could hear his low whistle, see patches of his black garments through the oak leaves. He lay in his tree castle, daydreaming.

It was as if no time had passed. Edmund was a boy again, and Kate the small girl who adored him, who longed to climb into his tree house and be with him. She did not know 'twas a castle at the time.

"Edmund!" Kate called softly.

"Kate?"

He must have jumped up at the sound of her voice. With the sudden, jolting movement, the last of the rotting tree-house boards gave way with a terrible splintering sound. The boards plunged to the ground. Edmund with them. He fell at Kate's feet.

"Oh, fie!" she exclaimed and sank to her knees beside him. "Are you hurt?"

He opened his eyes. Wide. And wider.

"Am I dead?"

"Nay, nay, Edmund."

"I am seeing visions."

"Hush now. Hush." In swift, light movements, Kate pushed and probed Edmund's body, examining him for broken bones.

Smiling weakly, he rubbed his head but did not speak. His lips quirked at the corner; his gaze swept over her in bemused pleasure.

Kate found no broken bones, only a warm, hard, muscled male body beneath her trembling fingertips. Edmund was not only not broken, he was magnificently all in one piece. She let out a whooshing puff of air, a heavy sigh of relief.

"Supplication is not necessary, Edmund. A simple apology will do."

He laughed, a deep belly laugh that echoed in the copse, that drowned out the merry splash of the stream. And when his laughter died, he pulled her down beside him.

"I have missed you, Mistress Kate," he murmured in a husky timbre. "I have sorely missed you."

"And I have been bereft without you, Edmund. I said things I should not have said when last we met. I know you only sought to protect me."

His burning gaze raked Kate from the top of her

head to the tip of her slippers, which peaked out from beneath her gown. Lifting his gaze, his eyes focused on her ears. "You wear the amber earrings still. I should have given you sapphires and rubies. I will."

Kate touched a finger to one ear. "I am verily pleased with these."

Edmund inclined his head, staring at her hand. "Where is your ring?"

" 'Tis with my mother. And that is a long story for another time."

"Can you ever forgive me, Kate?" Edmund asked, running a hand through his disheveled hair. "I was a jealous fool."

"No, never a fool . . ."

Edmund's eyes never left hers as he trailed the back of his hand gently along her neck. Goose bumps rose on Kate's skin.

"Never a fool . . ." she murmured once more as he nuzzled his lips in the hollow of her throat. Kate's mouth went dry.

"I did not know that love could make a man mad," he said, when at last he raised his head. "Fearing I would lose you, I thought I must possess you."

"But you do. I have always been yours, Edmund. You own my heart and soul for all time."

He pulled the pins from her caul, from her hair, and ran his fingers through the unleashed mass, gently combing it to Kate's shoulders.

"I am forgiven, then?"

"Aye," Kate whispered. She felt light-headed, as if she were floating away. Her heart drummed.

Framing her face in his hands, Edmund brought his mouth down on hers, and Kate knew with certainty she did not dream. 'Twas a searing, passionate kiss that left her shaken.

And when he raised his lips, his sparkling, evergreen gaze locked on hers. His voice was deep and hoarse. "I love you, Kate."

Hey-ho! He loved her!

"And I love you," said a breathless voice that was her own. "I have loved you for the longest time."

Edmund loved her!

The depth and width of his smile warmed Kate as she traced his jaw with her fingertip, pressed her finger gently in the cleft of his chin.

Bracing himself above Kate, Edmund lowered his head to kiss her with a passion that left no doubt of his love. The beating of her heart blocked all other sound as his lips next found the small heart above her breast.

At once Kate's gown felt too warm, too restricting. The smoldering ache curling through her forbade waiting for the comfort of a feather bed.

Beside the stream where they had fished in their youth, Edmund and Kate made love.

Her body hummed beneath his gentle touch. His whispered words of endearment tickled her neck and stoked the fire within her. Freed from hampering garments, Kate's palms caressed Edmund's arms, his broad chest. She marveled in his manhood, his strength and beauty.

And then they were one as they always had been meant to be. She knew no greater joy.

Later, as they lay silently folded in each other's arms, Kate listened to the falling leaves, the bubbling stream.

Edmund spoke quietly, a rich warm tone that wrapped around Kate like a gossamer blanket. "I saw stars, Kate."

"Lady Katherine, to you," she teased.

He ignored her. "Thanks to the planets, I have at last found you a faultless husband."

"You have not selected well in the past," she teased.

His lips brushed her forehead. "I am truly unworthy of you, Kate . . . Lady Katherine. 'Tis clear to me as the sun rising in the east. But . . . will you take me as your husband?"

"Hey-ho, Edmund!"

His dark brows dove into a frown. "Does that mean aye, or do you need to consult your stargazer before giving me your answer?" he asked uncertainly.

"It means that at last you have discovered the proper husband for me," she crowed happily. "I thought you never would!"

Edmund regarded Kate quizzically, as if fearing he may have misinterpreted her answer. "You do not require time to come to a decision?"

"I have known this answer all of my life." She grinned. Laughter bubbled up from her toes. "Ask me again."

"Will you have me as your husband, dearest Lady Katherine?"

"Oh, aye, Edmund. I will have you as my husband!" She lowered her voice then, murmuring seductively, "And I will have you again shortly in the rose garden."

As Edmund lowered his lips to Kate's and felt her fingertips splayed and tingling against his chest, he gave silent thanks that he had not destroyed the rose garden.

He and his wife were meant to spend many happy hours among the flowers. 'Twas written in the stars.

EPILOGUE

Nobles and dignitaries, including Queen Elizabeth of England and King James of Scotland, attended the October wedding of Lady Katherine and the Earl of Stamford in St. Paul's Cathedral, London.

Following the ceremony, the bride's father, Donald Cameron, Duke of Laird, made a stirring announcement. With newfound hope, he planned to launch a search for Lady Katherine's siblings. The duke was father to a son and another daughter, who were also abducted from him and are still missing.

The bride and groom repaired to Rose Hall where they would reside . . . in true happiness.